Praise for *Fishnet*

'Bold, sensual and unflinching, *Fishnet* lays bare a world too often misjudged and misunderstood. Kirstin Innes writes with courage, warmth and real insight. This is a hugely enjoyable and important book.'

Emma Jane Unsworth, author of *Animals*

'*Fishnet* is a determined debut from an inimitable talent. Kirstin Innes takes the reader on a remarkable, authentic journey into the contemporary realm of prostitution.'

Lisa O'Donnell, author of *The Death of Bees*

'It's dark and provocative, and it holds its gaze steady on the sex industry. Here's a new writer with huge talents and promise.'

Sarah Hall, author of *The Wolf Border*

'This book is utterly compelling ... a brilliant achievement.'

Janice Forsyth, BBC Culture Studio

'It's extraordinarily refreshing to find a writer on sex work actually consulting sex workers. Rarer than hen's teeth, in fact ... In places this book is harrowing, and brutal. We feel the abject despair of Fiona and will her to succeed. What really fascinated me was how Innes managed to capture the interaction between escort and client and get it so spot on ... *Fishnet* is set to be a massive hit, and it deserves every ounce of that success.'

Huffington Post

'Innes strikes sparks by rubbing a clandestine world (here, prostitution in Scotland) against the everyday. Unsettling and seductive, this tale of two sisters is moving, gripping and unforgettable.'

***The Independent*, 'Top Ten Debut Novels of 2015'**

'It's gripping, it's humane and it's the kind of novel that can actually make you investigate your own prejudices and opinions.'

The Guardian

Kirstin Innes

BLACK & WHITE PUBLISHING

First published 2015
This new edition published 2018
by Black & White Publishing Ltd
Nautical House, 104 Commercial Street
Edinburgh, EH6 6NF

1 3 5 7 9 10 8 6 4 2   18 19 20 21

ISBN: 978 1 78530 213 8

This novel is a work of fiction. The names, characters and
incidents portrayed in it are of the author's imagination. Any
resemblance to actual persons, living or dead, events or
localities is entirely coincidental.

A CIP catalogue record for this book is available
from the British Library.

Typeset by Iolaire Typesetting, Newtonmore
Printed and bound by CPI Group (UK) Ltd, Croydon, CR0 4YY.

Dedicated to the memory of Laura Lee

Past

The next morning, she's laid out there on the pillow beside you. Corn-yellow hair matted across her cheeks, crusty grains of makeup under her eyes and a sharp, feral smell rising from the duvet. You suspect maybe she's wet herself, but she looks happy as a baby. Half a smile stuck gummily round her mouth.

It rushes through your system as you sit up, toxic pressure on sinus, stomach. Still, you're awake, and still held together by skin. Underneath, though, that black emptiness of a comedown beginning. Pending holocaust of organ tissue.

The toilet flushes. Still here. At least he hasn't done a runner on you. Why would he? The club'll be paying for the room.

Tooth marks on your shoulder.

A towel or something on the floor near the bed. You pull it round yourself to cover up before he comes out, just observing formalities.

Water running.

Jammed stinking ashtrays and champagne bottles crowning the furniture, the cold slime of a spent condom underfoot; all that tawdry sort of carnage from other people's money that you don't think you'll mind the next day. Her knickers are hanging off the doorknob, yellow-stained gusset peeking outwards, dainty.

The mirror is balanced on the wicker coffee table so you have to kneel down and bend your neck over for a basic check, sweep away roach material and leftover coke to see yourself clearly. Hair still more or less in place, and a couple of rubs gets rid of the worst of the makeup. You're pinching anxious colour back into your cheeks when there are suddenly hands on your haunches.

'Ready to go again by the looks of you!'

Aw. You hadn't listened properly to his voice last night. Not to take in, anyway, not by the time you'd got out of the club, away from the speakers, in the taxi, up to the room. It's a boy's voice, is what you think, a wee boy playing at the big man. Reedy, nasal, south of England.

The state of your head.

'Heh. You look like I feel, babe. Glad you're up, though. Didn't want to run off without thanking you lovely ladies, but I've gotta catch this plane.'

Yes. A wee boy who still couldn't quite believe his luck, spouting lines he's heard playboys say on the telly. If you didn't know who he was, you wouldn't have looked at him; sagging jeans, music nerd's T-shirt, tinted hipster specs he doesn't quite believe in enough to pull off. This hand stroking your bum, this assumption he can; this is a man making up for lost time.

'Although, I could be tempted to miss it for you. Oof.'

The squeeze becomes a maul, fingers stealing up

under your towel. You try giving him a weak look.

'Aw, sweetheart! Look at you, you poor lickle thing. Come here and let Daddy sort you out.'

He kneels down beside you, pulling the pouch and his card from the pocket of his duffel coat, and chops you a small line, patting your hair as you bend back over.

'There we go. Breakfast time, baby. Yeah. Feeling better now?' You are, actually. He's unzipped himself and pulled it out, stroking fondly, casting it loving looks, this very average cock. Why not, you think. Poor sod. His next record could bomb, he'd lose his shine, and he'd be back to doing the sound at other people's club nights, now that much closer and bitterer to forty than before.

'Just a little morning fuck,' he's whispering, urging himself on. 'Just a lickle bit of joy in the morning.'

Across the room, an alarm shrills and he stops, pulls out, tries to batter it back down into his boxers.

'God. Sorry, my darlin. Sorry. Sorry.' As though it even mattered to you. Bless, you think. Bless him, running about now with a stiffy still poking out, throwing the last remnants into his bag and scooping up his massive headphones. God. You'd never see your actual major-league DJs this stressed about missing a plane, none of the ones you've met, anyway. Perhaps next year, if he made it through, he'd lose the jitters, the charm. But now, his jeans falling round his ankles, he's adorable. Bless bless bless. You sit back on your heels and beam up at him.

It's maybe the chaz, right enough.

He scampers over for a surprisingly sweet kiss.

'Right. Ready. Checkout's not for, like, an hour, so

13

you just take it easy, gorgeous. I will be sure to see you next time I'm up here. Ma wee Scottish lassieee, eh? And maybe Sleeping Beauty over there too, yeah!'

All the high-pitched excitement. He's pressing something into your hands.

'I'm sure Jez has got you covered, but have a lickle token of my appreciation, babes. I wouldn't have got that past airport security anyway.'

The door crashes shut and you wonder idly whether he'd remembered to zip himself up.

Wrapped round the half-empty coke pouch in your hand is what looks like – you count – £300 in crumpled twenties, soft and grubby to touch.

'Tell me he left us the chaz. God.'

Even half asleep, Camilla's accent cuts diamonds. She's wrapped the sheet round her skinny self, and you reach for the towel again, conscious of your stomach bulging. Camilla's hair rises out in a static halo. She's made that bed sheet look like a ballgown.

'I think I've pissed the bed, so let's scram before they try and charge us for it. But god, sort me out with a line first, lovely.'

The ritual scraping and chopping, scrabbling for grains, feels tinny and pathetic done in daylight with shaking hands. You only take enough to get you through, not tip you back over. Camilla leans her head back on her neck, letting the rush take her, wake her.

'Ooh. We might just make it. Anyway. How much has he left?'

'Cam, he left us like, cash –'

'Mm. How much?'

'Money. Like he thought, like –'

Camilla seizes the pile of notes and flicks, expert, croupier-quick.

'The facking cheapskate bastard. One-fifty each? For the whole night? For a threesome and a go-around with you next morning? Well, it's not going to buy a decent pair of shoes, lovely, so why don't we get the hell out of here and get some breakfast? Honestly. Jez can owe us this one.'

In ten minutes, you are slinking out of the hotel back door in skimpy bandeau frocks and last night's heels. Camilla pulls an enormous pair of shades from somewhere in that little clutch, and between those, the thin shoulders and posh-girl cheekbones, she looks like a movie star. You tell her that and the big sunglasses turn blankly on you, the words just sitting there.

She steers you round the corner onto George Street, its rows of fancy doors marked with portable topiary. Perhaps it's the drugs, perhaps that you've only had about three hours' sleep; but there's nothing awkward between you. And there should be, surely. After last night. Given that you can still smell her on your fingers. Surely. You'd first spoken about three months ago – difficult to pinpoint, just because Camilla has always been there. Always on the guest list, an air kiss for the promoter; sauntering behind the decks, waving across the floor; an air kiss for the DJ. 'Cam!' they all shout, all the well-off boys whose tables you sit at. 'Milly! Baby!' If Jez has an after-party in the dressing room or someone's huge-ceilinged flat, she arrives late and electrifies the whole thing all over again, perching on knees to distribute pills on tongues, her laugh chiming into whatever cold, soaring vocal is on the stereo. One night in a bar, one of those theme bars that are popular in this city, where everyone kicks off their shoes and squats on Turkish carpets, you'd ended up hunched beside each other, in separate conversations. A tap on the shoulder and Camilla's face, all bored and lovely, was up close.

'Mm. You went to Gordonstoun?'

'No.'

'Oh.'

She puffed out on her cigarette, blew it in your eyes.

'Oh fuck. Sorry. God, lovely, that wasn't deliberate, you know.' You're still new enough to this place that you haven't quite got used to the accents; that people your own age could open perfectly straight faces and make strangled, clipped Merchant Ivory noises. Something about this city, all its history and money, it pulls that sort of person to it. You can hear your own voice changing around them, adapting, but that's okay.

To apologise, Camilla had grabbed your hand and scurried to the bogs. You'd locked yourselves into a cubicle, shared a couple of lines off the toilet lid and danced together a little, arms round necks, getting off a bit on the close sensation of your bodies. The friction.

Ally, who does sound at one of Jez's nights, who you occasionally had a sweet, small fumble with after hours, little cuddle next morning, nothing major, Ally had pulled you aside. 'Listen, Rona, just gonny watch yourself with her, eh? Bad scene. Be careful.'

Mumbled out from under the trucker cap he kept pulled low on his forehead. It was his trademark; all the guys on the scene here seemed to have a trademark thing that they wore.

Aw, you told him. You're such a sweetheart. A genuinely nice guy, you told him. You kissed him on the cheek.

This, you know, this is nothing. Bad scene. You've been clubbing since you were fifteen, in harder, fiercer sets than this. Far badder scenes. The worst you're going to get here is a wee bit of well-meaning class snobbery, you'd told him. He hadn't got the joke.

With a vague nod at a waiter in an apron, Camilla has you installed at a table on a raised dais, surrounded by pot plants and gleaming brass.

'Bottle of Tait, two glasses, jug of orange juice and a couple of black coffees. Double shot in the coffees.'

She waves away the Sunday brunch menu as though it offends her. You realise you probably can't face food either.

Sunday.

'Shit. Shit. I'm supposed to be at work to open the bar up in half an hour, Cam.'

'God, lovely. Don't even think about it. For what, three quid an hour? Call in sick. Don't go back.'

She shrills out one chink of a laugh and spreads the manky notes on the table. A few of them curl back on themselves, probably the ones you'd used last night.

'One-fifty each. Fah. Straight down the middle less breakfast? Ugh. When I saw he'd clambered back on top of you I decided to play dead in case he wanted another round of Show and Tell. Absolutely did not have the energy, yeah?'

Last night. His set finished, the adrenaline reeking off him as he came back to the private section with a

17

stained towel round his neck, beaming with it. Everyone applauding as he walked in. 'Mate. That was absolutely bloody spectacular,' said Jez, arm round his neck in a sweaty hug. 'Seriously. I have, like, never seen the place go off like that.'

He was pulled in, into the circle, someone dispatched to get him a drink, and soon you and Camilla were sitting either side of him and Jez was saying: 'Let me introduce you to two very good friends of mine. Ladies, I'm going to leave our guest in your all-too-capable hands from now on.'

And you'd raised your glasses, the ice clinking, the ripple of bubbles, to toast him.

Present

I've stopped doing it now, but for a while, maybe three years after you went, I collected cuttings. *The Big Issue* was the best for it, because they have that missing person page; four faces a pop, the images all grainy and scanned in from their mum's ancient photo album. They're maybe red-eyed from the flash and smiling; there's sometimes a Christmas tree in the background, the boys with too much hair gel and a pressed, checked shirt on. Pearl buttons. The kind that snap shut.

It was the photos I went for, because the details were sparse: just height, weight, eye colour, and what they were wearing. Disappeared from her home on [date]. Occasionally a tantalising wee hint of motive: was said to be distressed. Had been suffering from depression.

Pretty blonde children with hair ribbons. Dead-eyed prostitutes.

I had a separate section for the ones they found, the ones whose stories had proper, satisfying endings. In a ditch. Floating up out of the river. In a dumpster. Then the manhunt, then the arrest. There is usually an arrest. Beginning, middle, end. But let me know. Let me see.

It might be that I became a bit ghoulish, just after. At my worst, I used to fantasise that you'd come back one day, just stroll into the kitchen and sit down and say nothing, and that I'd bring something heavy down on your head: a shovel, a frying pan maybe. I remember thinking that there would be an end to it, then, and I'd know.

Like I say, I've stopped doing it now.

ABOUT ME...

Meet Sabrina, a stunning 25yr old bombshell whose just packed with class!!!

A successful model and business woman, this elite courtesan loves nothing more than spending time in the company of a gentlemen who knows how to treat a lady.

Her stunning size 8 figure (32D, 25, 34) means she's both slender and curvy and her exotic looks and flowing black locks turn heads wherever she goes. She's a delight to have on your arm and as comfortable at large functions as she is up close and personal!!!

Whether your looking for a brief encounter or a longer date, Sabrina offers a truly sophisticated girlfriend experience!!!

HELLO GENTLEMAN. WELCOME TO MY SITE!

My name is Holly, and I'm an adorable, petite escort with a difference.

What you get is the real me.

I'm not merely selling sex; I'm offering you my soul. Please don't trample on it!

The experience I offer is sensual and intimate; lots of kissing, lots of stroking. I'm not your clichéd call girl as you can see from my pictures. I have my own unique take on fashion, and I love silky, vintage looking lingerie, soft satin sheets and a gentle kiss. Holly Golightly is my idol: really I'm just looking for a place like Tiffany's!

Please come to me clean, and freshly washed, as I promise I will. You can even have a shower at my place first, so we can have a lot of clean fun together! One thing I do not do is bareback!!! It's so dirty, please don't ask me. I respect my body and yours far too much to do that!

XXX

HI, I'M MARIE.

I offer incalls and outcalls in Ayrshire and, with notice, outcalls to city centre hotels.

I'm a tall, slim woman in my early thirties with long, red curly hair. I don't show my face on my site as I value my privacy as much as you do yours, but please be assured I am very attractive.

I'm afraid I'm a fairly vanilla escort, but that doesn't mean the time we spend together will be in any way boring. What I offer is the girlfriend experience: much more like going on a real date than acting out a porn film.

I don't do anal, insist on using condoms for everything, and my rates are not negotiable, so don't waste our time asking. I need payment in cash, in full, up front. Once that's out of the way we can relax and really get to know each other.

XXX

PRETTY PAULETTE, SCOTTISH ESCORT
I'm a mature lady who is ageing gracefully. I've been a lap dancer and a glamour model and I've kept my curvy, toned figure very well.

In fact, you could call me a bit of a cougar (although please note, I will no longer see anyone under the age of 40, and may actually ask you for ID to prove it if you're lucky enough to look that young!).

I'm a great listener, perfectly at ease in formal settings, and can probably cater to any sort of fantasy you might happen to have, you naughty boy. Why don't you get in touch and we can discuss what's possible?

By the way, discretion is my watchword. Rest assured that no one but us will ever know what happens behind our closed doors.

XXX

HAVE YOU BEEN VERY, VERY BAD? WOULD YOU LIKE TO BE?
I'm Sonja, a pierced, tattooed Scandinavian blonde who just wants to have fun. I offer a specialist fetish and domme service as well, catering to the kind of guy who likes his girlfriend experience with a bit of an alternative twist! I'm bisexual and love to play with women and men equally: my toybox is packed and I'm bound to have something that satisfies you (wink)!

I currently only offer incalls: my boudoir (and my dungeon) are in the city centre with easy access. I will sometimes go on tour, though, either by myself or with a little playmate – check my touring page to see if I'm coming to a city near you soon!

SCANDI SONJA'S FAQ

Can I take pictures of you, or film our encounter?
No, you may not.

How come your rates are so expensive?
Because I'm a highly skilled professional who knows her own value. You want Sonja – and believe me, many do – you pay Sonja rates.

I'd love to tie you up/handcuff you/share you with a friend.
That's simply not going to happen. I'm a strong woman with a big personality and a brown belt in Judo. I'm much more likely to be the one doing the handcuffing. I don't do submissive, so don't ask.

Will you have a threesome with me and my girlfriend?
Yes, but I'll need to speak to both of you on the phone at least two days in advance to make sure that we're all happy with the plan.

I don't like using condoms! They itch/spoil things/ are too small for me!
Oh no! Poor you! Looks like we won't be spending any time together, then.

XXX

LOOKING FOR AN ESCORT WITH A DIFFERENCE?

Well, hello there.

I'm a brunette with a brain, and I get off on showing off.

Want to make an appointment to see me? Click here.

I offer incalls to a discreet address in the city centre, and outcalls to major hotels within the local area. I'm happy to work with men, women, or couples, and I'm also an experienced domme. (Before booking please check my rates, and list of services offered, here. If something's not on the list, I don't do it, so don't ask. Condoms, like my rates, are non-negotiable.)

Need a little more convincing? Links to some of the utterly lovely things former clients have said about me on review sites can be found here.

If you'd rather we took things slowly, why not subscribe to my pay-per-view gallery, regularly updated with saucy pics of me at play. I'll occasionally take suggestions (from subscribers), so if you'd like to see me wearing/trying something . . .

I tend to post free taster pics in my blog, too, where you will also find my thoughts on sex, work, and sex work. One thing you need to know about me: I'm a very outspoken activist for sex workers' rights, and while I'm interested in having a good debate, comments that cross the line will be deleted with extreme prejudice!

And why am I an escort with a difference? Well, the sort of experience I offer is all about making a connection. Remember, my little pervs, the brain is the biggest sex organ.

ONE

VILLAGE

There was one other hen party in the only nightclub in town – the Fusion, it was called. A couple of boys at the bar, a few lone men prowling the circumference, scanning for the weakest ones in the herd, and that was all. A solitary puff of smoke leaking out of one corner to camouflage the mostly empty dance floor.

'And that was the luverly a-Destiny's a-Child with a-"*Boooooty*licious"!'

It was one of those places where they talk over the music, where the DJ croons in sleazy, transatlantic Scots. We dispersed variously to find seats, to check makeup in the mirror, to hit the bar and line up two rows of fourteen shots of lurid liquid, whooping, coughing as it caught the backs of our throats, chemical on our tongues. We were wearing the sashes over our regulation pink tonight, like beauty queens; *HEATHERZ HENZ*. Down the hatch, girls, someone might say if they were feeling particularly enthusiastic, and they were, and it was Samira this time.

Claire trailed behind us, features submerged under layers of powder and foundation that the other henz had forced on her after a few drinks at the cottage.

'C'mon, honey, you'd look so much better with a wee bit lippy. We'll give you a makeover.'

She'd clucked out a protest, but they'd closed in round her, wielding the old lanolin smell of their makeup bags.

The borrowed pink and silver vest top was stretched to bursting over Claire's wide, flat torso, tucked into her own black school-style trousers and hiking boots. Claire had a dodgy knee, sometimes, from years of athletics. She'd taken the makeup but refused to wear heels. My aching idiot feet admired her for that.

'And now it's time for Brenda's hens to get on the dance floor for the Slosh! Come on girls. Let. Me. See. You. *Moooove*.'

That last a throaty purr, so close to the microphone that you could hear the catarrh in his gullet. The other hen party squealed and roared and clattered on strappy sandals to the dance floor. It's always older women who do the Slosh. Sort of thing I can imagine my mum getting up to at a wedding or something, red faced, kicking off her shoes and clutching on to my aunty Linda. They looked genuinely happy, all of them beaming with it, helping each other into lines, folding each other's outhanging bra straps back into their huge sparkly tops.

'All right, *ladieeeez*, get ready to Slosh it up!'

They were counting, faces stern with concentration as the country tune wheedled its way out, and you could see them all mouthing the way they'd been taught it, years back: *one-two-three-kick-back-two-three-clap-right-two-three-heel!-back-two-three-under-TURN-TURN-TURN-and-one-two-three–*

I finished my chaser quickly and made a decision to get very drunk indeed. Someone tapped my arm, pressed gently, two fingers. I tried to shake it off, as you do in nightclubs, but it continued. I turned round; it was one of the older men, the prowlers.

He raised a glance at me.

'How you doing, darlin? Missed seeing you around the while, eh?' His hot nicotine breath on my face.

I shook myself free and moved quickly back to where women were.

Heather came tottering over. We'd dressed her in a white basque and pink fishnet stockings tonight, veil, tiara and a pink garter to hang her L-plates off. The men were watching her from their corners, watching her wobble and shake. She grabbed Samira and me, one under each arm. The bitter smell of her perfume and sweat.

'Mah oldest friends, and I love yis!' she screamed, her accent thickening, as Samira kissed her back. 'And listen, Fiona, listen, ah know we're not seeing that much of you these days, but it's always the fuckin three of us, isn't it? Three whatsit, muskahounds!'

She leaned heavy on my shoulder to take the weight off her heels, curled a lip at the Sloshers.

'God, would you look at the state of them.'

'Come on, Hedge,' Samira said. 'They're loving it.'

'I hope when I'm that age I've got the decency to stay out of nightclubs, eh!'

Two younger guys, pressed into dun-coloured shirts, had come in and a couple of the henz had already begun the signalling process: smile, look away, giggle to each other, look back, stomachs sucked right in.

31

Kelly, the one with the darkest tan and the French-polished nails, the skinniest, tapped Heather on the shoulder, took a breath in as she prepared to shout. 'We're gonny do a showcase of our own, wee wifey. No point in paying for dancing classes if we can't show off, eh?'

The Slosh hugged and clapped itself off the floor as music began to warp into something darker, squelchier, doomy hip hop pending and henz in heelz took over, three of them dragging a protesting Heather to her place at the centre. Kelly led the way with a prefect's wagging finger, assembling us in two loose rows, just like Cherry, the 'seduction tutor' with the tight smile, had taught us earlier. The bassline began to seep into our hips as the DJ slurred something over the intro. We all held two hands out at arm's length, gripped invisible poles, thrust our feet apart and ground like we were born to it. Some of the girls were giggling and snorting and checking each other – Heather kept turning her head and smirking at anyone who would look at her – but on the whole we were deadly serious, Claire most of all, her mouth ticking over the beat count as it went, as the song bent and raunched away and we splayed our legs wider, stuck our bums out-out-right-out and hip, and hip. Certainly, ladies, we had the room. The Sloshers tutted and turned their heads away across the generation gap, easy smiles gone.

Hip hip, thrust thrust, shimmy-six-seven-eight, titty-titty pump-left, pump-right, thrust thrust, hip hip.

I could feel it coming through the music, the fat electronic fart of the music, its meaty beeps. It began to make sense to my body, to bend my knees and rock my

32

pelvis on the beat, to stick my arse out back on a count of four and shake, and thrust, and titty-titty. All of us, moving as one. Like a tribe. The girls grew cockier, a couple of the ones with hair extensions flicking them from side to side – Andrea's hair got caught in my lip-gloss and I didn't care, I blew her a kiss – carving movements out of the stale air, all for the two, only two acceptable boys at the bar. Hip hip thrust thrust titty-titty. Body on autopilot.

Then I tuned into the words the DJ was grunting along with the rapper.

'Take it, take take it, baby. You're my ho, you're my ho, and I'll pimp you real good. Oh yeah, real good.'

You're my ho.

I was mid-thrust when my stomach went. I made it off the dance floor in time, so none of them saw me, but most of it still ended up on the toilet corridor carpet, silky, bile-green coils that glowed faintly in the strip lighting.

'You're my ho, you're my ho, take it ho, take it ho. Real good. Real good.'

I'd vomited so hard that I'd made myself cry great fat smudges of mascara, dripping down onto the cheap burnished metal trough that deputised for sinks here. The toilets were designed for female friendship in 1999; two pans to a cubicle, no lids. I suppose that made it harder to do drugs on. I heard three songs morph into different sets of beats while I was in there, carefully washing my face, scouring off every streak, squinting at myself in the crappy tin mirror, and starting again. None of my group came in to check I was okay, although I did get a motherly hug off a Slosher, gin on her breath and a smothering floral scent as she pulled my face in to her big soft bosom, rocked me, told me aw, darlin, it'll be all right. You'll be all right. We've all been there, eh?

I don't think we have.

Three henz and Heather were still on the floor when I resurfaced, repeating the invisible pole dance endlessly for a room that had moved on, to a song where a robot's voice had an orgasm: *ooh-ooh-ooh-OOHYEAH*. The others were clustered around the bar, around those boys in boxy shirts who seemed to have bred four more boxy friends. Samira was there, holding herself apart, stately, and of course attracting far more attention than the rest of the pack together.

The man who'd caught my sleeve materialised out of the darkness in front of me again.

'So, you not remember your old friends, eh doll? You too good for us now, eh?'

I made for the bar. He followed.

'Aye, well we remember you, though, darlin. We all remember you round here.'

He laughed. It wasn't an unpleasant laugh, but it ended in the long slow hack of a life-and-death smoker.

'There's precious few as talented as you around these days.'

I turned round. He wasn't so old, really, quite possibly still in his forties, although the drink had taken its toll, etched its years into his face.

'Oh aye. No forgetting you, hen.' I looked straight at him.

'I'm so sorry,' I said, over the music. 'I really think you must have confused me with someone else.'

XXX

That morning. Before.

Claire had done the dishes. Her martyrdom vibrated through the cottage, nipped heads, interfered with hangovers.

'Sit down, petal, you did them yesterday,' someone muttered with no concern at all.

She'd done them yesterday, after she'd marshalled us back to the cottage from the pub, handed Samira a notepad and had her count up the orders.

'Right. Fifteen fish suppers. Now, can everyone give me six pounds fifty? I'm not going all the way down there without the correct money. Not when I've paid for petrol.'

Being the only driver made her important. After she'd gone, we'd sat quietly.

'Claire's very organised,' we said, not wanting to offend Heather.

'Efficient. She's very efficient.'

'Yes. She's a do-er.'

We hate her. We hate her. We hate her. It pulsed beneath the weekend, the only thing uniting a disparate assortment of colleagues, sisters, college and school friends, stronger glue than the perkily fonted regalia we'd all had to pay twenty quid for. The HEATHERZ bit had dripped off the T-shirts into the loch after the canoeing session on Friday, when we'd also discovered that they went see-through when wet. We all squealed and tried to cover our breasts with our arms, as the fat-necked teenagers who were supposed to be instructing us leered.

Canoeing. Cocktail making. A screeching platoon of accountants forcing garters up the legs of an L-plate-draped someone I used to know. The pink furry hand-cuffs from a pound shop, the chocolate penises, these two people I went to school with and now email every few months.

Heather was brassy at school, shouting, rolling about. She attracted attention. It made her a target, because she wouldn't just settle down and accept her place in the grand scheme of things. Samira and I, neither of us having to learn to keep our heads down as we'd never put them up in the first place, would watch her careen about with anxious eyes, till the knocks came.

She came out the other side quieter, took the first place at the first university that would accept her, and continued to settle. When she got engaged to Ross, who is nice, but nothing, we wondered again, Samira, me, if she was just settling. It seemed very young to be settling. Maybe this is really all she wants, Heather. A hen weekend in a Highland village, cycling in the rain. A strapless white dress, two bridesmaids, a chance to get on the property ladder. First kid before she's thirty.

Heather will have invited Claire to her hen party because it's what you do; it's how you behave to your fiancé's sister, because she's basically decent, good, and doesn't hate people just because they're efficient. Do-ers. Heather will have invited me to her hen party out of long-fused loyalty. Because I held her hair back

36

in pub toilets, because I dumped Andy Oliver for her when we were fifteen. Because we've kept in touch, just. Because these tiny past connections mean things to her.

Claire clanked china.

'I'm going to go for a walk,' I said.

'Don't be too long,' she buzzed, from the sink. 'The bike ride's booked at half eleven: twelve miles, which will probably take us up until two, seeing as some people are feeling a little dozy this morning! We have to get the bikes back at half past, so.'

The terrifying cheer of a Brownie leader. 'It's going to be FUN,' she said.

It was Claire's idea to come to this village, this grey-brown holiday camp for outdoors enthusiasts, pivoting on one small street of theme bars and sports equipment hire shops. Heather had been dithering. Prague? Paris? And Claire had said, Look, my friend has a house that she rents out up there. It sleeps ten. I'll book it. In doing so, the organisation for the whole weekend became hers. She quickmarched us round the supermarket, set up a production line for cocktails. She supervised.

It was Claire's idea to come here. She didn't know.

I phoned home, and Dad picked up. The nerves of him, still, after six years, on answering. Just in case. Just in case. Always twice.

'Hello, hello?'

'Me. Is she there?'

'Fiona. Yes, yes. Yes. I'll just get her. Yes.'

The noise of that house in the background. The noise of absence not even blocked out by the blaring colours of cartoons.

'Bethan? BETH! It's your. It's the phone. It's. Mummy.'

She came to the phone and breathed into it for a second.

She's always shy with phones at first. 'Hi Mummy,' almost whispered. Flash and fanfare, for my girl.

'Hello, my darling! How are you feeling this morning? How's your tummy?'

'It's fine today. Well, there was a little bit of it that was sore when I woke up but then I had some cornflakes and it all went away and Grandad said it was probably just hunger, so I was being silly!'

'So it isn't bothering you? It isn't hurting? Are you able to run around and play?'

'Yes! I've got Barbie today and we're watching the princess film and then we're going to make boiled eggs for lunch and dip the shoulgers!'

'That's good. That's good, darling. Do you know what Mummy did yesterday? Mummy was on a boat, on a little canoe all by herself in the loch! And then she fell in the water! Silly Mummy, eh?'

'Silly Mummy.'

'Are you fidgeting there? Okay, darling. Go and watch the princess film, and put Grandad back on.'

'Bye, Mummy.'

'Bye, sweetheart. Mummy loves you, remember. Very much. Very much.'

Some breathy scuffling, then Dad again. 'Hello.'

'Hi. Can you make sure and tell Mum to give her another spoon of Calpol before bed? And she says you're having boiled eggs for lunch? Has she had some vegetables? It's important when she's got a sore tummy, to make sure she's getting a balanced diet. The doctor said.'

'All right, no problem.'

'Okay. I'll phone again tomorrow, but make sure and call me if it gets any worse.'

'Right. I'll let you get back to it then.'

'Right. Bye.'

All the things that we don't say to each other any more.

I noticed one of the girls, one of the henz – Jenni? Andrea? – slouching against a wall, smoking. Has she been watching me? I was just talking to my daughter. I wasn't doing anything wrong.

She nods, gestures to her cigarette, also guilty.

'I was supposed to have quit,' she said, with a half smile.

There's one main strip in this town. Glass-fronted family friendly bars and the sign to the ice rink. I came once on a school trip, when I was fourteen, because it is a place you go to on school trips. On hen weekends. Not a place you live in, surely.

Imagine my sister, aged nineteen, walking down this street back from the supermarket. Waving at a neighbour. Having a drink in one of these pubs. Six, nearly seven years ago.

We assumed she would have come back here, afterwards. This was the first place we looked, just because it was the last place she'd been. She'd had a job in a glamorous Edinburgh bar for a while after leaving school, surprised us all one day with an email saying she'd moved north. She lived here for about seven months; settled, we assumed. As much as Rona could settle.

In her low-ceilinged kitchen, Christina had disabused us of that one.

Christina had been at school with Rona, was her only real reason for having come up here in the first place and was our only real lead afterwards. Christina was a ski instructor: it made sense for her to live here. Rona had never really been that interested in outdoor sports.

'She just turned up one day, said she'd had it with Edinburgh, was looking to start over somewhere else. It was a surprise, sure: we'd not kept in touch that well since leaving school. I asked her why she didn't go home to youse and she said she wanted to do things her own way. I could understand that, I suppose. The rent was – the rent was handy.'

She was clipped, formal with us, uncomfortable in our distress.

When we'd asked, Christina had shown us the room my sister had slept in, which was just a room, mauve, uplighter shade over the bulb. Bed. Mirrored wardrobe covering one wall. We sat in the kitchen she must have cooked her dinner in, on mock pine plasticky chairs. We drank tea. The mugs had cats on them.

'I don't know that she had any other friends, as such. There were girls she w-worked with, but they were all transients.'

We'd looked at her, me and Dad and Mum.

'Transients,' she said again. 'Temporary bar staff. Up for the season. People pass through this place. It's just a stop.'

'What about boyfriends?' we'd asked. We were

especially keen to find out about boyfriends.

Christina took a breath in, and something crossed her face. 'There were a couple of guys she saw. A couple of guys she. Brought home. But nobody, really. Not recently.' Another breath.

'What you have to understand,' she said. 'I don't know how much Rona told you –'

'Let's just assume nothing,' Mum said. 'Anything you can tell us, Christina. Anything at all.'

'Well. We fell out. We had a fight.'

She looked away, looked anywhere but us.

'It's okay,' Mum said again, her voice gentler than I'd heard in years. 'We all know Rona can be, ah. Difficult. We don't blame you, Christina.'

'I haven't spoken to her for about five months,' she said. 'She moved out. She lived in other people's spare rooms, I guess. I never found out who she was staying with. I mean, I would see her around town. We saw each other, and we'd just ignore each other. But I haven't even seen her. Not for a few months.'

I leaned forward.

'When you saw her. How did she look?'

Christina paused again.

'The police have already been here,' she said, through a tight mouth. 'They didn't think I had anything to tell them that they didn't know.'

'We know,' Mum said. 'We know. We just wanted to hear it from you ourselves.'

'Well. It was difficult not to notice. And she didn't look happy. She was always distracted, the last few times. Didn't even register me enough to give me a filthy look, you know.'

She laughed and we didn't, and she looked terrified again.

We sat in this bar right here, afterwards. The Ochil. The three of us. We got Cokes and pub meals, picking at scampi and chips, cottage pie, not really eating as the speaker above our table blared songs about patriotism and hearing the call of the old country, going back to Caledonia. Sentiment welling up in the damp patches on the ceiling.

'What's the point,' Dad was muttering into his beard. 'What is the point of even being here? Tell me that. Nobody's got a thing to give us.'

'I know,' Mum was saying, in this strange soothing voice. 'I know, darling.'

She patted his hand a couple of times.

'It might help,' I said. 'Later on. It might help us understand, just from being here.'

'You're maybe right,' Mum said, not meaning it, not really. All the spark dreeping slowly out of her, out of all of us, evaporating into that smell of smoke and frying. A month later Mum and Dad were living together in the old house again. Two months after that, Beth and I had moved into the vacant flat upstairs.

The official reason is that we all want to be in the place she's most likely to come back to. Really, it's because with all of us mostly absent, together we approximate a whole person.

We'd sat there for a bit, staring out the window at the paint peeling off the ski shop, the people. Most of them seemed to be aged sixteen to twenty-two, marking time up here, making money then leaving again. The smell, the music. The empty fourth chair at the table we were at. The uneaten food.

They've got the same tartan carpet as they had six years ago in the Ochil, and the frying smell's stronger since the smoking ban came in. The same sort of music, playing loud for hypothetical tourists who are the same nationality as the staff. A man at the bar, older, the sort of stubble that looks painful, caught my eye as I stood in the door, started, then recovered himself and winked. There were no other customers, just a girl behind the bar who couldn't be more than twenty. She had pretty skin, her hair pulled back with a ribbon. Transient. Another transient.

CITY

This is where I work. The International Financial District. The Call Centre Capital. The Graveyard of Graduate Dreams. And after dark, The Notorious Drag. The Red Light Zone. An awful lot of names for an uninhabitable slant of tarmac so steep it'll give you a stitch if you can make it up in one go. There's not a single growing thing in the whole grid, not by design anyway. Weeds, maybe, between the cracks in the paving, between the designated areas of ownership, because nobody cares enough to root them out. Lots of pickings for rats, between the sandwich crumbs of office workers and the detritus of night-time activity, in this proud new area intended to attract free enterprise and the glories of capitalism to a former industrial city.

Nobody lives here. They work here; they drink here, some of them fuck here, but they don't live here. That makes it perfect. Eight, fourteen, twenty storeys of hard new architecture behind which there's probably no sky; buildings designed to suck in the sun, channel it into money.

The shift happens at around seven, later in the summer

months, if you're working evenings. The girls emerge from wherever they spend their daytimes just as the last of the suits disappear. They must just be ants from the seventeenth floor, ants on the march out of the zone, before the concrete is reclaimed by slaters scuttling in and out of the corners. When the cuts started, we had an email from head office: could female employees stop taking on overtime after dark, because the company can't afford the taxis.

One of my jobs every morning is to check the car park gutters for used condoms.

'Did *you* see that bloody carry-on outside?'

Norman doesn't bother with *hello Fiona, how was the hen weekend* because Norman is furious, his already pouchy eyes distending even further. He mutters in headlines: *no respect* and *shameless hussies* and *it's just gone too far. Too far*! And his hair crackles with static indignation.

Over at the window, Moira is closing the blinds.

'Ach, it's just a protest,' she says with her soft voice. 'Just a couple of daft buggers. You'll not have seen them, Fiona – they look like they've been camped out in the car park since cock crow. We'll just pull these shut and get on with our day, eh? How about you put the kettle on, darlin?'

'One of them called me a traitor, do you know?' Norman is incensed. 'Me! Me, who served fourteen year in the Territorials!'

'Norman'll have a cuppa as well, hen,' Moira says.

Here is how Moira and Norman work together, how they'd got on sharing the same corner space of RDJ

Construction's Surveying Office for fourteen years: if you make the tea for the two of them, you always pour the water over the teabag in Moira's special oversized teacup with the flowers on it, then pull it out immediately and add it to Norman's mug (bright blue, says World's Best Dad! in red), which already has one bag in it. You let Norman's tea stew for the time it takes to go to the fridge and get the milk, pull the sugar down from the cupboard with the anonymous notice that we all know is Elaine's work:

Would Everyone wash up there own Dishes and Cup's please!!!!!!!!!!!!!!!!!!!!!!

Three sugars for Norman and a splash of milk. The tip of a spoon in the sugar for Moira. Then, and only then, you take the two teabags out of Norman's mug. This is how Norman told me to make the tea, exactly this way, when I was settling in on my first day.

'Moira doesn't like it strong. Not at all. Me, I'm the opposite, see. I like brickie tea! Tea to put hairs on your chest! But Moira, it's just delicate for her.'

His voice softer, more reverent, as he told me this than I've ever heard it since.

Moira and Norman are both married to other people, have been for years. Only when they go home, though. All that time they spend together in the day, looking after each other, smiling affectionately at each other, checking that the other one gets their tea right. And it would never occur to either of them.

Graeme is already in the staff kitchen, on his knees in front of the fridge, trying to find the perfect spot for his sandwiches. 'It's because of the new development,' he's saying. 'They announced that we'd won the contract to do it last night, and it was all over the papers this morning. They gave the full address and everything, but the protesters still didn't work out which entrance was ours till Elaine arrived.'

'What's the new development?'

'Oh yeah. We were keeping the bid a secret, and Ian mentioned it to the office on Friday, but you were away at your hen weekend. I've had my sister on the phone this morning giving me a total earful of it, and she's never usually up before twelve.' He's still smirking.

'What's their objection to it? Ach, is it the Christians again? We're not knocking through another church for those bloody style bars?'

He passes me a tabloid, folded open, the ink of it grainy on my fingers. I read and flinch.

JACKSON GROUP BUY OUT VICE GIRL BASE

'The new development is on the site of a brothel?'

'Heh, heh. No, I think it's like a shelter, actually. Just down the road, that's hows we got the contract. You know, where all the, heh, eh, prossies go and hang out. On the night shift, eh?'

Chuckle, chuckle. He's blooming under the idea of it now, the fur coat and nae knickers of it, lads-mag innuendo nudging away at his little boy smile.

'The Sanctuary Base? So presumably, that mob outside are the people who work there?'

'Well.' He lowers his voice, leans into me so I can get a better smell of his Lynx. 'I heard Elaine saying that, actually, some of them are the *hookers*!'

The word has me before I realise. *That dirty hooker.* Three days ago I wouldn't even have paused.

47

It takes Graeme a couple of seconds to realise that I'm not sharing the joke, by which time I'm working on an encouraging half smile so as not to hurt his feelings.

Graeme and I are the only people under thirty in this company. I know that because I've got access to his files. He turns twenty-six next month. There's not much to him, not to look at, but I think about having sex with Graeme, some day, just because he's here. Maybe in the stationery cupboard, when the office is empty. I won't. His desk is across the way from mine, and if he's on the phone, concentrating, I look at his crotch sometimes, trying to see what's outlined under the folds of Topman smarts. I rub myself, guilty, frantically, in the toilets, under cheap hard lighting. I wash all trace of it off my fingers with the rose-smelling liquid soap Moira buys in bulk and stores in the cupboard in the kitchen. Sometimes I look at him and think, surely we are too young, we are both too young to have given up like this, to settle our bones in this halogen-lit tower. On Mondays he grins and sits on the edge of my desk, tells me about nights out he's had 'with the boys', always 'with the boys'.

'Not got a girlfriend yet, eh?' Moira says, listening in, playing matchmaker.

I don't think of Graeme at all when I'm not there. Graeme, going out for drinks with the boys, playing computer games with the boys, wouldn't really understand my world. The spaces, the silences, the waiting. The childcare.

I'm not sure why I'm angry at him now, though.

'Where are they going to go, Graeme? The, eh ... the prostitutes, if we knock down their sanctuary?'

He's doing that thing with his face again. He looks like he's laughing, but it's actually nerves. Or wind.

'Eh, well. Not really our thing, eh, problem. It's the council sold the place. They should be taking it up with them, those women outside. We're just doing our job. Eh. And it's not just like we're knocking them down. It's the whole block. Leisure complex. Possibilities for multiplex, eight bars or restaurants, bowling, casino –'

'And you're okay with that?'

This is further than we've gone in conversation before, and he's reddening, shifting to the door, glancing back over his shoulder.

'Do you not need to take the bag out. Moira's cup.'

Then he turns around properly, in the doorframe.

'I've seen the blueprints. It's going to be an exciting project for us, you know? For, ehm, for me. Good opportunity. Big one. We'll make a really beautiful building out of it.'

Glass, crap techno, cut-price cocktails on Thursdays, I'm thinking to myself. He's running off. Moira's teabag is bleeding scorches of tannin into the cup. I'll need to start over.

XXX

'They've got stamina, I'll say that for them. Well, they'd have to, eh, in *their* line of work.'

Norman has kept up a muttered commentary all day. There's a judgemental wind shaking the building, and even the diehard smokers like Elaine and big George from Maintenance haven't made it all the way down to the car park today. The protesters are still going, though, hours on, their faces whipped scarlet under cagoules, and we can still hear the chanting over the weather and the air con and the wheeze of Moira's old computer.

'SHAME ON THE COUNCIL!'

'SAVE OUR SANCTUARY!'

I had a look at them earlier, peeking through the blinds like a spy in an old movie. They must have been waiting for any sort of motion at all from our floor, because they all pivoted on the spot to face me, turned their heads up to the window, synchronised, eerie. Five women and a man, earnest-looking middle-class types for the most part. Tomorrow's paper will tell me that they aren't all prostitutes, that one of them was a well-known independent local councillor whose outspoken views on *women's issues* had made her a target for that paper for a while, that the man was a noted Socialist Worker agitator, that one of them was Suzanne Phillips, the former 'masseuse' who runs the Sanctuary Base. The paper will take pleasure in those quotation marks. The rest will just be given names and ages. Anya Sobtka, 27. Michelle McKay, 24. Carla Forlorni, 32.

A fierce-faced girl had made eye contact with me, mouthing some words I couldn't have caught, white-bleached hair and a little bolt glistening between her nostrils. The rest just glared up, damning me by association.

'Oh my god they've been on the phone all morning,' Elaine, the office manager, is saying as she comes in to bring files and get Moira's sympathy. 'My ears were ringing! And I just told them, a hundred times if I told them once, I told them, the boss isn't in today. We are not available for comment. I do not know what all the fuss about it is, I swear. It's what this area needs, a big new development in there. It's crying out for a bit of a smartening up. And property prices will rocket! Maybe bring a few decent folk into the area for once. These people. These people, eh.'

I want to shut her up, shut her ignorant mouth up, but all I manage to say is, 'What about the, eh, women, though, Elaine?'

I'd borrowed Moira's soft voice for cowards, but she heard me anyway, turned the full force of her thick lipstick on me, the minty fug of her nicotine gum breath. You could look at Elaine, strip twenty years off her and know exactly what she was like at school.

'We've not got a wee red in here, have we?' There's an intense little catch in her voice, like she's laughing. She's not laughing.

'Just leave her, Elaine,' Moira's saying. Elaine is a straight-talking gal from her own private movie. She courts applause in her head.

'Listen, missy, you'd better work out where your sympathies lie on this one, and fast. This is the biggest contract we've had in years. We need it. Are you going to get hung up over a few old bricks? A few bloody hoors?'

'Elaine!' Moira's saying. 'There's no need for language.'

'You've got a wean, Fiona. Keeping hold of your job should be your first priority. And in order to do that, you might wanty show a bit of company loyalty, all right? I'm just saying. And I'm not the first to say it, eh.'

51

'She's had a stressful day, hen,' Moira says as the door slams, Graeme and Norman looking straight into their computer screens and nowhere else.

Ian, our department head, arrives at two, brings storm clouds in. The protesters had mistaken him in his big sleek car for the boss, had obviously been holding eggs very carefully in their cagoule pockets all day.

'Fiona. Get my clean suit immediately and call the police. I'm disappointed that you've indulged these idiots even this long. Norman, Moira. I'm going to want you in my office for briefing. We'll all be spending the rest of the afternoon on the new site. We need to get moving fast. Graeme, if you could begin bringing Norman and Moira up to speed while I get changed. Fiona. Call George and have him bring the people carrier round the back entrance. The back entrance. You and Elaine will be holding the fort here for the rest of the day, and I want these people gone by the time I come back at six. Understand?'

Ian disappears off to the toilets, then sticks his head back round again.

'And all personnel visiting the site should ensure they've got protective headgear with them. There's another party of this lot down there, more of them, and because the site's not been handed over properly yet, we don't have the power to have them removed.'

Norman, jaw set like he's going into battle, is pulling out all his official RDJ Construction-branded equipment, grimly folding his reflective jacket and setting his hard hat on top, just so.

A whole afternoon. A whole afternoon with the office to myself. I'm weighing up Elaine's dislike of having nobody to talk to over her hatred of me, and betting on a succession of crabbit phone calls but no actual state visit.

I'm not going to let myself think about my sister, though. No. No. For distraction, I walk under the flickering light in the corner, feel the bad, harsh crackle of it beam down on me. I slip my finger inside my bra and rub my nipple till it hardens, just because it's the sort of thing I wouldn't ever do here. This movement usually happens constricted, under covers, in toilet cubicles. I pace. I notice the light still on standby on Graeme's computer, and I move behind his desk, just intending to switch it off. The mouse is greasy to the touch, layers of pastry flakes and 3 p.m.-biscuit in the gaps between the buttons. I move it gently and there's that half second of high fuzz before the screen lights up again.

Internet Explorer. Hotmail. Personal use of online privileges on company time? Bad boy, I tell him, in my head. Bad, bad boy. And he hadn't even thought to hide it.

Two unread, presumably from his sister as they shared the same last name.

SENDER	SUBJECT
Carly Bain	FW: SAVE THE SANCTUARY BASE
Carly Bain	graeme you are a wanker

Eight notifications from three different social networking sites, all of them read, even the one that came in an hour ago. Naughty. I click to the next page, and there it is, right at the top.

SENDER
Dominant Femmes
Subscribermail

SUBJECT
Your picture of the day!

He'd read it. Which meant it probably wasn't spam. Click.

A thin woman in a black leather jumpsuit which cut away just under her breasts was standing over a supine, guilty-looking man. One long elegant leg was extended over his face, the spiked point of a heel in his mouth.

Graeme. Vague, timid Graeme.

My phone rings, on my desk on the other side of the room, and I almost knock Graeme's chair over trying to catch it in time.

Elaine, tinny, disapproving.

'Fiona, Ian's just been on the phone. He said you're supposed to have called the police about those, eh, people downstairs, and as far as I can see they're still there.'

'I was just about to do that. Ian did actually give me a long list of items to be taken care of this afternoon and he has only been out of the office twenty –'

'Well, I'm fairly sure this is his top priority.'

'I'm Ian's assistant, Elaine. It's my workload to manage. Calling the police is the next item on my list, as it happens.'

'Well, it had better be done. If they're still there in fifteen, I'm making the call myself.'

'All right, Elaine. I'm on it right now.'

I don't think I convinced either of us with that performance. Norman has the numbers for all local amenities,

54

including the police station, taped to his desk, because of course he does.

Getting the tray with six mugs downstairs and out the heavy fire door is tricky, but I manage. They see me coming through the glass, and a couple of them tense up. I indicate that they've all got to keep their distance before I fob open the security door, and they do. The tray and I go out quickly, let it slam behind.

'Thought you might like some tea.'

This isn't what I imagined prostitutes to look like, I'm thinking. These faces. Their jeans. But until last weekend I hadn't really thought about them much at all.

It's the fierce, bleached, pierced girl who speaks. She's got an accent – Scandinavian? Polish. It'll be Polish.

'You haven't poisoned it?' She's smiling, though, which is more than can be said for a couple of them.

'I haven't poisoned it. I have had to call the police, though. Mr Henderson, our chief surveyor, who was the, ehm, the. You hit him with the eggs. So. I've just come down to give you fair warning, really. You've got about ten minutes.'

'We appreciate it,' says the girl.

There's something stark and intense and beautiful about her face.

'I'm afraid we're staying put, though,' says one of the other women, the one I'll find out is Suzanne, the former 'masseuse'. She's nice about it. Motherly.

'Look, everyone's gone. There's nobody on our floor but me, the maintenance team and the other PA. Everyone else left by the back entrance for a site visit about half an hour ago, and they'll be gone all day. And

Elaine can't even hear you from where she's sitting, so it's just me, really. You could make a run for it? You could make a run for it and go down to the main site? To the, eh, Sanctuary? Lots of action there.'

'We appreciate what you're doing,' says the blonde girl again. 'We're going to stay where we are, though. Thank you. And maybe you might want to go back upstairs? So you are not caught fraternising with us.'

Her voice slow over the longer word, sounding out each syllable. Frat. Ter. Nis. Ing. Ting. Ting. Ting.

'So sorry to have interrupted your workday,' says the older woman. 'Really. And thanks for the tea.'

I convince myself I can feel the heat of the pierced girl's eyes on the small of my back through the glass, till I turn up the corridor. I take a detour past the Ladies, push myself up against the cubicle wall and slide a hand inside my knickers again, concocting flash fantasies that she's in there with me, that it's her hand and it's forceful, that she's baring her breasts through black leather. I think about her nipple between my teeth. I think about the two of us masturbating each other with a foot each on Graeme, who's lying there, hard. I come. I come. I scrub with Moira's rose scented soap.

By the time the police get there, of course, they've all handcuffed themselves to the drainpipes and have to be cut away and formally arrested. Elaine officiates, buzzing around the policemen while I watch through the blinds. She calls my phone as soon as they've gone and I let it ring out, realising too late I've left the mugs down there, and realising I don't really care. After a few seconds the voicemail button begins flashing angrily. I move a notepad over the top of it and go back to my computer, with no Norman looking over my screen, his wet accusing eyes. Finally letting it all back in. Personal use of internet privileges on company time indeed.

In the years after Rona left, I padded out every dull temping job typing variations of her name into search engines. Flickr-tagged pictures. Blogs. Myspace pages. More recently, reading down the friends lists of everyone I could remember she knew at school who was on Facebook, going back to her year group's Friends Reunited page for fresh names and starting all over again. Nothing nothing nothing. If you want to disappear these days, disappear completely, then the first thing you need to shake off is your name. Why be Rona Leonard when you could be xxcutiexx, or Asriel1983, or Glitzfrau, or Kittylover, or MsStiletto?

It's supposed to be easy now. It frightens people, how easy it is. You can find the girl whose house you played at when you visited your gran, that guy you sort of fancied from the bar you worked in for five months during your second year of university, a man you met through friends one night, three years back. You can bind all these people to you for as long as the internet lasts, on a page that exists nowhere tangible, look at who their friends are, watch their lives. And this small, small country we live in. Graeme-at-my-work used to go out with Heather-from-my-school's cousin. Beth's best friend's mum was a former pupil of my dad's. I went to university with a guy whose brother was my gran's home help. Blips on a radar, spreading out across the country, across the world. I'm here. I'm here. Everyone knows someone who knows someone who knows someone, and yet my sister has found a way of removing herself completely from this matrix of nosiness, has wiped her fingerprints off the world.

Computers are wise, though. Computers learn things about you and use that information, and after a few days in each office, each new machine started to offer me solutions, clusters of one-line-one-link adverts sprouting around my search, her name filled in by automemory after I'd put in Ro–. Clean, bold typeface.

Trying to trace family members?
Missing persons found!
Track your genealogy!
Families reunited
Looking for someone?

I followed every link. I paid for trial membership on every single scamming site. There was one that looked properly genuine, though. Findastranger.com. A well-designed webpage laden with testimonials that had email addresses attached. I decided to go for the deluxe package.

'I've found a way to trace Rona,' I told Mum. 'I'll need your credit card. It's just a payment of about two hundred pounds a year, in dollars.'

She looked at me.

'Don't you want to find her?' I said.

Mum feels the most guilt, about all of this. She's sat up nights weeping into a bottle of wine and blaming herself for having left us. She's the easiest touch.

I had to create a profile for her. Not just name, age, sex, last known location, but interests and favourite movies, favourite songs, subjects taken at school, names of childhood friends, childhood pets. Favourite actors. Favourite curse words. Favourite musicians. Teenage crushes on celebrities.

They would use this, they told me, when the confirmation email came through, to source her. They had technology, they told me, that would track through hundreds of message board users and bloggers, people commenting on other people's web pages, look for people who declared interests in these things, who quoted from these films, who adopted usernames and passwords with similar configurations of letters.

I scanned in every photograph I had of her, from childhood up: dressed as a tiger on the bench in our old front garden, scowling at the camera on a beach somewhere. I zoomed in on school pictures where all the girls in the front row had their hands crossed nicely, one on top of the other. A couple from her high school yearbook: cheeks sucked in, arms round boys in nightclubs, pouting. I eased my mouse around the wild fuzz of hair sticking out from a paper hat on the last Christmas before she left, when she drank about three quarters of a bottle of Dad's crap wine even though she must have been – god, it still makes me angry sometimes. I uploaded them in the box on the secure link. Facial recognition software, the confirmation email said. If there are pictures on any of our online sources featuring subjects with similar features, we will send them to you for review. If you have samples of your loved one's writing style, or feel that you are able to approximate their speech patterns, please use the form provided to attach examples in Word document format.

At first I was just putting in stories, things I

remembered that I thought were significant, but then I started actually trying to write *her*. That last year, I thought, when she was living away from home. Try that, try reconstructing that, out of the little clues she'd given, accidentally: four bar jobs, three changes of address, the last after she fought with Christina, the boyfriends she mentioned. Jez? Cammy? The crappy presents she bought that Christmas, the long, long interviews we'd done with Christina and her last boss, both of them sleekit at the eye, worried we might be trying to blame them, might be suspecting them.

She haunted me. The way she'd started saying 'god' and 'like' as though they were punctuation. The way I could hear her laugh chiming in my own, tainting the things that made me happy. My palms had permanent nail marks from clenching, because I was coursing with anger at her, all the time. In my dreams, she lost her face; I couldn't see it. Only the idea of her, height and hair, present again in the corner of my eye, just out of reach.

Rona on a computer somewhere. Working, doing something, typing her own name in, again and again until her own adverts bloomed. Want to be found?

We didn't hear anything from Findastranger. Mum had to cancel the card, and I began to wonder whether I'd given them enough to create a fake her, out there, for money. And slowly, when my searches and searches threw up nothing new, I managed to numb that part of me off, and let her drift away.

This was where my head was at when I got Heather's email. *We've got the hen weekend booked!* it said, and gave the name of the village my sister had lived in, six years earlier.

VILLAGE

I was pretty sure that was her door, two down from the Ochil Bar. It took me a couple of seconds to get the nerve up to press the bell. A single note, and the sound of footsteps.

People don't just turn up unannounced on doorsteps any more. Visits are arranged on Facebook, confirmed by text message; you pick and choose who you open your door to. That's why the young man in the socks and boxers holding a coffee mug with cats on it looks confused.

'Hello?'

She's moved, of course she's moved, everything does.

'Hi. Sorry – I might have the wrong address. I was looking for someone who lived here a long time ago. Christina?'

His face breaks, relaxes.

'Aw, she's up at the slopes just now.'

'She still lives here, then? Are you her boyfriend?'

The smile gets bigger, a whole headful of happiness.

'Husband. As of two months. I'm Craig. Do you want me to let her know you called, eh . . .?'

'Fiona. I'm an old friend – well, we were at school together. Sort of. There was actually something I wanted to ask her, and I'm leaving the town tomorrow. Do you know what time she finishes?'

'Not till six today, and then, well. We have plans this evening.' He's just smiling to himself, now. 'Actually, hang on. We've got the schedule pinned up –'

He disappears back down the hall again, and I can see that Christina has decorated the place since last time I was here. I'm thinking, Christina is the same age as Rona, and that age is still ridiculously young to have a husband. Craig returns, head bent over a sheet with official-looking crests and a terrifyingly organised grid.

'She's doing early learners today – the eight-to-tens, then under-fives after that, but they don't start till twelve. You'll probably be able to catch her on a shift break if you hurry.'

'Right. Where's that, exactly?'

He wrote it down for me, the ski slope, and pointed across the street to the bus stop, described meticulously where I needed to get off. He was nice. A nice boy. He and Christina were probably very happy together.

She'd clocked me right off, when I'd scrambled off the chairlift, stared and then nodded curtly in my direction. I had been thinking, wow, her memory must be good, we only met a few times, but of course, her husband would have texted her, warning her of the unannounced intruder. I also remembered that, from a distance, I look quite a lot like Rona. From a distance. She flashed a hand up: ten minutes, pointed all the way back down the hill at the cafeteria and mimed drinking a cup, then turned a far less irritated face back to the padded children strapped to boards she was helping down the bristle slope.

I stood there for a while, watching the faces of those people on the brink, about to take the plunge. Christina's kids were certain, set, determined, under their too many layers. It was the older ones who showed fear, those few flashy adults who were on this slope this morning, designer sportswear more suited for a resort in the Alps than a wee Scottish mountain town. Their eyes going extra white against their fake tans just for that point-nothing of a second before they went over, stuck in that tiny hesitation between still and slope, a moment where they didn't definitely trust what they knew would happen.

Beats me why anyone would want to do this at all, this ungainly freefall, all your faith in two planks of wood that could snap your legs apart. For the rush? Surely it can't be that good.

I called Samira from the cafeteria.

'Hey hon. Listen, something's come up and I'm not going to make the bike ride.'

'Yeah, we'd figured that one out, actually. Where are you?'

'I'm just – look, I'll tell you later.'

'Okay. Can you get back to the cottage for four, though? Kelly and Andrea have paid specially for a surprise for Heather. Pole dancing. They've paid for all of us. '

She hung up.

Christina shook her hair out from the imprint of her hat, making huffy theatre of throwing it and her gloves down on the table, not sitting down at once, going straight to the queue for her cup of tea. Staring at me.

'So. Long time.'

'I know. I'm so sorry to barge in on you at work, and thanks so much for taking the time to talk to me. I'm just – I came up here on a hen weekend, and it's brought a lot of memories back, and I just wanted to check a couple of things with you, like –'

'Right. So I take it she hasn't turned up, then?'

It took me by surprise, that. That some people wouldn't know.

Of course she hasn't turned up.

'No. No, she hasn't. Not a word in six years.'

'Ah.'

'Anyway. Sorry – you're married, aren't you? Congratulations! He seems very, ehm. Nice.'

'He is. He's moral.'

I remember thinking, that's a strange thing to say about your husband, these days anyway.

'I thought you might have moved. I'm amazed you're still in that flat. Stroke of luck for me, eh?'

That came out as one of those jokes that isn't a joke, all upward inflection and slapped on jollity. Christina did not take it as a joke.

'Why would I move from the flat? It's my flat. We'll be paying off the wedding for a while yet, and then we're going to need to start saving for children. It's home. Listen, I've not got long, and you didn't come all the way to the top of a ski slope just to find out how I've been doing.'

'Right. Sorry. Ehm. This is probably just paranoia on my part. Actually, of course it is. Sorry. But being back up here has been strange. I just thought – and I don't want this to sound like an accusation – I just – thinking it over, was there, maybe, something you didn't tell us? At the time? Just maybe to save our feelings?'

She blew air out of her nostrils, stared straight at me. There was no trace of a thought process on her face; the thing she was about to tell me had been decided as soon as she saw me clambering off that chairlift. Maybe even sooner, when her husband had texted.

'Okay,' she said. 'I didn't want to say this in front of your mum and dad. I don't want to say this to you, actually, but I will 'cause you're here.'

A couple of seconds, then it came out in a harsh whisper.

'Your sister was. Was, eh. She was turning tricks from my flat. That's why I threw her out.'

'Turning –?'

'Having sex with men. For money. You know.'

There was breath between us, hot breath. Slightly sour. She spoke the rest very quickly, looking into her tea.

'I thought at first she was just having a lot of men back and I didn't like it but I didn't think it was my place to, ah, judge. Ha. Although I couldn't work out how she was managing to pay the rent after she got fired from the pub. But anyways, I didn't twig until I was sent home sick from work one day and there was a. A man in the sitting room. With his thing.'

Christina's tiny sitting room, its functional, cheap uplighters. How ordinary and dull a room it was, how unsexy.

I could still hear her talking, though.

'Anyways, it turned out she was advertising. She'd

65

been taking out adverts! It wasn't just something she'd done for tips with a couple of guys she'd met in the bar or anything, not that that would have been excusable – I don't know, maybes that's how it started – but by the time I caught her she was advertising in the local paper and on the internet! On web forums! High demand, 'cause she was the only one, eh, servicing the tourists, but only working while I was out the house! It was my house, Fiona. My. House. I had to bleach everything. I got cleaners in, professional cleaners, and I moved in with a friend until it was done. Everything.'

'Ah –'

You're in shock, I thought. This is shock. I actually put it in those terms to myself. While I was doing that, I asked the only question I could cope with.

'Why didn't you tell this to the police, Christina? It could have helped us find her. They could've tracked her online. We could have got them to look at arrest records or something.'

'Look, I understand that you want to find your sister, and that that's your main concern.' Her voice had been very tightly controlled, but suddenly she let it go, that tiny whisper pissing through the room.

'She was using my flat as an – an *effing hoorhouse*. I thought they'd think it was me, too, that I was her – pimp. I mean, I own that flat. I own that flat and I took her in when she bloody rocked up on my doorstep in tears, and she – she put my entire livelihood in danger, that dirty – *hooker*! After we'd been friends for years – oh, god, sorry. I didn't mean it like that. Please don't – look. I'm sorry for you, for your family, Fiona. But I just couldn't. Still can't. Sorry. I'm really sorry.'

CITY

These were not the women I was looking for. These bosoms, matronly and welcoming, these round backsides, puckered flesh spilling out and around suspender belts. These knowing winks from eyes beginning to wrinkle at the corners, these bodies that weren't slim, or that young, or toned. These were vocal women, mainlining opinions and their own businesses through their blogs, on Twitter, organising themselves in unions, advising each other, protesting their rights.

They didn't tally with the story I had in my head. I went further, searched deeper into recommendations. I wanted younger women, women my sister's age or less, women looking frightened, coerced, or just gone. Women who were being wronged by the system. Girls. I wanted girls, who men were using, girls who were doing this out of desperate necessity.

I can find all these things, of course. Anyone can find anything they want, instantly, any story they want to believe in, any pictures they need to see. It's all there. Almost.

I'd had this picture in my head of Rona prowling

round the streets, one of those ghosts dropping condoms outside my office, but that doesn't seem to be how it happens these days. All you need is internet access and a picture with your face pixelated out.

Just a couple of clicks and I'm back in the right narrative again. I've found a forum where the girls and men both go, where the girls advertise themselves and the men critique them. Where be dragons. Where be young women photographed from behind, a lipsticked grimace and a splayed, waiting arsehole on every individual profile. Where be punters, and the opinions of punters. Field reports, they're called.

Her tits were really disgusting. Once I got the bra off they just sagged all over the place. They were flopping in my face.

She's back on the scene after a long break and I'm thinking she must have had a kid cos my god, the stretch marks on her. Boobs not as pert as I remember either, and it was like a fucking tunnel up there.

She went down on me and it was all right, but not anything special, and her hand moved on my shaft just mechanically.

Holly is a real gem, who should only ever be treated like a lady.

Wow! What a technique! And that's all I'll say ha ha. Afterwards we cuddled for a nice long stretch.

I certainly didn't get the idea that she was a "clock watcher" or anything like that.

I eventually fucked her doggy while trying to ignore the disgusting smell coming from her fanny. But then the most repulsive thing hapened, my cock was suddenly covered in blood. It even ran all over my sheets!!!! She said she didnt know she was due well poor excuse if you ask me, how can you not know??? It was like something out of a horror movie!!!

She's also a great conversationalist, can talk about any subject really well.

It says on her blog she likes to wear boots and so I was pleased to see she'd come dressed in them and her fishnet stockings, just like I'd asked. She has the most beautiful legs, too.

We did it twice: i was so anxious about pleasing her that I maybe finished a little bit quickly the first time, fortunately Angela is a lady and was very nice about it, and let me go down on her for some time. She certainly seemed to enjoy herself, too, she's a real sexual adventuress.

Tiffany is a really sweet girl. Now I truly understand the meaning of "girlfriend experience". I'll be back.

XXX

By the time I left the office, it was dark outside. The station is at the top of the hill; the concrete felt treacherous, slippery in the rain. We'd all had to stay late, cover for work lost in the protest mess, and I realised I'd missed my window for leaving before the transfer happened. These streets were no longer my place.

It was the first time I'd seen it happen up close, though. The woman walking across the road from me, skinny jeans, eyes ringed and her hair up in a high band, the tail twitching as she walked, hitting her shoulders. Probably not even nineteen. Her limbs were thin, very very thin. A car pulled alongside her; she looked, indicated her head round the corner to a lane with a dead end. The car blinkers turned smoothly and she carried on, catching up with it without ever breaking her stride, although she looked over her shoulder at me. Alley cat flexing and spitting on a wall.

Oh.

Even the click of my heels on the concrete was full of meaning, suddenly, the noise of them. Another set of footsteps cut over my beat. Speed up, head down, grip knuckles round my handbag. Keys in my other fist, in my pocket, ready to strike at someone's face, but it passed.

I'd got halfway up when headlights smeared the wet tarmac ahead and around me, the noise of brakes cranking together at my back. The car made warm animal noises as it pulled in, waited for me.

Me. The fucking cheek of it. Me in my work clothes, my plain trousers and heeled boots, my fitted coat. Me, a woman in this area, a woman who works here. Did the very fact of my being female and in this patch of real estate after dark mean that they think I'm –

The car purred sexily, a hot gust on my legs, and a sudden bad bit of me thought, what if I did it? What if I turned round to meet this car, the man inside, leaned in at the window? What if I got in, pulled my trousers down to my knees, climbed on top? In one minute, if I wanted to, I could have had a stranger's cock inside me.

Instead, I broke into a run, up the hill. The scuttle of an outraged, virtuous member of society. Every noise in the dark, every shadow on the empty platform once I'd made it to the train station was a threat. I'd shrunk my muscles in on myself, tensed up and waited the train out, those agonising seventeen minutes counting down in yellow computer font on the screen. It was a fright when the recorded monotone began, in an itchy burst of static:

> *The train now approaching*
> *Platform two*
> *Is the*
> *Seven*
> *Twenty-three*
> *To*
> *Helensburgh*

The car hadn't followed me.

I took my bag and coat off at the door, put my shoes in their place on the rack, began the sort of comforting bustle that helps the brain short-circuit back to home mode. Mum nodded at me from the sofa, began to gather her things, retreat back to the flat downstairs.

'She's asleep?'

'Like a light. About half an hour ago.'

'Great. Thanks. She wasn't any trouble?'

'No, no.'

She made her way to the door. I heard it close. Beth was pouting in her sleep. I propped her door a little more ajar and moved to the computer, without really thinking. You want to know a thing, you type it into a white, blinking space.

prostitute scotland

And now the clock says 02.14. I'm probably going to be late for work tomorrow again. I take my clothes off and the mirror looks at me, red eyes, faded cotton pants around its ankles, and I'm not sure what I was supposed to do with that, so I go to bed.

DO YOU REMEMBER THE FIRST TIME?

Early forties. Thin, short, unhemmed like his edges had been gnawed. Something feral about him, but not bad looking. Not really.

I'd thought he would be ugly. Old and fat and ugly. I'd thought about fucking someone repulsive, fantasised about rolled lolloping flab that'd shake as he shagged, kept my fingers and brain in place on the transaction, the power, tried to train myself into it.

Old skin touching me.

Instead, just this little vulpine man, smell of dead smoke off him. His mouth was dry, smacked as he opened it to say hi, white flecks in the corners.

I said hi back, and he let me in.

Just two of us in a room, a very ordinary hotel room. 'I'm Jimmy,' he said. Irish.

'R__,' I said. (That was the name I used, when I was starting out.)

'Yeah – I guessed.'

'Of course.'

'So.'

'So.'

That's when I realised it was my job to break through this. My job, this, to ease him out of the nerves, to take his hand. Maybe it was his first time too.

All I had to do was smile at him, and say, in that voice like it was a normal thing to say: 'So. Shall we discuss services?'

And I smiled at the end, again, so much smiling, like we both knew how awful a thing it was, to have to ask, to have to reduce it down to money.

'Just the basics, please. Just the hour.'

The words flat, no expression.

He handed me an envelope without me having to ask.

It probably wasn't his first time.

My phone rang, before I could check the amount.

'I'll just need to –'

'Of course,' he said again.

No, not his first time.

'So?' she said, down the line.

And I thought, well, I'm not sure. It was something you were supposed to know, by instinct, she'd said. Well, my instincts weren't telling me to run. They weren't telling me anything at all. I was just in a room with this expressionless man, and he was skinny.

'I'm here, and it's fine,' I said.

'Okay. I've got the hotel on speed dial anyway,' she said. 'Two rings as soon as the hour's up. And good luck, my honey.'

If my instincts had been telling me anything, the code was: 'I'm here, and he's really lovely.'

We both stood there in the silence again, and I remembered that this was also part of my job.

'Give me two seconds,' I said, taking a step towards the bathroom, 'while I go and change into something, eh –'

'Just do it here,' he said, gesturing to a space on the floor. 'I'd like to see you undress.'

I was thinking, I haven't been able to count the money yet. I was thinking, I haven't done the lube yet.

He sat down on the bed, looking at me, and I stood in front of him, and pulled at the zip on my dress. It stuck for the first few seconds, and I had to wrestle with it, trying to keep smiling, swaying my hips a little to distract him. Cheap fucking thing. It came, eventually, and I let it swish down around me, stepped out of it. See through panties and a half balcony bra, so this man, this stranger was now pretty much seeing me naked.

He didn't say anything, his face didn't change, but he unzipped the front of his trousers and pulled himself out, already mostly hard.

'Would you like me to suck your cock?'

'Yes,' he said. 'I'm right in thinking I don't need to wear a condom?'

'Not for oral, no,' I said, like that was what I always said.

Eyes closed, and it's just like giving any other blowjob. Could be someone I'd met in a bar.

Could be a new boyfriend. I was touched that he'd washed it.

We spoke in these clipped, formal sentences, both of us. Like neither of us was there for the conversation, so what was the point in pretending? Made sense. He helped me in a way, that wee skinny Irishman, because my response would have been to crack jokes, to ease things through a bit. And of course, with some clients you can do that, and it's great, but the first time, this one, he helped me pare everything right down, establish a rhythm and a way of being in the room. It wasn't a kindness to me, he was just a customer, waiting for a service; I was the provider, that was the point.

It didn't occur to me until afterwards that I'd crossed over, that I'd actually done it, that I was now not one of us.

Anyway. Ooh. Yowza, has this blog got serious, right? For being such good and patient little pervs, you can have a sneak preview of my new panties. I do love my bum.

Tags: <u>clients memories</u> <u>irish</u> <u>outcalls</u> | **Comments (3)**

TWO

BACK

The first time I noticed what Rona could do was the year after the divorce. Mum was renting out the house while she travelled; Dad had moved to a tiny suburb on the outside of the city. The sort of place that had probably once been a village in its own right, co-opted into the city by bypasses and Tescos and housing schemes.

It was February, the air was sharp and good for you; we'd just started having to put an extra jumper on under our coats. Thirteen. She was thirteen, for fucksake, probably hadn't even started her periods yet (not that I'd know).

There were five of us at my school who lived out that way, the only ones. Me and Rona, Jenna Anderson in the fifth year and her wee brother, and Malcy Lamont. If we made it in time, which we usually didn't, we could catch the school bus, the one put on by three city centre schools for a disparate bunch: kids from village schemes and the part-timers staying with the parent who made less money.

Anyway, that day we were on time; weren't going to shamble shamefaced into first period as usual to everyone mock tutting, James Gibson pointing and going oooooh! Crossed the road and I went to grab her hand out of instinct. She glared right up at me.

'I'm not a baby,' she hissed. 'And there's no bloody traffic.'

Screw her. I was in a good mood that day. We sat down in the wee shelter and I leaned out the one window where someone had punched the scratched Plexiglas away completely, grinned up the hill, still a bit heathered, the sky above it blinking off the last of the sunrise.

Rona was thirteen, but she already had more chest than I'd ever get. Not that I knew that at the time, still clinging to old Judy Blume tales of hope and late development. Even in uniform I was nobody's fantasy of a schoolgirl; I've never really worked out how to stand. But this was the day I realised it.

Dad lived at the last stop before the bus turned and ploughed down the bypass. It usually filled up at the five earlier stops and we almost never got a seat together. Not that Rona would mind that day. After a few seconds she got up and marched down to the verge, glaring into the road, hood of her duffel coat pulled up in the sunshine, shooting the odd glare back at me. Still all pissed off because I'd tried to take her hand. Oh, get over it, you stupid kid, I muttered at her in my head.

Just the two of us there, that day. Looking up the hill again, I saw him coming.

Malcy Lamont. He was in my year, but we never spoke. What would we say? He'd been in trouble ever since he arrived, just turned up one day about six weeks into second year. I think it was just the way he looked at the teachers, default expression of solid, nasty insolence. Eyes deep set with a shock of long fantasy girl's eyelashes, greasy gingery curtains over a round head, fat lips always wet and half open. Not sixteen and already sexed, sizing the female teachers up when they told him off, just standing up there, itemising them – breasts, legs, back up to the crotch, where he *stopped* – till they backed down, every one. There were whispers about who he'd poked round the back of the science building, who had let him get three or even four fingers up, who he'd gone all the way with. Nobody really mentioned whether the girls had had much say in the matter. It was Malcy Lamont. He just happened. My plain girl's invisibility cloak didn't work on him, either – I'd had to pass him in the corridor on the way to PE once and he'd put his arm up, not let me through till he'd had a good, slow look. No words. Just letting me know that he would, if he felt like it. You dreaded getting anywhere near him during country dancing, in the progressive numbers, but you dreaded it silently.

Malcy Lamont was coming down the hill to the shelter now. Soft flop of cock at the crotch of his tracky bottoms, sour smell coming off him downwind. Malcy Lamont was only physical. The times before, when we'd made the bus, hulking Jenna Anderson and her brother had been there, the two of them like a barrier, soaking up some of Malcy. Not today. And he was coming over. I curled into the wall of the shelter, carried on staring out of the window frame, ready to flinch, wondering after what never-ending length of time the bus would come.

He didn't come into the shelter, though. I turned

around and saw him standing in the grass, him and Rona facing each other. Her hood was down, the coat open and slipping off her shoulders, her hair blown back from her face. Just staring right back at him, eyeballing, keeping his sightline level with hers. Her jaw was set; not the way it would be when she was going to start a fight.

I didn't understand what I was seeing, really. I'm not sure I do now. No idea what their two bodies were saying to each other, what sort of silent conversation happened there. Malcy Lamont didn't move. I didn't move. The bus came and Rona broke it, stepped past me and told me to come on, commanding, making her point. Schoolies spilled and burst all over us, jeering across the aisle, warmth and the fart stink on my skin. Somebody's tinny transistor playing that Robert Miles song 'Children', scratching and fuzzy at the strings. Rona was three paces ahead of me, cutting briskly through the tangled limbs of the aisle. She got a seat beside a smaller girl in her year, turned to her and started chatting.

'Are ye getting on, then, son?' the driver was asking.

Malcy Lamont walked quickly down to the back seat, where his mates were whistling at him. Head down. Didn't stop to brush his groin up against any outstretched knees, didn't look at Rona. I looked at her instead, through the seat behind. Her and thin, lank Donna Bruce nattering away, the same age except one of them was a child and the other one wasn't.

Next time I got a chance to talk to her was after lunch, passing her on the way to French.

'What was all that about this morning?'

'All what? You just need,' patronising voice, full height, 'to remember that I'm not *actually* a baby, Fiona.'

'You know what I mean. With him. With *Malcy*.' I whispered that bit, didn't want to get caught saying his name out loud.

'No idea what you're talking about,' she said, peeling off and away from me, her hair whipping out behind her.

I wasn't even surprised when the knock on the door came that night. Dad was out at the shops and Rona was in the toilet, so I went, already half-knowing who it would be.

'Eh. Is your sister in?'

He was wet through – it had just stopped raining – huddled up under a man's coat too big for him. I looked down on him from our steps and thought it was maybe the first time I'd ever heard him speak. I wasn't really sure what to do, so I just closed the door on him, softly, and went back into the living room, turned the telly up louder.

That was it, for Rona, though. I heard her new laugh in the corridors and on the bus, bright and healthy. From nowhere, she had boy friends and then boyfriends, mostly third years but once, for two terrifying, glorious weeks until the slaggings from his friends got too much for him, Chris Wood in fifth year, captain of the football team, lead actor in the school plays. Never Malcy Lamont, although I'd sometimes catch him staring at her cheek on the bus, immobilised. She was untouchable for the likes of him now. She walked taller than me, bunched her school skirt into her belt, stretched her legs out at break times to pull her socks down into thick rolls over each ankle. She started staying out late, crashing home at one and three and four. Her clothes and makeup got much, much cooler than mine, quickly. I'd pass her in the playground, screeching and flirting and petting with an entirely different set of friends from the ones she'd had before. I just stood back and watched her, got my grades, told no tales to either parent. They were busy finalising the divorce then, anyway, didn't notice, didn't want to.

FORTH

I am beginning to know this world, I think. It's like a soap opera. I tune into them every day, when I get home, when Beth's fed and the telly is on. There they are, listed, all the women working in my city, reports on them, their own blogs, their new pictures.

I check the forum to see if anyone has posted a new field report, any of the ones I follow, the ones who seem sort of famous with the men, the personalities. Sabrina. Tiffany. Casey. Shiny American names. Bubblegum exotica. I think I've found the blonde girl, the one with the piercings, from the protest. Anya. She calls herself 'Sonja'. Her website says she's Swedish, and specialises in fetish work. Her face is blurred out, of course, but you can still see the piercings. She has another one through her nipple, little silver bolt, the skin all bruised and puckered around it. Not for the first time I think how strange it is that most of these women will show every little part of themselves but hide their faces.

Holly has a new blog up; it's short and boring, complaining about women in the game who lie about their age. Holly is nineteen, and she doesn't understand why anyone would ever want to lie. What's the point, she says. When I'm thirty-five, I'm going to tell everyone I'm thirty-five. I'm going to be proud of it.

Holly is one of the ones who is either far too trusting or knows exactly what's she's doing; I haven't worked it out yet. There's nothing blurred out here – there are only a few who do this, and they're mostly young, very young, late-teens-grew-up-on-Facebook young. Holly also pours out her soul, though. Where the others blog about irritations with clients who don't read their websites properly before calling, or use their sites to draw attention to political rallies, pulling for sex workers' rights, she writes about her hatred for her mother; her college courses, her compulsions.

> If there's one thing I just can not stand it's bad hygiene. I am OCD and proud of it! If you want to play with me, gentlemen, I'm always always going to insist that you shower first.

Her father. She writes about her father, sits it all up there alongside the pictures of her, modelling dresses and lingerie, spreading herself wide for the camera. With just two clicks I could book an appointment with her, this fragile bird-thing who I know far too much about.

> Its Fathers day so I wanted to write something about my favourite man in the world, my Daddy!!! Its no secret that me and my mum don't get on coz she's an abusive bitch who ruined my childhood with her selfish behaviour. My dad couldn't stand

to live with her, she drove him away just like she drove me away by the time I was sixteen. I went to look for him and we had the most amazing reunion ever, it was like getting a second chance to be a little girl. After years of a jealous woman on a campaign to brake down my confidence, it was amazing to have someone tell me that I was actually beautiful and that I was his princess.

I imagine the men who come to her, having read this, spent time inside her bruised head, and I hope it's a ploy, that she's cleverer than this. Her face is not quite pretty – she missed being pretty by a hair's width, a blink; everything individually is, but not together. She's trying to look like Audrey Hepburn in *Breakfast at Tiffany's*: the eyeliner, the plastic tiara and underfed bones. The other one who goes without pixels is young and posh and beautiful, a student, through in Edinburgh. She calls herself Felicity and for all I know it's probably her real name. Edinburgh's not her hometown. Why should she care what they think of her up here?

All this I know, because it's right there in front of me. Click, click. Felicity charges three times as much as Holly, and is less up front about the services she provides, although both make it clear that anal sex is not a problem. I look at their skinny bums, Felicity's beribboned, in satin, Holly's naked, her hands pulling the cheeks apart, blue-polished fingernails digging into scrappy flesh.

I am not even ten years older than either of them, but their display, their lack of shame, their sex makes me feel like I'm from another time. You see, Rona? People like to be visible these days. Completely visible. Everything on display for the whole world to see. You're doing it all wrong.

I worry about Holly. I worry about her like I worry about the eighteen-year-old girl who lives near me and advertises on the site, doesn't blog, only hosts two grainy pictures, one of her breasts, one of her shaved crotch, both taken on a mobile phone, and says she does 'bareback'. No condoms. I want to write to her and warn her.

I forget that they don't know me, no matter how much I can read up about them. I wonder if their clients, prospective clients, faceless men at computers, feel the same.

They are exciting, these lives, though. They are. That they can list, on a site, the things they will do, and men will pay to do those things with them. I find it exciting in spite of myself. In spite of the bits of me that are repulsed.

There are no new field reports on any of my girls. I go back to the search page.

Search by Lady's name:

Search by Location:

Search by Services:

Outcalls Incalls Fetish/Specialist

This computer is wise to me too, fills in the o and the n and the a after I type the R, and although I've broadened it out to search the whole of the UK, it only returns the one in Manchester.

Manchester, I'd thought, when I'd first found her, my skin prickling, Manchester was the last place we had any sort of sighting. But it isn't her. Wrong skin colour, wrong age. I could tell from the first reports.

Not that she would be using her own name anyway. What does she go by, now, I wonder again. And then, back on the search page, without knowing why, I delete the R and put in an F and an i, my own name.

Field Report 15/03/08
On: 'Fiona'
In: West End

Her place: Clean new flat in West End. Nothing much to say about it.

The punt: Went well. She immediately put me at my ease. A stunning girl in her mid-20s. I would say about 25. Curly dark hair. Looked like a young Raquel Welsh. Needless to say I was delighted. Started off with amazing blowjob. Let me come all over her beautiful tits. Then some petting until the half hour was up. Perfect lunchtime treat. I will be back for a longer session!!

There was a link to a website. West End Girls, it was called. Listing the finest independent escorts in your local area, it said. There was faceless 'Fiona', all thin shoulders, big breasts, fake tan, blue French knickers and a head full of smoothed brown curls. It was definitely our hair.

BACK

A peace of sorts, damp-smelling and resigned, has settled about our family these days. In the evenings we usually group together downstairs, in Mum and Dad's tenement living room, let the dramas of made-up families wash over us. They sit on the sofa, together but not touching, I sit in the single matching chair, Beth scuttles about the floor. One two three four.

The room could do with redecorating, to be honest. It's looked like this for well over a decade now, ever since Mags Leonard, thirty-five and with two teenage daughters, married to a man almost ten years older, walked into it with her hair all different one day and screamed that she was feeling stuck, that she'd never asked to be a mother. Soon after that, the walls were painted in pale, inoffensive colours for the tenants who would come in, while the two teenage daughters and the floundering confused husband moved out to a chewed-up suburb. The room we shared in Dad's rented house had Care Bears on the walls and was never repapered. Every second weekend we'd share the sofa bed at Mum's new flat and make formal conversation with her young-looking boyfriends about our school subjects over dinner. When we moved back in, first Mum, then Dad, then me with Beth in the flat upstairs, which had been on the market for months, we didn't talk about doing the place up. The agreement we didn't need to voice was that we were only here temporarily, so Mum's strange wall hangings and ornaments collated from her travels, Dad's stodgy watercolours of Scottish island landscapes, and the cheap cotton throws and cushions of my student life have stayed in their boxes in the cellar space. We put up Bethan's nursery and then school pictures, though, in their free cardboard mounts. Not on the walls: she ages along the mantelpiece, from two to six, the face thinning and the eyes widening and the teeth disappearing.

Mum was seeing that Andrew guy; Dad and Jackie had been awkwardly coupled for a couple of years. Two sets of lives beginning to be lived together, neither bond strong enough to absorb the gap Rona left. Their grief not only pulled them back together again, it finally gave them something in common, beyond having been a pair of idiotic romantics who worked in the same café together that summer when she left school and he was trying to finish his first play and I was conceived. They've never said anything out loud, not to me, and perhaps they only had the conversation telepathically with each other, but we are all aware of their sticky puddles of shared guilt. His selfishness, preferring to write plays than earn money for his bloody kids, the ongoing affair with that woman. Her martyrdom, taking on three jobs and bullying him for his inadequacies, making him feel small and bloody stupid all the bloody time. Those things they shouted at each other in this room, their faces purple and ugly, while I flinched and Rona, blank-faced, turned up the volume on the TV.

FORTH

All this week, I've been nipping downstairs in my lunch breaks, calling from the alley, scuffing the same shards of glass under my toe as I wait for the answerphone to kick in. She never answers her phone, it seems. Not during the lunch hour, anyway. A breathy Hi, leave a message in a voice that could be anyone's; too quick to tell and she might be putting that accent on like I am. Muffling it through my coat, a bit of an Irish twang to keep her from guessing.

'Hi, I'd still like to make an appointment to see you. Could you call me back on this number, please.'

I imagine her playing back her voicemail, gruff requests from regulars, first timers full of nerves, and then me, bell clear, from nowhere. Maybe it would feel tight at her throat, my voice, or it might make her dizzy. I know why she isn't answering.

Fresh condoms in the car park today, I notice. I'd need to make another call to street services or Ian would be on me.

I don't get out till six, those musky patches of no-light

already waiting up the alleyways for the girls, and a text message on my phone, glowing there, waiting for me.

Please stop calling i dont do women thx

'Graeme, would you be up for doing me a wee favour?'

I lean over his desk a little and his eyes fidget over my cleavage for a second, coming back to my face then flicking down again. He's going to make himself dizzy. I've dressed up for this; astonishing the amount of planning I put in, I'll think later, hot with shame.

'It'll not take two minutes - I just need a – well. A man. Through in the store cupboard.'

'Eh. Aye. No problem. Sure. Now? Right. Eh.'

Moira's face disappears into the wrinkles of a knowing smile above her computer as he follows me through and I feel suddenly mucky, like I'm deceiving her.

Inside the cupboard, I let the door close behind us and he flinches at it, arranges each nodule of his back against one side of the wall.

'Boxes, is it? Which ones?'

He's putting on more of an accent than usual, staring somewhere around my shoulder.

'Boxes?'

'Aye. Can't you reach the boxes?'

'Oh, no. Actually, it's a little bit of a strange request, and I'd appreciate it if you could keep it from the others, just for now.' I've thickened my voice to match his.

'Ehm.'

I take a half step nearer to him, we both breathe in

92

the three extra scooshes of perfume I'd put on, and something alien begins to speak with my lips.

'Oof, it's warm in here, isn't it? Anyway, hon. I'm trying out a new system for arranging Ian's meetings, using a programme I found online. If it works, I'll buy it for the office and it could make everything a lot easier, but – you know what the older ones can be like with changes – I'd rather present it to them as a working model, you know? I'll not bore you – you need to get back to your work and I don't want to hold you up.'

I'm talking very, very quickly. His face says he's scolding himself for every look he's stealing down my top. Naughty boy. I know what's in your inbox.

'Basically, I just need to record a man saying a few things, so I can try out the answering system. It doesn't seem to be working as well with my wee girly voice! So I've got this recorder here. You okay with this, yeah? You'll be back at your desk in a second, I promise. Thanks, hon. You're such a pal.'

The skin under his old acne scars reddens. I ease my weight forward again, stroke his shoulder, hold up the recorder. Later, I'll be shocked at myself. I've known this man for three years and never been able to advance our relationship between the odd awkward shared joke. I don't know if I've ever flirted in my life, for sex or any other reason. Not with him, not with anyone. Certainly not for years. Later, it will terrify me, what I can do when I want something.

She didn't answer her mobile in the evenings, either, I'd noticed; that was all to the good, though, as my plan would probably work better.

I'd put a tenner into the new SIM card, and fiddled around changing them while Beth was doing her homework that evening. The card got stuck under my fingernail for a second while I was trying to shove it in; the metal edge pricked me and I worried that it would have come out, that I'd have to go and do all this again tomorrow. I needed it to happen now, this evening.

Beth seemed to pick up that I wanted her out of the way, too; she whinged and put on baby voices when I tried to rush her through her bath.

'Me want to stay in, Mama!'

She began to punch the water and a torrent slopped up and hit me in the face, lukewarm, stinging my eyes and giving me the excuse I needed.

'Bethan Camilla Leonard. If you don't get out of this bath and go to bed right now, I will skelp you till you're raw, so I will, you little madam. And stop speaking in that stupid voice. You're a big girl now. Act like it.'

She went tiny and silent then, shrunk away from my hands as I tried to wrap the towel round her. But she went to bed.

In the living room I pushed cushions from the sofa into the crack from the door, and took the corner furthest away from her room. I thought she was probably awake still, lying there, but I couldn't wait any longer.

It always rang seven times before the voicemail clicked in, her phone. I had the little recorder held right there at the mouthpiece, as she garbled her message.

'*Hello, my name is Graeme Bain,*' said Graeme's voice, flustered under this morning's tits and perfume. '*I'd like to make an appointment with you at half past eleven next Friday, for an hour. Thank you.*'

He has a nice voice, Graeme. Polite. Middle class, middle management. Well trained by his mammy. You'd never guess he liked it kinky.

I held the phone close to me for the rest of the night, like I was waiting for a message from a new lover. At one point, Beth coughed and I went through to check on her. There were tear stains dried on her face, but they were old ones. She looked sleepily at me through one eye.

'I'm sorry, Mummy,' she said.

I sat on the bed and her warm legs curled around my haunches.

'Here, here, sweetheart.' I leaned in and stroked her hair. 'Mummy's sorry too. She shouldn't have shouted at you like that. Bad Mummy, okay? We'll get ice cream on Saturday to make it up to you. Would you like that, darling?'

She burrowed her face into the pillow a little more, affected apparently neither one way or the other by ice cream, which is a new state of affairs.

'Mummy, who was the man?'

'What man, baby?'

'The man who was talking in the room.'

'Oh. I don't think any man was talking. Did you maybe have a dream about a man? There are no men here, baby. Just Beth and Mummy.'

I moved my thumb back and forth above her hairline, like my mum used to do for us when we were kids. It gets her every time, eyelids battling heroically as her face settles back into sleep – and my phone beeped. She stirred back up.

'Come on, lovey. Go to sleep now.'

I moved myself as gently as possible up from the bed, but it still disturbed her back up, eyes open. I whispered one more *sleep* at the door, but three-quarters of my body was already in the living room.

XXX

An appointment. An address. I've walked to it three times over the weekend just to be sure, but there it is, every time, number 28, the numbers on the buzzer going up to the fourth floor. A five minute walk from Beth's school and less than ten from my flat.

Good view. You could probably see Beth's school playground from up there.

It couldn't, couldn't be a coincidence.

Has she been here, right here all this time? Moving around the same routes to the supermarket, the bank machine and the train station, feeling her muscles relax in the way that meant *almost home* when she saw the rail bridge and the church? Watching me take Beth to school every day, leave her there in the playground?

I know the people who live in this neighbourhood. Sure, there's probably thousands of them in the tenements, but you learn to recognise familiar shapes as you live here. I know the woman who walks her dandruffy spaniel to the bottom of the road and back, three times a day with her feet encased in blue plastic bags; I know the skinny businessman whose suit is always in the checkout queue just before mine; the polite boy at the deli, the broken veins in the old men who smoke outside the Victoria Arms, the melancholy woman who runs the corner shop and each angry commuter on the 8.15 to Airdrie. I would have recognised her, on a street somewhere; I would have seen her back, her walk, and chased after her. You can't spend six years looking out for just one person only to have them living under your nose the whole time. You just can't.

But it makes sense. The flat looking over Beth's school. It made sense that she would expect me to fuck up, would be checking in, poised to intervene. God, what if she'd been planning to take Beth from the school playground one day? I spoke to the worried-looking splinter of a woman who ran the afterschool project.

'I'd like you to be very, very careful not to let Beth home with anyone claiming to be a relative,' I said. 'Nobody but me or her grandparents will pick her up from school from now on.'

'Mrs Leonard,' she said, insulted. 'We never let the children go home with anyone other than their designated carers.'

'Not even if they are visibly a relative,' I said. 'Not even anyone who looks like me. Especially not.'

I read and read and reread those forum reports, what her clients have to say about her. Every nuancè. They go back to 2007, so she's only been here for a year, and there was no trace before that. I copied them into a Word document and emailed them to my work address so I could go over them in the office when Norman was out at the site, or in the toilet, or talking to Moira, while Graeme slunk around me, avoiding my company but burning holes in my back as avidly as though we had actually had sex in that cupboard, rather than just recorded a ten second message.

That's how I fill my days until Friday.

I drop Beth off and stare up at what I think must be her window. There was someone up there, I was sure of it, a shadow. I bent in to kiss my daughter, hold her closer and harder than I usually do.

'Ow, Mummy! Stop it!'

My head is throbbing after the run back up the hill home, so I take a bath, and then, without knowing why, shave my legs and the stubble under my arms. A razor cut under my knee I hadn't seen in the water begins bleeding as soon as I step out, great scarlet streams of it loose on my wet skin and dripping onto the tiles, and I swear at myself, realise my hands are shaking.

An hour and a half later, I'm calmer. I'd spent a lot of time smoothing down my hair – it's complicated, doing that, and I'd had to concentrate – and applying all the products in my little-used makeup bag, one after another.

I put on my most expensive clothes: the red cashmere sweater, the pencil skirt, the leather boots. I put in the little gold earrings Gran had left me. I want her to see them.

And I leave my flat. I walk down the stairs like I always do, and steady myself on the rail at the top of the hill. The noise of my heels clipping the macadam as I turn left, like I always do, for the station and the cash machine, where I withdraw £200, feel it in my hand for a while.

Number 28 is a pale, new-build row meant to blend

in with the Edwardian tenements, although its poky, plastic-bound windows will always give it away even after the too-clean sandstone succumbs to the grime of the main road, of life. Its squares and angles are too neat; its fronts too flat. I couldn't live somewhere like that, somewhere with no history, although I imagine it would suit Rona just fine.

The buzzer at 2/3 doesn't have a name on, not like the others. I fumble in my handbag with one hand while pressing the button with the other.

A pause.

A click.

A crackle.

A scuffled, deep 'Hello', and I hold my new voice recorder up to the intercom.

'*Hello, this is Graeme Bain,*' Graeme says.

'Mon up,' says the voice.

She could be putting that accent on, too.

The stair smells of new carpet, of showrooms and polythene, of summer holidays chasing each other round floor-mounted tiling samples while Mum hissed Dad's name and he flushed. The door is cheap wood, varnished up. Gold bell. Brass knocker. There's a joke in there, somewhere, surely.

I ring.

Footsteps, coming towards it.

As it opens, I realise I haven't thought for a second what I'm going to say.

BACK

At first, the TV was just there to distract us from the billion questions and worries flickering back and forth in our heads. He had to go back to work first, then her, and we were no nearer to working out what was happening. I began to take up residence in this room when they weren't here, and I was haunted.

The health visitor said the baby was picking up on my anxiety, on theirs, that's why she wouldn't settle. That's why she cried. I could be changing her, or playing with her, or out in the park with her held safe in front in the pram and she'd sense Rona coming into focus and me tensing up, and it would scare her.

I made a promise to my baby, one day, to stop her crying. I promised her that when she was around I wouldn't allow myself to be haunted. So we improvised, the two of us, just like we always do, with the gleam of Mum's old television. I didn't have one of my own then, so at the first sign of trouble we'd lock the door and move smoothly down the concrete stairs to the living room, switch on and curl up, the small softness of her on me. She came to know it so well that just the noise of our door shutting behind us and the different smell of the stair would calm her.

We looked out together, from this blank room, into the lightweight opinions and overwrought acting of daytime telly, and soon she was annotating my sarcastic commentary with her own babble, and I'd talk right back, and we were in perpetual nothingy conversation all day, Miss Bethan Leonard, me, the telly. The health visitor said I should be proud of the progress she'd made, how advanced her speech was, and I swelled with it. Keeping myself limited to one space and concentrating everything into her was working out well for both of us.

They'd come home, first Dad, then Mum, and not ask why I was always there. He'd sit down beside us for an hour and when Beth grew able to she'd sometimes curl into him and he'd feel the same peace from her, I could tell. The telly stayed on, always, there for us, offering respite from having to think or talk to each other. The Leonards are a television family, now. We have our regular viewing schedule, agreed upon silently. In the first year, when a soap opera plotline would veer too closely to our lives – teenage runaways, missing girls, single mothers, violent divorce, abandoned children – one of us would cough, shift, press the remote. At some point we stopped doing that. We let them smart out, those stories, now. Just pressing the old bruises to check they still hurt.

Eight o'clock is bedtime. Probably it should be earlier, but the health visitor hasn't been for years, and it seems to fit us all about right. At 7.45, in the last advert break, I tell her to pick up her toys and she does, usually without too much complaint, scoops them into a box behind the sofa. Most of her toys have found their way down here. Then there are kisses, for Granny, for Grandad, and we climb the stairs, me and my girl. In the bad years I would only let Rona back in after Bethan was in bed, after I'd checked the sweet rhythms of her breathing twice, almost breaking with a love that worked as anaesthetic.

Mum came home early one day, before Dad was there, and she switched the telly off, and the pudgy, napping toddler on my lap shifted and moaned in her sleep. She spoke smoothly and gently and didn't raise her voice, and neither did I. It was time, she said.

'I never wanted this for you, love, but you're going to have to look for something. You know your dad and I don't make enough to support all four of us and both flats. Not indefinitely. And Bethan needs to go to nursery and meet other children. She needs to play. It's important for her.'

The guilt that had kept them supporting me, prevented this sort of conversation, slowly losing its adherence, peeling off. I was to ease myself back in. Just take a part-time job. A few hours a week helping out behind a reception desk. Odd shifts in a call centre. The same sort of work she'd done when we were small.

'But you have to come to me. You have to promise that. The second you start feeling any sort – any sort of resentment. Towards her. Or us, you know. Because it can come. The second, you talk to me about it.'

Knowing I wouldn't. Talk doesn't happen between us. Not like that.

Without the noise of the telly and a baby in my arms,

Rona had insinuated her way back in. She found her way everywhere. Monthly dinner with the girls always started with cold pulsing dread through the small talk, knowing that just after the main courses arrived and the eye signals had been exchanged, one of them – usually Samira, with her well-bred tact – would tilt a cautious head to the side and say something with long, sympathetic vowels like *So. Any news? How are you holding up?*

And what would I say? No, no there's no fucking news and there probably never will be? Shut up, I don't want to talk about this – in fact, I never want to talk about it again? Yeah she's back; can't you see her – she's sitting right there?

They were acting out of love and concern, those friends of mine; out of the perfectly logical deduction that anyone whose sister had gone missing would be frantic and worried and want to talk about it. She began to occupy the fourth place, the empty chair at any table when the three of us were out. So I stopped going out.

FORTH

The woman behind the chain looks at me, and I look back at her. 'Sorry, pet,' she says. 'I think you've got the wrong door.'

I must have, surely. Her big body blocks the gap, bulked out in a checked housecoat; the flat grey perm of hair that had given up at least two decades before curling round the door frame. A respectable wummin who probably had no idea that a house of ill repute was being run from her building, or if she did, would probably hiss at the gentlemen callers as they made their way back down, blank her hussy neighbour if they met in the street – and yet, the enamel numbers on the door quite clearly say 2/3. Surely not. Okay, pictures could be faked, but the men's drooling reviews had been unequivocal. *A right tasty piece. Total wee darling. Wanked thinking about her all week.*

She's still looking at me, but her eyes are darting occasionally over my shoulder, looking for something else in the stair. She's looking for the man, for Graeme Bain.

'Is this, ehm, Fiona's house?'

Her eyes narrow behind the thick specs.

'It is. And I'm telling you, dear, you've got the wrong door.'

'I don't think I have. Look, I made the appointment. I'm the half eleven. I just wanted to – I've maybe made a mistake.'

She looks at me again.

'I'll just go and have a word with her,' she says, and the door closes in my face.

A madam? I wonder. I think of glamorous older women in films, Dolly Parton's cleavage wrapped in silks and feathers, welcoming in leery cowboys.

The gatekeeper opens the door-crack again.

'What is it you're wanting?'

'Just to. To talk to her. Nothing, ehm, else. I've brought the money. She'll still get paid –'

The door shuts. Behind it, female voices tango blurrily. What sort of prison is this? Even from the crack, I'd been able to see that she was big. Strong. Fifty years ago, the sort of woman who'd have been scrubbing stairwells and lugging her family's washing back and forth from the steamie. Rona had always been delicate, small-made, bones like a bird. This woman could snap her neck under one meaty arm if she wanted.

They were supposed to be men, the traffickers, the pimps. According to the headlines. Sleazy men. Vice kings if they were British; monsters and immigrants if they were not. This was not a thing that women did to other women, this crime. It couldn't be –

The door opens all the way, and the auld monster stands there in her pinny in the hall, beckoning.

'Okay. In you come. But I'll warn you, she's no happy about this.'

I think for a second, I could take this woman right now, do enough damage to keep her distracted, scream 'RUN' – but what if she's tied up, or if there's someone else in there, some big bruiser paid by the pimp to keep her down –

My feet tread fluffy carpet and I'm ushered into a small living room. Sunny. New sofa. Mirrors on the walls, china ladies on a stand in the corner. Uplighters. A woman's face, suddenly, right in mine, its pointed teeth.

'So are you the one that's been phoning, then? For fucksake. I'll just tell you this one last time, doll, to your face, so you get the message. I am not a fucking lezzy. Okay?'

She's wearing a silky, bum-skimming dressing gown, sheer black, with something purple on underneath. Flip-flops, dark blue toenails and a deep, even tan. Dark eye makeup. She's the right height, right size, her hair has been straightened but was probably pretty similar to mine. I knew her from somewhere.

She's definitely not my sister, though.

Of course she isn't. Of course of course of course.

The room smells too sweet in the heat, is beginning to lurch about me. The woman who is not my sister is still going, her voice getting louder, her face redder.

'– absolutely wasted an hour of my fucking day. I mean, this might be a wee joke to you, hen, or it might be some great big moral crusade, but it's my fucking job and you've just cost me a perfectly good paying client, do you get what I'm saying? Do you? Ho. Doll, are you all right?'

I come to on the sofa. There's something cold and wet on my face and it's being held by the older woman.

'There she is. There you are, madarlin. Okay. Okay now.'

The dressing gown material shushes against itself as the younger woman – Fiona – comes to sit beside me.

'All right. Come on, I'm not gonny shout at you. But want to tell me what all this is about?'

'I'm really, really sorry,' I say. 'I've made a huge mistake.'

'Aye, you have. But you're here now.'

'I thought you were my sister,' I said. 'She's been missing for years, and your – your pictures on the West End Girls site. You look like her, a bit.'

She breathes out.

'You're not from the council, then?'

'The council?'

'Aye. The council. Their Ways Out hingmy. Ann was hearing that they've started coming round the women in flats now, as well. As though we were criminals or something. Buncha interfering auld biddies.'

'No. I'm not. I'm not from the council, and I'm – I'm not the police or anything either. I was just looking for my sister.'

The older woman comes in, presses a hot mug into my hand and leaves again. I hadn't even noticed her go the first time.

'Wouldn't care if you were the police. I'm no breaking any law here. Your sister – is she a working girl?'

My sister is many things, I think, feeling suddenly lucid. A flirt. A dancer. The beauty of the family. A fucking bitch.

107

'She was, about seven years ago. I've just found out. I thought I could maybe find her using the sites, maybe. Sorry. It was a stupid idea.'

She makes a soft noise in her throat.

'And was she working from a flat, or on the streets, like?'

'A flat, but it wasn't hers. Up north, in a wee village – she's not there any more. Obviously. Sorry.'

'And she looks like me?'

'Not really, no. Not now I see you. But in the pictures. And you were so nearby.'

'Is she called Fiona, aye? Is that why you thought it?'

'No. I'm called Fiona.'

Her breath comes out in something that had probably originally been a laugh.

'Right. You thought your sister was working, right by your house, and using your name to do it? I mean, I'm no saying it's impossible, but that's pretty fucked up, likes.'

She has a point.

'Look, I'm really sorry for wasting your time. I should go. I just – I just wondered. Her name's Rona. She looks like me, a bit. Prettier, but there's a resemblance. Do I look familiar to you?'

A thin wee smile for a second, and she looks away.

'*You* look familiar to me for the same reason I probably look familiar to you.'

She pauses again. I stare over at her china figures, elegant long white statues with skirts, no faces. She coughs, starts.

'Our kids go to the same school, doll. I've seen you at the gates before – I think your wee one's the year

108

behind my Adam. I'd appreciate it if this went no further, because if it does you and I will seriously have words. You get me?'

'You've got a child?'

'Aye. It does happen.'

'I didn't realise. Of course. I do recognise you now.'

'Yeah, well. You forget you recognised me. I'm a good mum. I'm doing this for him. Okay?'

'How does it ... Sorry. Do you mind if I ask: how does it work?'

She sighs, she nods. She breathes in.

'Ann through there,' she jerks a thumb back at the kitchen, 'comes round when I'm taking him to school, lets herself in and gets the place cleaned up. My first punter comes in at ten, leaves at eleven. Half an hour to tidy before the second,' she snorts, looks back at me, 'usually. Final one's out by four unless I've driven out to see one of my disabled clients, and Ann gets the last of it tidied while I go and pick him up from afterschool, get back to my flat. I don't work weekends or evenings and I'm trying not to do school holidays unless he's in playscheme.'

She's been looking over my shoulder, at the mantelpiece, at nothing, while she says this. Now she stops, fixes on me straight.

'I was a cleaner, doll, when he was a baby. Manky minimum wage work – getting up at four every morning, living with my mum so there was someone to watch him, knackered by 10 a.m. Scum under your fingernails that doesn't come out. But there areny that many cleaning jobs that only take up school hours, you know? And when they cut the benefits –'

109

She recovers, something in her face pulling back, returning to a place where she doesn't have to justify what she does. Not to me.

'They don't know about him, he definitely doesn't know about them, and nor do the teachers at that school. And I want it to stay that way, all right?'

She bares tiny, pointed cat's teeth at me again.

'As for having seen your sister about, I really wouldn't know. It's no like there's a working girls' social club or anything, eh. The street girls probably know each other, but I'm just a mum who does a job from a flat, that's all. The only non punter I see in my working life is Ann here, and she's just my next-door neighbour.'

'She's not your, ehm, pimp, then?' The word sounds stupid and prissy in my mouth.

'Fucksake, no! She's been round the block enough to suss the time-wasters out at the door for me – *most of the time* – she's a help with the cleaning, she's handy to have around in case any of them get funny, and she'll sometimes sit in and watch for a wee bit extra.'

'Watch?'

'Aye, watch. Some of them like that. Doesn't bother Ann. She's seen everything before.'

Surely this is all a dream. Surely. The room is still too hot, and I need air.

'Look. I really should go. I'm sorry to have mucked you about like this and wasted your time.'

'Okay. Did you say to Ann you'd brought the money, but?' She laughs at my face. Probably I was looking confused. 'No point pussyfooting about, is there?'

I nod, reach for my handbag.

'Just make it fifty, eh. You've only been here half an hour. That's the quickie rate.'

I count notes. The numbers, the famous faces and the smell of money are reassuringly familiar things.

She takes it and her face gets younger again, eyes bigger.

'And I've got your word you'll not let on? Imagine if it was your kid, if the other parents knew that about you. They're fucking snooty enough as it is, some of them. I'd have to move him schools, the teachers would probably get the social work involved. I'm a good mum, eh. And what I do – it's legal. I even pay my bloody taxes, for chrissake. Okay?'

'I promise,' I say, feeling the strange bend and flex of power between us. 'It's none of my business, anyway. Really.'

She sighs.

'Look, there's a group of them. Scottish Union of Sex Workers. They got in touch a wee while ago, looking for new, eh, recruits. The sort that want to get rights and that. Campaign, eh. Just attracting a load of trouble for themselves, if you ask me – anyway, they've got a website. I'll write it down for you. They have meetings every couple of months.'

At the door, Ann hovering in the background, she puts a hand briefly on my shoulder.

'I hope you find her, eh.'

It closes, and I run down the stairs, out of the main door, trying to get to the air. I lean over the gutter for a second, wondering if I'm going to retch, but nothing comes and in the end, after a couple of deep breaths, I just make my way back home again and the world goes spinning on.

Later that afternoon I see her at the school gates. Jeans, glasses and a ponytail, face scrubbed, hugging a little boy in a green coat close. We make eye contact, and she flinches for a second. I nod, smile a bit to reassure her, then walk inside to pick up Beth.

BACK

Okay.

We had opened the window the night before because we were drunk and the room stank, and we thought it was a good idea. The skin on my arm was pricking, cold, and the binmen had got me up two hours early. Trying to prise my numb hand out from under Simon's vicious cheekbone, I woke him up. He rubbed his erection into my hipbone twice, then wandered off to the bog to try and piss rid of it.

I was twenty-two years old, working in the most junior position there was at a publishing company. I took minutes in meetings. I got coffees. They were starting to remember my name. My nights were spent in a fusty flat in the West End with a privately educated final-year medical student. Simon had sublet me his spare room until one night – two bored, horny young people who hadn't been touched in a long time – we fell into bed. We read books on the sofa at night and sometimes went out to watch rock bands in sticky-floored pubs. We had a favourite café we got scrambled eggs in on Saturdays. We'd tried to have sex in the shower once, but the smell from the mouldy grouting put us off. That was my life. Not a grand romance, not a great job. But both of them had potential. I'd liked them, and I'd liked who I was beginning to be in them. Maybe if I'd had longer, one or both of them would have survived it all.

Beth and I eat cheese on toast for tea and then she reaches for the kitchen roll and, finicky, wipes every crumb away from her mouth before sending her tongue out – one, two – into the corners. She washes her hands a lot, too, doesn't like being dirty. I don't know where that comes from. *What will you say when she asks about her father?* my friends said, my parents said. I didn't know. I still don't, because she hasn't asked, ever. Maybe she hasn't worked out that she has one yet.

None of them ever ask what I'll say if she wants to know about her mother.

You're a *good* girl, Gran used to say, pressing a twenty-pound note into my hands like she used to do with coppers from her pension when I was younger. My mother's helpless, fluttering grip on me, her deliberate, teary glances. My father turned off, tuned out.

Okay, here goes.

The phone rang. I was at work and the phone rang, and it was my sister. I didn't answer it, my boss did. I was told it was an emergency.

'I'm at the station,' she said. 'I'm at the station and I need your help, Fi.'

I told her not to worry, I told her I'd be there in twenty

minutes. I took my lunch break early, not realising that I wouldn't be back to work for weeks, and then just to collect my stuff. I ran almost all of the way.

I had lived away from home for five years by then. In that time, Rona had phoned me three times, only ever looking to enlist my support in her ongoing war with our parents. She hadn't come to my graduation. She was not particularly attached to ideas of family, my sister, and she'd only turned up at Dad and Jackie's Christmas dinner under particularly heavy duress.

She'd put on weight. Big smudgy makeup eyes. Cheeks pink with the cold. Layers of textures and wraps all over her.

'Fi. Thank you. Thank fuck. Make it stop.'

As I went to hug her, I realised there was something in the way, something warm. And she thrust this something at me and it started to cry and so did she.

That evening. Simon was stunned, quiet, decamped to a friend's house, more because he didn't want to deal with the situation than because he needed space. I don't remember what we said to each other, or even if she could say anything, or if I could say anything worth saying, anything more than *oh hon. Oh hon, it's going to be okay*, which was a lie, one of those little lies you just tell people.

Because we had got to sleep that night at around ten, nothing asked, nothing revealed, just hugging and stroking and crying. I'd pulled out all the blankets we had and wrapped her with them. I'd counted out plastic spoons of formula, as though this was something I always did, trying to keep the panic out of my movements. I'd held both of them, separately, rubbing my thumb back and forth across their temples.

The baby started crying at about half four, before the sun was up. I padded through after a couple of minutes. The shape on the bed didn't stir, so I picked the basket up off the floor, and said something comforting and instant like shhh, shhh, let's let mummy sleep, and then I thought about what I'd just said, and who I'd just used the word 'mummy' to mean, and I wrapped myself in Simon's smelly dressing gown and carried her through to the kitchen.

In all that time, the fifteen consecutive years we spent breathing the same stale air of the same house, I don't remember once having shown her how to put on makeup or insert a tampon. I was an inadequate big sister, a geeky gawky spotty thing who didn't speak and didn't ever help her out, not that she needed it. Ever. Rona always had the skill of mixing with people, but coming out whole and still herself. If I was ready to tell her the secrets of our flesh she'd have heard them, and heard them some years before I had even known. I hadn't ever fulfilled a need, so she had grown up not to need me. Until now.

After I'd fed her, the baby stirred and fretted for a while, then I felt her growing limp, watched her tiny eyelids flickering down, felt her nuzzle in to the softness of my chest and fall asleep on me. And I just sat there, overwhelmed, as still as I could. I was scared that if I moved I'd spoil it, this huge, beautiful feeling. My breath slowed to match hers, and everything about us was perfectly in unison.

Half past seven. I needed to have a shower and get

ready. So we made two mugs of coffee and we went through to wake up mummy.

I know Rona, though. I know her. And so I don't know why I was surprised, as I pulled back that convincing-looking hump of duvet to find a faked body – blankets and a couple of pillows. Like a bad joke from a bad film.

I wasn't that old, not really. I might have managed three more years on the planet, but I wasn't ready for this. I wonder if it even occurred to her whether I would be or not. And I needed to pee, and there was a baby beginning to cry again because I'd gripped her too tightly. We went through to the bathroom, and one-handed I pulled out towels enough to make a softish mat. I laid her down on the floor on top of them, and then turned her away so she couldn't see me. All this seemed very logical. I sat down on the toilet and breathed in and almost collapsed. When I was done I washed my hands for about two minutes so that she wouldn't pick up any germs. I looked at my palms, my fingertips, and imagined them encrusted with bacteria, so I scrubbed and scrubbed. And the baby started to cry again. And I said oh shit. Rona left my flat sometime between two-thirty and four in the morning, six years ago. She left behind the bag she'd brought, which only contained the baby's things. There was a possible sighting at the bus station at 5.30 a.m., but the person wasn't sure. We had word that she might have been seen in Manchester four years ago, but it came to nothing. She hasn't used her bank account since that day, although she'd cleared it out three days before. Her phone was a pay-and-go, which hasn't been used; her passport hasn't left the country. I have no way of screaming at her, or slapping her, or telling her to take her fucking baby and give me my life back.

After that morning, Beth would only sleep on me. Not lying down. Not on anyone else. And I thought, fine. I'll take her. You've given her to me. But you don't ever get to have her back.

THINGS NICE GIRLS DON'T DO

Difficult to know, really. When does it slide over?
When do the walls rebuild themselves around
you? The first time you have sex for money?
It's not as clear cut as that, though. Before the
act, itself, you have to market yourself into the
mindset. Before that, even, you must have sensed
something flexing in yourself, a relaxing of the
codes you were brought up with, the easing away
of all those hard-drawn pencil lines around Things
Nice Girls Don't Do.

Does it start to happen the first time you laugh
at a dirty joke, because you mean it, not just
because you're being polite? The first time you
have a wank over a really dirty fantasy you've
made up, kind of thrilling at the fact that you're
getting off on things you couldn't talk about in any
sort of company? The first time you watch porn?
Bed a stranger? Because things have changed;
they're supposed to have changed, right, but

there are some things that women, nice girls, even liberated, modern women, still just aren't supposed to be into. And undercutting it all? It's still the assumption that we don't like sex, isn't it? That we don't like sex and men do, and male desire, as it concerns women, is shameful and oppressive.

Nobody ever talks about what nice boys do or don't do. We all know that men like sex. It's written into the laws of sex. A man who has sex and is paid for it is a lucky bastard. A woman is a victim. That's written into the laws of sex too. Because what underwrites these laws is a truth universally acknowledged: that every act of heterosexual sex (a thing, let us not forget, that happens to a woman, upon her) fundamentally damages the female partner in some way. Is there a time, ladies, when you might have gone to bed with someone who, perhaps, you weren't particularly attracted to? A little act of mercy – you wanted to make him feel better, maybe, or you were just horny and didn't really mind who it was? Or has an act of sex happened upon you that you didn't really enjoy? It went on for a bit too long, maybe; your mind wandered. He seemed to be having a bit more fun than you. He just wasn't very good.

Perhaps you barely remember these events. Perhaps you shrugged them off and haven't attached any significance to them since. Wrong! Under the laws, the sex laws written out by Those

Who Know Better, these happenings of sex upon your person will have scarred you. Irrevocably. You are now damaged, because of them. Or you are if you accepted payment for any of them.

And this is what gets to me. Why can't we save the worry about damage and trauma for those who actually have been damaged. If you blur the lines between my job, or some boring sex some bored girl had once with the old guy from the shop because there was nothing else to do in her town – if you keep on maintaining that these things inflict the same amount of psychic damage as actual acts of rape and abuse, you trivialise those acts. And you make criminals and victims out of people who are neither.

And as long as we keep those laws, the men and the women both will think and act like that. So here we are for now, perfectly legal outlaws.

Today, my camera and I are just in the mood for a very simple leg shot, in my favourite stockings. Sure, fishnets are a bit of a hooker cliché, but look at me. I'm making them work.

Tags: <u>politics activism sexism</u>| **Comments (17)**

THREE

PUBLIC

The strangeness of another person in the bed. I didn't sleep well, all that alcohol dehydrating me, every alien mutter and twitch causing me to start, awake, on the defensive. Realising all too late that I haven't done this since Bethan for a reason, half hoping I'll wake up alone, before Mum brings her upstairs, before she opens the door and –

Daylight, the grey beginnings of it on the backs of my eyelids. The body beside me easing up by centimetres, small calculated movements of limb. The shufflings for clothes, the agonising hushed noise of a zip done slowly. Then the nearness of warmth, then a hand on the side of my face, stroking my hair away from the temple, gently. A small, dry kiss on my forehead, then the door opening, closing. I'm pretending to sleep, so I don't see any of this, but the smell of sadness left in the room is almost overwhelming.

There's always a kid skiting about the dance floor on its knees at a wedding. If its parents are too pissed by the time the dancing starts it runs the risk of being mown down, or being hit by a flying shoe, because there's always women kicking their high heels to the side and dancing on in their stocking soles at a wedding.

There's always country dancing at a wedding, too, so of course there's country dancing at Heather's, the bride first up, pulled by her kilted nothing of a husband in her strapless floor-length white number, same thing every bride's been wearing for at least the last ten years, since sleeves went out. It's on a figure like Heather's that you really see the limitations of this style, because her tits are too big to stay in easily, are already bulging and rushing out the sides, under her arms. That bride could have your eye out in a Strip the Willow, I'm wanting to whisper to someone. But hey. It's her Big Day; her chance to be a princess, and how will people know you're a princess if you don't dress exactly like all the other princesses.

The band plays a loud chord to get everyone's attention. It takes me a second to realise that it's actually my daughter on the floor, and I need to rush up and grab her off, two great dirty marks on her white lacy knees.

'Look at you, poppet. Look at what you've done to your pretty tights. You're all over dust! Mummy's goingty havety wash them for you! Come away and sit down for a bit or you'll get hit by the dancing.'

'You're speaking funny,' she says, and she's right, I am. I'm talking clucky and my accent's got stronger, manhandling her off the floor in big, plump mother hen movements.

The other mothers we used to meet at Tumble Tots, the first-time mothers, would always stop themselves at something like that. Oh god, I sound like my mu-um, they'd moan. Tonight I appear to be acting the part of a mother. Like a pantomime dame, I find I've muttered out loud.

'Mummy, I think you're drunk,' Beth's saying, solemnly.

I mean, the thing is, I look good tonight. I know I do. I've done everything that could possibly be required of me. I had a hairdresser iron down my frizz so it hangs sleek, and my dress is new and blue, dark blue, and I've borrowed Mum's pearls.

It works well.

That fuzz sinking in already, the bit when you feel the welch and warp of the booze around the limits of your vision; that's happening. I noticed it beginning about half an hour ago and decided to go with it, not to counter the acid sharps of my cheap white wine saliva; another glass, another.

That guy is looking over again. Everyone else is staring at Samira, the sharp green of her dress and the brown of her skin snapping your eyes to attention in a sea of whey-faced bores in pastels; she's been snapped up for the first dance by one of the two anxious-looking friends of Ross's who flitted about her during the buffet. But that guy is looking at me, peeking out from under his weird baseball cap, which actually looks pretty good with a suit, shy, turning away, looking back again.

All the girlz from the hen night are getting up, Claire's big face turning, nodding at the man beside her, just as dull and awful-looking as she is. I have to say, I think it's a bit off of Heather to have put me and Samira at different tables, I really do. It's not like either of us know anybody here, although Samira's clearly not bothered by that. I had one of them and her boyfriend beside me, and it was a bit embarrassing because I was sure she was the one called Kelly, but she wasn't, she was the one called Andrea, and it even said it on a card in front of her, although I didn't notice that until I'd called her Kelly twice and Bethan's right, I am drunk.

I'd had a chat with Heather's dad, Beth straining and twisting at my arm because she was only interested in staring at the bride as hard as possible, trying to absorb those fake Swarovski crystals by osmosis. Beth hadn't quite got over the hug Heather had given her earlier, bearing down on her, cooing.

'You look great, Heather.'

'Aw, thanks. And doesn't Beth look cute, eh? Who's this beautiful girl, then? What a pretty dress!'

Heather is transformed, in Beth's eyes, at least, into a sparkling, scented celebrity. A brief, paranoid flash, from nowhere: did it seem like she'd made the fuss over Beth so she wouldn't have to talk to me? No, no. Probably just drunk.

Beth's in a foul mood, too. She's decided to start whining. 'I want to da-ance. Mu-um. I want to da-ance!'

I smile at the older couple sitting it out on our table, one of those mother smiles. I pick her up on my lap and crush my arms in round her.

'I want to da-ance with Aunty Sameeeera!'

'What we're going to do is we're going to watch Aunty Heather and Aunty Samira just now, and see how the dance goes. These dances can get very rough, and I'm not wanting you getting hurt in there. Can you see Aunty Heather and Aunty Samira? See where they are? What we'll do is, we'll go and dance alongside them if it's not too fast. We'll go in and dance at the sides.'

He's not dancing, just looking over again, the guy in the cap. The idea that people are still attracted to me. One person, but still. I could kiss him, later. I could pull him away, find a quiet corner of the hotel, a corridor somewhere, push him up against a wall, take him home –

A tug on my bodice.

'Mu-um! You're not watching!'

The immense rustling that fights with the music as everyone turns, a mass rotation. Like a machine in Dorothy Perkins formalwear. The spinning is the best bit, actually, all those skirts, all that hair birling round, the men hemmed in at the centre with their arms raised like cranes. Heather's got her free hand jammed across the top of her bodice, her flesh spilling, bouncing; but Samira is just flowing, the loose, bright green material of her skirt like conical water, her fanned hair rippling. She's spinning so quickly you can't see her face.

'Look at Aunty Samira,' I whisper to Beth, and she does, she's silent.

Something suddenly clicks between her and her partner as she lands back into him, and he pulls her out from the filed shuffling circle and into the centre, where they dance a faster polka all the way round the circumference. You can do that, in a Gay Gordons, you can break out of the circle if you're both clever, if you can feel it in the music. They take turns about, leading. Her forward, two three. Him back, two three.

I sit Beth up on the table so she can still see, tiny Samira in danger of disappearing behind all these anonymous bodies. She gets up on her knees, and I perch up there beside her.

'Aunty Samira's like a fairy princess, isn't she?' I whisper. She nods.

'Your breath smells of being drunk.'

Flat disapproving tones just like my dad's – actually, no. It's exactly the sort of put-down Rona would have used.

The older woman at the table gives me a funny look and I smile another mother smile at her.

'Would you mind watching this one for a second? I just have to go to the loo!'

PRIVATE

There are days when I feel like I've stepped through the looking glass. That the days before that hen weekend – before that conversation in the ski slope cafeteria, before the smell of tea on Christina's breath – that they were part of some other life, other world. A world where I was aware of prostitution, course I was, but only in the same way that I was aware of, say, accountancy.

Now it's everywhere. It's like being given goggles that allow you to see another dimension sitting on top of the one you live your normal life in. Rona used to love this story when she was a kid, in a book of world fairytales one of Mum's friends brought her back from somewhere, about the djinns. Indian spirits, living their own spirit world, one that lies on top of our own. There were connections between the worlds – at certain points in time and space you could feel the djinns' presence, and most people, fearful, would call them ghosts and run. There were those who could see the second world for what it was, though, and now I'm one of them.

I turn on the telly and a former teen pop star in expensive lingerie, playing at being a high-class call girl, fellates a lollipop and flirts with a handsome man who just happens to want to pay her. Old school friends on Facebook post links to furious online debates, where angry voices claim that all prostitution is violence against women. Shopping on Saturday, I pass a face that I know on the high street, and my mouth smiles, says hello, before my brain kicks in and it's Holly, the young one, the Audrey Hepburn wannabe who shows her face. Her thickly linered eyes crease in panic as she realises I can only know her from one place, is turning, scuttling off into a thicket of sale racks. I watch her go, delicate moves, bad posture, and she turns a hardened stare back over her shoulder, gives me the full fuckyoulookinat.

They've been here all this time, walking amongst the city, running their businesses, doing their things, completely unseen. This other world, off grid, and Rona a secret corner of it. I heard implications in every stranger's conversation on the street, every wisp of the radio from the office next door.

'No darling, don't touch yourself there. Only dirty girls do that ...'

'A third prostitute was discovered dead in Suffolk last night ...'

'No better than a common hoor, so you are ...'

'Of course, Jonathan thinks I'm prostituting my art.'

'Patricia Arquette plays the tart-with-a-heart ...'

'MP's £500-a-night romp with vice girl ...'

The late-evening gloom of having worked too long means I catch a taxi back from work. I use my own money.

'D'ye read in the paper? They're knocking down the old Sanctuary Base down the road from here,' says the taxi driver. White hair, moustache. Grandfatherly. 'Crying shame that, if ye ask me. Crying shame. Used to work this area, back in the nineties, ye know. I wis in the polis, for a time.'

'Were you in the vice squad?' I ask, thinking of grim-faced cop dramas from the telly.

'No, no. And I don't know that they would call it a vice squad, the ones whose job it wis to charge the girls. Mibbe now, right enough. Aye, they might well now. No, we were just a unit working the area. The girls trusted us cos they knew we wereny goingty book them; they'd tell us things, not the others. Some of those others, they just treated they lassies like they were scum.'

'The, ehm. The punters?'

'Naw. The other polis. Shovin them about, screaming abuse at them, you dirty slag this – aw, sorry, mind ma language, pal. Ye just needed to treat them wi respect and they'd gie it back to you. They'd tell us about any dodgy punters they'd had, help us out catching the odd dealer; in return we could sometimes fix it so if the lassie went down an alley wi a punter, we could turn up just after he'd handed the money over, but before she had to do onything for it, chase him aff.'

This whole other world. I take my daughter to school, go to work, sit at a computer for eight hours, pick my daughter up, go home, eat dinner in my comfortable flat, watch television, pick over celebrity gossip on websites that make me feel bad about myself, sleep.

'At the end of the day, ye know, it's somebody's job.

It's always goingty be somebody's job. And you've got tae respect that. This is how some of them support their weans, make their money, and there are laws set up that dinnae even treat them like they're part of society?' He pulls up at my flat. 'Sorry, pal. Here's me been talking all that time. Ye have things that just get you up on that soapbox, eh?'

'No, not at all,' I say. 'Thank you. Really.'

'Anywey, that's how I came to leave the polis.'

It's like the world won't let me stop thinking about it. The next morning the condoms in the car park drains seem terrifyingly important.

XXX

I'd started spending a lot of time on Swedish Sonja's site; the one who I thought was almost definitely that blonde, foreign girl from the protest, Anya. Her blog was updated daily at the moment, short, righteous bursts of anger directed at the council, at the demolition of the Sanctuary; longer musings about what this meant, about why street girls were such easy targets for the sort of disgust that underpinned this kind of action. We think of them as victims, not real humans – disposable people, she'd say. She talked a lot about stigma. About the way sex workers were regarded in society. 'Sex workers' was what she said. Not 'prostitutes'. Sometimes, she'd call herself a 'hussy' or a 'whore'.

It confused me, this website. The force and blast of her intelligence shining through, the fact that it was designed on clean lines, no jiggling GIFs of sexy silhouettes, no garish fonts, no adverts; that the photographs in her 'private gallery', the one you had to hand over your credit card details and pay for a week's access to, were beautifully shot and lit, framed in unusual ways, felt more like art portraits than pornography, even as she spread her legs, displaying the sharp titanium bar through her clitoris, head thrown back in apparent ecstasy so you couldn't make out her face.

I poured out the last of the bottle.

If you were that smart, that conscious of the world; possessed of that much taste and dignity. Women who had these sorts of choices, whose brains gave them that, they didn't have to do this. Didn't have to sink this low. *Rona* didn't have to, for fuck's sake. Shot from behind, her pale-bleached crop rumpled, the shiny black corset nipped in on her waist. Bare arse, bare legs, long, sturdy platform boots. The white-golden length of her, from raised fingertips to heels.

Close up on a breast, the nipple pierced through, sturdily obedient to the bolt.

Short black nails paused mid-air, flicking powerfully over her genitals. There's nothing crude about this show; none of those stretched holes, not the smallest wisp of exploitation about it. She's just very, very beautiful, and aroused, and she wants to share that with me –

'Mummy?'

Bethan, nightmare-mauled, at the door. I swipe the screen away in time, rush to zip my jeans back up, stand, confused. The room is thick with sex and guilt and I hope she's too young to detect either. I curl round her, warm her back to bed, stroke her damp temples till she drops off. I shake myself; I think, what the hell are you doing?

I need to bring this under control. This new world; it all exists in my head. I find out more and more every day, and I don't talk to people about it. It's going to become too big for me. Maybe it already is.

There's a contact email address on her site.

Dear Sonja,

Really, really sorry for the out-of-the-blue email, and a hundred apologies if I'm wrong. But were you one of the protestors outside the RDJ Construction office last week?

If not, I'm so, so sorry for the intrusion. Please ignore me. If I'm right, though, we met there. I was the employee who brought you all tea.

You have no reason to trust me, I know – especially not me – and I appreciate that you probably won't respond to me.

But, the reason I'm writing to you: the weekend before your protest, I discovered that my sister, who has been missing for six years, was a sex worker before her disappearance. It's taken me some time to come to terms with this. I'm not sure I have, still. Anyway, I found that out, then I came to work and saw your protest, then I read your blog. And I think I'm on the wrong side. I'd like to not be.

I would very much like to buy you lunch at a convenient time, and talk some things through with you. I understand that you are a very busy person, but I think, given my job, I could be of some use to your campaign.

I will understand absolutely and utterly if that isn't possible. I just need to help in some way. I need to talk to other people in this world. I need to understand.

Yours,
Fiona Leonard

At the end, hitting send before I could sober up and take it back, I was gasping. I opened it up again immediately, read, reread. You fucking idiot, I rail against myself through wine-blacked lips in the bathroom mirror. Of course she's not going to respond. She can't confirm what her real name is. You've fucked it. You've fucked it, I'm muttering.

But oh. Actually writing it down and sending it away for someone else to read through me. Seeing the words take clean black shape.

I woke up on the sofa, soaked through with sweat. High electric fuzz in the room. Beth had come through, switched her morning cartoons on.

There was a new email, sent at four in the morning:

Fiona,

You are right. I wouldn't usually answer this sort of email. It goes against all of my better instincts. But you were kind to us, and you didn't have to be, and so I'm going to take a risk and trust you. Please, please be deserving of my trust.

She was quite happy to meet me for lunch. She suggested a restaurant about fifteen minutes from my office, expensive enough that nobody from my office would be there. I couldn't really afford it, but I'd manage, somehow. How does Tuesday afternoon, 1 p.m., suit you? she said.

The world throwing a rope out, letting me grab it. A pull. A connection with something, anything.

She'd signed it Sonja. I'd need to remember that.

PUBLIC

It's cool down here, refreshing. I rest my hot forehead against the marble wall between the Ladies and Gents doors, just for a second. The wedding party creaks and thumps into the next song upstairs, louder as someone opens the door. Footsteps.

'Oh. Are you all right?'

Claire. Nosy bossy Claire, makeup already melted off her scarlet face, although to be fair she does look all right in the plain blue bridesmaid dress. Nothing fancy, but all right. She sees it's me as I turn round and the concerned smile ossifies.

'I'm fine. Just trying to cool down. Hot up there, eh?'

She nods, moves past me to the toilets, uneasy. After a couple of beats I follow her in, lock myself in a cubicle, listening to the stream of her forthright piss and a hearty, unabashed fart. She rustles. She flushes. The lock clanks open and the tap water runs as she scrubs, thoroughly. Oh Claire, you're so healthy. So clean. So good.

'Claire! Hi! Well done up there, by the way!' Samira is here, suddenly, outside.

'Oh, thanks. Thanks. Lovely to see you. Nice dress.'

'You too. Well bridesmaided.'

Weak laughs all round and the door slams. I flush, come out. Samira is patting her shine away with powder, the contents of her makeup bag strewn between the sinks.

'Has she gone?' I pull a comedy face round the side of the toilet door.

'Oh. Hiya.'

'Oof. Hot. You looked bloody gorgeous up there, by the way, Meer. Loving that frock.'

'Mm. Thanks. Bethan looks adorable. Anyway, I'm off back up –' and she's trying to scrabble her various powders and liners back into the bag.

'I mean it. Gorgeous. A cut above that buncha boring fuckers up there! I mean, a bit predictable, trotting out the same old dances, but it's a by-the-book wedding, eh. And you were making it work for you.'

Her face in the mirror freezes for a second, and her rich voice is clipped-off at the ends when she speaks.

'It's tradition, Fiona.'

'Yeah, but you know what I mean. It's just so safe. Exactly what you'd expect at this sort of wedding. I'm not getting at Heath –'

'I've been having fun. *I've* been enjoying it. Maybe you should get up there and dance yourself instead of just leering away at everyone else. Even your six-year-old is having a better time than you.'

I'm not sure what's going on here. My brain sloshes, cheapwinely. I try to make a joke.

'S'one of the pleasures of a wedding, though, the bitching about people's outfits!'

137

She whips round, not talking to me in the mirror any more. 'Could you just say something nice? Just one thing?'

'Eh?'

'D'you know, I'd actually been meaning to meet you and talk about this after the hen weekend. But I thought, nah, just leave it. You probably wouldn't even show, anyway.'

'Meer, what –'

'I was going to ask you to apologise to Heather. You ruined that weekend for her.'

'I – what?'

'Okay, I know, I know the choice of place was a bad one for you, but you didn't make much of an effort to get on with it. Couldn't hide your contempt, could you? And you were downright rude to poor Claire –'

'Poor Claire? Everyone hated her, Samira.'

'*You* hated her. And you made sure we all knew it. You made such a big point of not going on that fucking bike ride, too, and then you just disappeared, turned up an hour late to the pole dancing class and wouldn't look at anyone! I mean, why come at all, eh? Why come at all. Me just left there, all of Heather's workmates staring at me, wondering what kind of freaks she called her oldest friends. Why come?'

'For the same reason you did. For Heather. Loyalty . . . the past.'

'Loyalty? You've been staring at Heather's dress with this horrid little sneer on your face all day. I know it doesn't fit her, hey, but what if she'd caught you? How would you feel, seeing someone looking at you like that on your wedding day? Just couldny be bothered to hide it, could you? Don't think I'd want your sort of loyalty at my wedding.'

'Did Heather – did Heather say this to you? Did she send you?'

'Of course she didn't. Heather? Come on. I saw it with my own eyes well enough. My own eyes saw quite enough to get this angry, on my friend's behalf.'

Samira's face, this redness, this spite. I don't know it.

'Listen, I had a lot of stuff going on that weekend that I have no intention of apologising for. Bethan was ill, for a start, and as you said, the place isn't exactly good for me. As you don't have kids you won't understand . . .'

'I won't understand how hard it is for you, as a single parent, yeah yeah. Know what? Heather and I have done nothing but understand. For six fucking years. We've offered you solid gold support whenever you've needed it, and we've done that without expecting anything, *precisely* because we know how hard it is for you. We've reminded ourselves of it every time you've turned down invitations, cancelled on us at the last minute, or been fuck all use when we've had problems of our own. But after that hen weekend, I think we both realised we're gonny have to admit to ourselves that you just don't actually like us that much. In fact, you don't like anything, do you?'

Upstairs, applause as another dance finished. Footsteps on the stairs outside.

'Come on, Samira. Of course I like you. I like you fine. You've maybe had a hard week. We've both had a lot to drink. This isn't you talking.'

'How would you know this isn't me? How would you know? Because we send each other emails once a month, see each other what, three, four times a year? Because we went to school together a decade ago? People have kids all the time and they don't just *disappear*!'

'Yeah. Nice choice of words there. Thanks.'

'Oh, for – you know what? Let's just leave it, eh? Let's just go. I won't email you again, and you won't respond two weeks later saying sorry, you totally meant to get back to me sooner. This isn't a friendship. Let's just leave it.'

She scoops up the last of her makeup and storms out of the door, nudging past the person who's coming in, muttering a quick sorry.

'Ah. There you are.'

It's the older woman from the table, the one I'd left Beth with. 'Your daughter was wondering where you'd got to.'

My big flushed face, in the mirror.

PRIVATE

The café Sonja/Anya picked is written in a language I don't speak; there's some sort of awful thrashing girly punk music on the stereo, all the people in here are thin, and there's something strange about their clothes, their hair. Some sort of structured fashionableness that I just don't get. It's not like those places Samira likes, where even though the people are all thin, they're gelled and groomed and manicured. Sure, the, ah, *clientele* are still beautiful, but there's something just *off* about the cuts of their fringes, their shabby knitwear, their makeup.

Their spectacles, where they wear them, seem to have been cast off by Deirdre Barlow from *Coronation Street*.

She is keeping me waiting.

The abrasive music stops, fades into something lisped in a Scottish accent. At least it's quiet. I look at the menu. There is no meat on the menu. Beside me, a boy with the raggedy beginnings of beard types into a silver Apple laptop, his face glowing with electronic purpose. Under masses of eyeliner and coiled, streaming black hair, a girl picks at her phone and a salad, intermittently.

'Hi, what can I get you?'

A tired, skinny girl with a faint twang of something Australian, a stripy T-shirt, a pen behind her ear.

'I'm waiting for someone,' I say. 'Just a white coffee, please.'

'No probs. Just to check – you know we only serve soy milk here?'

'Oh this?' says a woman's voice. 'Vintage. Fleamarket in Brooklyn.'

My lunch hour ticks away.

She is definitely keeping me waiting. Playing trust games.

Look at these people. Look at them closely. I'd assumed at first glance that they were all art students, loafers, killing time in their inoffensive vegan play-rooms, their dressing-up boxes, before having to come out, blinking, into the Drag and assimilate, join the rest of us at our imitation plywood desks, our wheezing black computers. But they're not. There are wrinkles here, grey streaks. And they aren't just here for pleasure. The woman with the salad takes a call.

'God, darling, if they won't move on the matched funding we're going to have to ask them to reduce the number of performers they're flying over. Could we ask a local choir to do the choral number?'

Across the way, there's a couple I'd assumed were out on a date, the boy with thick specs, sharply quiffed like he's Buddy Holly or something, the girl with fake eyelashes and a fur coat draped over her seat. But he's asking her questions and there's a digital tape recorder sitting between them. She's got a tiny blue sequin stuck on the end of each flick of her eyeliner. It's a Tuesday lunchtime.

I'm suddenly overwhelmed by the idea of other people my own age, getting out, experimenting, making things new for themselves. Not just surrendering to a box and a screen and the first steady income they're offered. A great long line of twentysomethings, thirtysomethings even, with their eyeliner and their strangely cut pretensions and their vintage and their Brooklyn and their laptops and their busy, busy lives. The instinctive sneer and bristle in me melding into something else, and I'm ashamed of the thin, plasticky material of my supermarket-bought work trousers. That's what I'm aware of. The slight itch around my thighs and knees from it.

But then. None of them have children. I bet none of them have children.

'You are Fiona, aren't you?'

Suddenly, she's just there, in front of me. Eighteen minutes late, my phone says. She doesn't mention that she's late; there's just a small smile, guarded, and I'm rushing the words out, absurd supplicant I am.

'Yes, yes. Yes. Thank you so much for coming. Thank you for this.'

'You did not have too much difficulty finding this place, then? I like the atmosphere, the vibration in here? Also, it is very difficult to find good vegetarian food anywhere else in the city centre.'

I nod like I know this, like I understand the way these sentences are sliding into questions. I am very, very conscious suddenly that I don't understand anything, and we look at each other for a second before I realise the onus is on me to talk, explain my purpose, juggle, dance, be something.

'So. Yes. So. I just – thank you for coming. I just wanted to, needed to talk this out, with someone. And. I found your website by accident – I was just looking for people who had been writing about the protests at my work, you know. Eh. Because I wanted to understand it from another perspective.'

This is what I had decided I would tell her. I thought it would go down a lot better than saying 'since we met I've become obsessed with you to the extent that I'm now confused about my sexuality'.

'Through there, through your blog, I found the punter forums, and the various sites the other girls use, and . . . Well, with all this in mind, and knowing what I know about my sister, that new knowledge. I'm just – phhh.'

I exhale, trying to indicate confusion, blown minds, appealing to her with my eyes.

That guarded smile again, but before she can say anything, the waitress comes back over, and while Anya/ Sonja is ordering, I take the chance to actually look at her properly. With her clothes on, face unblurred, hair longer and smoother than in the pictures. Her tiny waist is obscured by the bulk of a battered-looking leather jacket that she hasn't yet taken off. Tight jeans tucked into glistening biker boots – all hard angles, but at her neck, under the jacket collar, there's a flash of something ribboned, soft, red.

They're both looking at me. It's my turn to order. I'd planned jokes in my head about supposing they don't have any steak, then, but stop myself just in time. There is a thing in my eyeline on the menu, a grilled courgette and pine nut salad. I would absolutely never order that, ever, usually. I point to it.

Anya/Sonja, this enviably cool woman, her accent and her fine, clear skin, leans across the table at me, as the waitress nods, smiles, scurries off.

'So, my god. You have been on the forums?' She sighs. 'We are very public, all of a sudden. If I am on the forums, I can look up and there will be a counter, it says there are maybe fifty, sixty "guests". People who don't register, they just watch. Like ghosts, you know. Silent. Maybe getting their kicks, who knows.'

Her laugh is a deep hoot, one burst.

'People are fascinated by us. I think you must be feeling very confused now. I can understand why you would need to talk to someone.'

'Yes. Yes. I thought I could maybe, maybe if I pay for lunch, you might, there might be questions I could ask you?'

'Maybe,' she says. 'It depends on the questions.'

'Of course. Of course.'

'Okay,' she says. 'Ask questions.'

'I think the main problem is that I don't understand. I don't understand how my sister – how anybody ends up doing this. How you – you're so intelligent! I've read your blogs. You're not even writing in your first language and it's fluent, well reasoned –' I'm tailing off because her eyebrows are knitting disapproval.

'You are new to this, and you are in grief, I think, so I give you this one pass, just once. But please understand, I do not answer this sort of question.'

I want to just look at the way her lips move, how sure she is of the words they make, and so I almost miss what she's actually saying. Almost.

'This question, it comes from a place where for a

woman to work in the sex industry, it's shameful, wrong. I don't think like that. I know many, many women who don't think like that. It is maybe not your ideal job, but you have to realise that you don't know anything about what it involves, what it really is. What you know is horror stories of rape and powerlessness, that teach us to prize our virtue, to keep our legs closed, that nice girls don't do things. What you think you know is stereotypes about drug addiction, about desperate girls out there on the street. About the bodies that they find, whenever some fucking lunatic goes on a killing spree. And yes, this is all there; I am not so stupid as to say to you these things don't happen, and that they are not awful, but it is not a complete picture. This is not my life. It may not be your sister's life, how it was. If we are going to talk, if we are going to be of use to each other, you are going to have to accept this one very vital point that I am making; that what people call "the sex industry" is not always, not completely, a bad thing. That just because a person sells their sexual skills, it does not mean that their life is – bam! – forever ruined.'

Her eyes are sharp on me.

'Do you think you can begin to consider that a possibility, for the time that we are here? There is no point to us talking otherwise, because you will be always in the back of your head pitying me, maybe wanting to rescue me, and therefore nothing I can say will have any sort of effect on you.'

I get the impression she has had this sort of conversation many, many times before, the weariness in her voice. And I think that I'm going to need to accept that, in order to accept the brick-built reality of this woman sitting in front of me. I'm going to need to try and think like that, just for just now, just to get through this.

'Yes,' I tell her. I try to sound like I'm as firm and confident as her, like I'm an equal. 'Yes, I can do that.'

Her eyes. We look at each other for a long time. Glaciers move. Species die out.

'Good. That is good,' she says suddenly. 'I am not going to sit here and pretend to you that it is all wine and roses, that every woman who does this job does it because she just loves sex. We make a distinction. There is a world of difference between someone like me, who has chosen this job, actively chosen it, who made an informed decision, who works from a flat or hotel rooms and manages her own advertising – you know, there is almost nothing the same with me and someone who is forced out on the streets to fund her addiction. I mean. I do it, still, because I need the money. I am a student! But the vast majority of the world, they will run the two lives together in their heads, you know? It all comes under the word pros-ti-tute, and oh, that means bad things.'

The waitress is hovering by, staring, two big plates in her hands. They come down on the table suddenly, like she's frightened of us, and this woman, my lunch companion, this person whose clitoral piercings I've seen but whom I don't know what to call – Anya, Sonja, hey you, anything – flashes me a killer smile.

'That salad,' she says, pointing over at my plate, 'is amazing.'

She's right.

I don't know what to ask. I didn't really think through a list of questions.

What – what do you do? With the men?'

Stupid. What do you think, idiot? She's patient with me, though.

'There are limits. There are some limits. French kissing, for instance. I remember when women who did that were looked down on. Nowadays, most clients want the "girlfriend experience". Even the ones who come to me, with all my piercings and my leather, mostly they are just wanting very sweet, plain, vanilla sex, lots of kissing, lots of cuddling afterwards. It's just like, making contact with someone. Touching base, hah?'

That hoot of a laugh again.

'Touching base for an hour. Just reminding yourself that the world exists again, and that you exist within it, hey. I think we all need to do that sometimes. But no, there are limits. I mean, I have a client who is eighty-five. A regular. And I am not going to French kiss him. I'm not. He knows the limits. And there are the awful ones, yes. The really unattractive ones. You get around that by just giving them lots of oral. You can shut your eyes, for oral.'

I want to ask something about the sex, the act of it. Your body, and another one, one that you haven't selected, aren't attracted to. The feeling of sex of that sort. I want to know how she does it, and to try and phrase it in a way that does not imply that I think she's degrading herself. I want to try and think that myself. Instead I ask her how this all started for her. She tells me about when she first moved here from her home country. She doesn't say what her home country is, and I think of her website, the Scandinavian Sonja headline.

148

She was trying to fund her first degree, which was in Manchester, and I start again, think Manchester, always Manchester.

'So, I think, I'll get a bar job. Easy, no? Pfff. Bar job. Hotel job. None of these pay me enough money to cover my big fat international student fees, let alone my rent, my living – no rich parents for me, hey? I have to do it myself. So this girl on my course, she says well, there's a job going where I work, and where she works is a massage parlour.'

I must be looking blank, because she expands, in the sort of voice used for tourists and fools.

'A massage parlour. The men come in and pay for a massage; it's very cheap. Anything they want extra, they have to tip for. You wear a tight T-shirt. They maybe have a sauna afterwards. You know? And hey, it suited me. It offered a way to make the sort of money I needed to be earning. This system, you know, it will keep us trapped if we let it: pay you the smallest amount so you never dream bigger. Me, I got out.'

It isn't what I meant. What I want and never manage to ask her is the stages in her head she'd had to go through to turn herself into a person who does this. Maybe I'd never know; maybe it was all there in the first thing she'd said. The gaps between us sag.

'Then I come here,' she's saying. 'And I am looking around for decent fetish clubs, for my scene, and I don't really find anything too much here, so I started thinking, surely, the desire is still there. I think there must be some demand for it, no? So I set myself up as an independent. As a specialist. I had no desire to go back to working in a parlour – there were two older women there who were great to me, who talked me through it, but it can be a very bitchy environment, that one. I prefer to go solo, ha? But it was a valuable apprenticeship. It helps to learn things in a controlled environment.'

The strange taste of the food, oily and green and new.

'You need to learn to trust your instincts in this job. You always sense when something's wrong. It's something that grows, the more of them you see. I am a buddy: you know we have a buddy system, we women? We help each other out. Any new girl coming up who makes herself known to us, she always works with a buddy. There is always a person on the other end of the telephone. My new girl, she phoned me up once and said, Oh it's great, I've got my first booking! Two guys, in a Travel Inn! and you have to grab her, you know, say no, no, no. We don't do that.'

She's not – I don't think she's deliberately trying to shock me. If I am shocked it's a by-product, of the distance, is what it is. Yes.

'Do you think you could ever be with a man again normally, though?'

'Ho! That is another one of those questions. I have a boyfriend.'

Obviously my face didn't hide that one. She screws up her mouth in imitation of me.

'Oooh. Look at you. This is not what you were expecting, hey? We have been together for a couple of years. He knows my job, knows everything. He is cool with it. I pay him to come and be my minder with new clients. Just to check. You can have sex with different people and have it mean different things. I like sex. I have sex *normally* with my clients. Yesterday I came four times and got paid for it, more than you'll make in at least three days.'

The exoticness of my salad. Of the people in here. Of the frankness. This whole other world, other way of thinking and being. It sort of bursts out of me when she says that.

'I just – you don't really, really think this is an – an uncomplicated choice, do you? A job that anyone could do? I just – sorry. No, I'm sorry.'

I expect this to be the final straw, that I've lost her now, that she's going to get up and stomp out, those thick-soled boots beating angry holes in the floorboards. I'm surprised that she leans towards me, says more gently than she's said anything: 'Listen. I have a little half-sister at home. She is eleven. And that is the question they always ask, all the anti-prostitution campaigners, would you want your sister to do this, your daughter to do it? And I think about her growing up and going with some of these guys. The really sleazy ones. And I say no, to that, in my head. It is not hypocrisy, though. Do you see? I can want to do it for myself, still, and not for her.'

I think about the only other person I've had this sort of discussion with, 'Fiona', the not-Rona. Her defensiveness, the need to apologise her way out of the job to another woman, and it hits me that this is absent here. This is shamelessness in the true sense of the word. She exudes it. And it's why I'm compelled to keep looking at her.

'So,' she says, finally, as soy milk curdles in my

151

second coffee. 'You mentioned being able to help us. Do you mean, you will be able to give us information from your work? Are you, basically, proposing to spy for us?'

My brain has been racing through so many things I trip, need to double back on myself. Yes. I suppose that was what I meant. 'I have answered an awful lot of your questions. What do you say to mine?'

The air sharpens into transaction.

I'm forty-five minutes late back to work and I creep in like a traitor. Norman, sour faced, turns cold eyes on me. I seek absolution at Moira's desk.

'I got a call from the school: Beth had got into a wee squabble with a classmate. Nothing big, really – bit embarrassing. It knackered my phone battery, taking the call, so I couldn't phone you, let you know. I'm going to make the extra time up this evening – my dad's picking her up. Is Ian angry?'

In my head, I apologise to my little mouse-girl, to her quietness. Moira is not sure that she believes me. 'He's still down at the site with Graeme, love.'

'I never got a call from the school with my Toni. They'd tell you afterwards, when you picked them up. If anything was wrong.' Norman releases his proclamations into the air with the gravitas of a preacher, and I'm not sure if he's calling me a liar or berating a feeble newfangled school system, but I find myself turning round anyway, snarling at him.

'You maybe never got a call, Norman, but I'm pretty sure your wife would have done!'

I type up data from manila files for the rest of the

day, in self-righteous silence. I give myself a paper cut. Occasionally I flip open my diary, stroke the new entry for next weekend. Scottish Union of Sex Workers meeting, Glebe St. Hotel, 4.30 p.m.

PUBLIC

'I hope she wasn't too much trouble,' I'm saying, auto-pilot mother.

My face still feels hot from the encounter with Samira. I'm absolutely not equipped to deal with the judgement of the older woman from my wedding table just now. She's marched me up from the bathroom in silence, back into the body of the kirk. Samira's over there at her own table, talking with forced sparkle at the man she danced with earlier, radiating shrapnel.

'No, no, we had a lovely chat, didn't we, Bethan? Bethan was telling us all about what *her* wedding's going to be like.'

This is all directed at Beth, for Beth. Not for me.

'She's going to have a pink dress! Can you imagine? A pink wedding dress. And all the bridesmaids – thirty of them – are going to be covered in sequins, and there'll be a pink horse to ride in on. Isn't that right?'

'That sounds lovely, Beth.' I'm picking up the woman's sugary tones.

'Anyway,' and her voice drops back to flat,

contemptuous adult-speak, her head flicking at her husband, who is holding their coats, 'we need to be going, now. Nice talking to you, Bethan!'

'We should probably go home too, darling. It's getting late.'

'It's only late because you were gone for *ages*. And I haven't been allowed to dance yet.'

'Mummy's not feeling so well, Bethan.'

'Is it because you're being drunk? I wa-ant to daa-nce! You sa-aid I could da-ance!'

'I'll dance with you.' It's one of the henz, the one from our table. Andrea? Andrea. 'If that's all right with your mummy?'

She gives me this smile, this smile of camaraderie and friendliness, this we're-in-it-together smile, and I almost burst with something, almost want to hug her or cry or something. Then she bows low to Bethan, who is star-struck again, and asks her formally for the pleasure of the next dance.

I get out my phone, tap out a hurried rescue message to Dad.

Come and get us. Please. She's overtired, and it's a nightmare.

Thirty seconds later.

Okay.

I sink back into my chair.

'Eh, hiya.'

It's the guy, the one in the weird baseball-cap-and-suit

155

combo. I must look a state. I try and manage a smile, anyway.

'Mind if I sit –'

'Go for your life.'

I reach for one of the not-empty bottles on the table, shoogle it at him.

'D'you want a glass? We've still got half the bottle over here.'

'Eh. Are– No. Sorry. Thanks. Sorry to bother you, man. It's. Eh. You just look like someone I used to know.'

Could be.

'My sister,' I say. 'I look like my sister.'

'Is your sister called, eh, Rona?'

'Yes. Yes. Oh god. Have you seen her?'

I'm pouring out those words, but my brain's ticking, thinking, he called her by her actual name, so he wouldn't have been one of her – punters.

'When was the last time you saw her?'

I can't make that come out casually. It's not small talk and he knows it, pulling back from me as I realise I'm clutching at his wrist.

'Oh. Eh. Dunno. Must be, like, five years ago, easy. More.'

'Five? Are you sure?'

'Naw. Hang on. Ehm. It would have been before I left Edinburgh. Probably more like seven, eight years, now.'

I let him go.

'Sorry. Sorry. Rona – Rona went missing, six years back. We haven't heard anything since then. Sorry. That must have come on quite extreme, there, eh?' I do a little chuckle to try and brush it off; he stares like I'm madder than ever.

'No, no, it's understandable. I didn't know that. That she was missing. Sorry, man, eh. Fuck.'

He sucks the sweaty air in through his teeth, reaches for the wine bottle after all.

'What, eh. What happened? Was it when –'

'When what?'

'Naw, eh. She just kind of vanished one day, wasn't around any more, didn't answer her phone and we all thought she'd just gone back home or something, man. Had enough. I'd hoped so. Was that it?'

'When you were living in Edinburgh – did you know her well?'

He wishes he hadn't sat down, I can tell. I'm making him uncomfortable, because that's what I do, tonight.

'I did. Aye, I did. I was pretty fond of her, eh. She was nice. She was a nice lassie.'

I resist the temptation to snort. *Nice* is an interesting word, I want to say. Swallow it, swallow it. He could have said no, there, fudged it, walked away from the intense drunk in the low-cut dress and back to the warmth and skirl of his family. He didn't.

'Did you know she was – how she made her – sorry. Sorry. Hi. What's your name?'

'Ally,' he says. 'Ally McKay. Cousin of the groom.'

'Fiona Leonard. School friend of the bride.' And we shake. 'Right, Ally. Did you ... When you knew her, was she working as a – as a hooker?'

Not the word I was going for. Just the one that came out, sitting there between us, full of what feels like judgement. A tut, in the air by my head. Claire and her boring man are making for the exit, coats in arms, and it seems she would like me to know she disapproves of my language. I gulp wine, probably not from my own glass, ignore her, try and suppress that burn that happens when you realise someone doesn't like you.

He doesn't look surprised, though, this Ally McKay, with his pleasant, handsome face and his trucker cap.

'No exactly, eh. No, like, the girls you'd see in the street. But aw, man. That's really shit. Sorry.'

He'd really, really cared about her. His face, like someone's emptied it out. I do the gentle voice, the police officer delivering bad news.

'Were you her boyfriend?'

'Ach, we had a fling. A wee tiny thing. I was more into it than she was, eh. We were mates though, I thought. I'd tried to –'

'Did you see me, Mummy? Did you?'

Andrea is being led by the hand back to the table. She looks worn out.

'Yes. Yes, you were beautiful, sweetheart. You're such a good dancer.'

Beth nods, pleased, and looks up at this Ally McKay.

'Hello,' she says, and she is so inescapably Rona in that moment that I almost break up and I can see he's thinking the same.

On the table, my mobile flashes.

Outside.

My father is not a garrulous communicator.

'Stay here,' I say to him. 'Please. Five minutes.'

I have her coat picked up quickly before she knows

158

what's happening. We're out, fresh air kniving my skin under flapping chiffon layers.

'Oh look! There's Grandad! Am I going *home*?' She's disgusted.

I open the back door. Dad is in his pyjamas in the driver's seat.

'Dad, I want to stay out. Please. Can you take her? Put her to bed at yours tonight?'

'Fiona, come on. I'm ready for bed myself.'

'Da-ad. It's my best friend's wedding. I never get a night out to myself. Please. Please.'

The car drives off, Bethan's fury steaming up the windows. Lying seems to come much more easily to me these days.

Inside, the party is already fading and it's not even 10 p.m. yet. The band is on a break; couples cling to each other and sway limply to the love ballad on the PA. Heather and Ross are nodding at an elderly relative. Samira and her gentleman friend are not in the room.

He's still there, though. Ally McKay, where I left him. Frozen to the spot, maybe.

'She looks so much like Rona, eh, your daughter.'

'That's because she's Rona's daughter.'

It strikes me that I haven't admitted that out loud to anyone for ages.

Poor fucker. I don't know that he can take much more of this. He's living out a concentrated dose of my last six years. I pat his arm.

'I need something stiffer than wine. There's a bar next door. Fancy nipping out for half an hour?'

PRIVATE

I'd been expecting, I don't know. An amphitheatre rustling with PVC and lipstick, maybe. Pillars. Glitter. Something.

Rentable meeting room in a chain of budget hotels. Corporate-purple carpet, pale wood-toned plastic on the tables. Projector with laptop connection up front, paper cups of coffee from the machine out in the hall. On the door, a printed-off sheet of A4 said SUSW. A table outside with a man behind it, starched shirt, spiked hair, so clean-shaven he looks like he can't actually grow stubble.

'Hi. Sorry, don't recognise the face – what's your name?'

He's friendly, but I have no doubt I will not be allowed into the room if I don't pass.

'Fiona Leonard.'

'Ah ... yup. Sonja's accounted for you.'

'Sonja', then. I wonder if any of them know each others' real names.

The spikes of her blonde hair over someone's

shoulder, in the front row. A skip, somewhere near my stomach. About thirty people in the room.

Why am I always surprised by how ordinary they look? Do I expect them to be perpetually in fishnets, lubed-up, damaged and hollow? Yeah, I've realised. I do.

Jeans. Shirts. Business suits. Jumpers and skirts. Sure, there are a couple of girls up the back with suspiciously buoyant breasts, teased hair, false lashes, but for the most part these are just the sort of women you'd see in a supermarket. Not sex dolls, not desperate smackheads. There are men, too, three of them, well groomed, two younger and the one from the door, probably around forty. Pimps? I think, rent boys?

There is so much about all of this that I don't know.

I take a seat in the back row, by the two heavily made up girls. They're about my age, run their eyes quickly, appraisingly, over my clothes, find me wanting, and settle back into their conversation.

'And have you seen her new set of pictures? I was like that, eh, hello! Photoshop!'

'Yeah, would those be the ones where she's claiming she's a size ten? In what universe? Or does she mean an *American* size ten?' I glance around, checking to see if any of the ones whose blogs I've read are here, trying to tease out the faces from behind the pixels. Holly, the young one who I saw in the street, Holly is absent.

A tiny woman in her fifties with elegant, streaked hair and a very beautiful face stands up, facing the rows of seats. She has the presence of a schoolteacher and the talk in the room ebbs its way to a respectful silence, at which she smiles.

'Good afternoon, and thank you all for coming.' Her tones are strong, clear, almost accentless.

'Not a problem, Paulette. Anythin for you, ma darlin.' A smoker's cracked voice from the row in front of me. Paulette smiles at it, moves on, delicate, professional.

'We're going to hear from a number of different speakers today, and I trust that you'll treat them *all* with the respect our speakers are accustomed to. First up is a familiar face both to our meetings and to the, ah, local media recently: Suzanne Phillips, director of the city centre Sanctuary Base.'

Suzanne Phillips stands up, and I recognise her as the motherly woman from the protest at my work, the one the papers had outed as a 'former masseuse'.

'Hello, everyone. I'm going to keep this short and – well. It's not going to be very sweet, I'm afraid. As you've probably read about by now, if you weren't actually there, we staged three simultaneous protests the week before last: outside the council offices, at the building company who'll be in charge of, em, of knocking us down, and at the vacant warehouses next door to Sanctuary Base, which the Jackson Group intend to be the cornerstone of their new ... Well. *Leisure* complex.'

A laugh I don't quite understand moves softly through the room.

'To be honest,' Suzanne says, 'we were always on borrowed time with the council. You know, they encouraged the street workers to move into the Drag, originally: made them easier to contain and keep track of than when they were spread out up east, and there

162

were no residents around to complain. But they can't pretend it hasn't buggered up the whole idea of people investing in the area, or of business coming in.

'They've been wanting to get rid of us for a while – they cut the tiny wee bit of funding we'd got from them at the first sniff of credit crunch. The council have made it clear they're going for zero tolerance on prostitution. The girls are making their International Financial District look a wee bit shoddy, eh? No offence, Ms Buchanan.' She smiles thinly at the woman sitting beside Anya, no, Sonja.

'They didny say there wis somewan from the cooncil here,' mutters the troublemaker in front of me.

'They've cracked down on everything, the fines have gone up again as much as they can manage, and the women are getting heavy treatment again. We're nothing. Skeleton op these days, surviving mostly on volunteer help for the last few months. And I think we're going to have to concede defeat.'

A few hisses through the room. The girl beside me is picking at her nail polish.

'They're going to finally move us out of the Sanctuary Base on Thursday next week. Obviously, we're going to resist that right till the end, and it would be great to see as many of you as possible helping us out there, but I understand about other commitments. The police are already aware that we're planning a peaceful protest. There may well be photographers there, too.'

The woman sitting in front of me pipes up again, turning her head around to bring us all on side with her. Late forties, a creased, grizzled face.

'Suzy, you know I'm all for it, doll, but I'm just not

163

goingty run the risk of ma weans or thur teachers seeing me in the papers. Aye?'

'Thanks, Helen. I appreciate that. I know it's going to be difficult for most of you, and I also appreciate that we're asking a lot. Anyway, anyone who is interested please have a quick word with me after the meeting. That's all. For now. Thanks for listening.'

The applause is well behaved, downhearted. The older woman, Paulette, stands up again.

'So. We've got a bit of a surprise guest here today. We've spoken a lot about the campaign to close down the Sanctuary Base recently, and so we were delighted when the council proposed that a representative from the service they're intending will replace it come down here and speak to you. That representative has, of course, promised that anything she hears today in this room will be kept absolutely confidential. Now, I would like you all to join me in welcoming Claire Buchanan from the Ways Out scheme, and I can trust that she will be allowed to speak her piece. There will be an opportunity for questions at the end.'

'Ooooh. Got awffy formal in here aw of a sudden,' says Helen in the row in front of me, to no one in particular.

The woman sitting beside 'Sonja' – stubby, unstyled brown furze, navy blue suited shoulders – is standing up, turning round.

Claire. Heather's now sister-in-law Claire. Claire of the cycling and the time management. Claire who I'd last seen just over a week ago leaving the wedding, tutting at me.

This country is so small. So small. So crazily small.

164

She's gripping a set of cue cards in both hands, presumably to curb the shaking. Her neck hooks over them, and she reads word for word, in what's almost a monotone, phlegmy with nerves.

'I – Hem. Hem. I am here today on behalf of, and as one of the leading figures behind, the council's new Ways Out scheme. We believe that no woman should have to suffer the degradation of prostitution for a minute longer.'

More muttering.

'Oh, you and me are going to get on just fine, honeypie,' Helen hisses, her whisper deliberately audible.

Claire goes on, staring down at her speech as though nothing had happened.

'The Ways Out scheme will replace the current and soon to be demolished Sanctuary Base with a mobile unit, staffed and maintained exclusively by council employees, operating in the city centre. The mobile unit will have a greater degree of flexibility and be able to cover a wider area than the Sanctuary Base was limited to, and will offer exactly the same sort of refuge to any women forced into prostitution in the area. Women coming on board the mobile unit will become part of an active monitoring scheme to make sure their, eh, way out of prostitution is clear and accessible.'

Anya/Sonja stands up. She raises a hand out of courtesy, and talks gently, but there's no sign that Claire has acknowledged her, or that she was waiting for acknowledgement.

'So, street workers have now got to demonstrate that they want to leave the industry, before you'll offer them basic shelter, free condoms or allow them access to the Ugly Mug sheet? They must be monitored? Like tagging animals or criminals – sex offenders, no?'

'Sounds like the fuckin Joab Centre tae me!' Helen says, barking out a laugh, looking around again to share it.

The girl beside me calls out.

'Look, no offence, right, but is this all going to be about wee junkie street walkers? I just do not see how this stuff affects those of us who work for agencies. Or even like youse independents. If the punters canny get it in a red light zone, they're going to have to come and find us, aren't they? More work! Good. Business. Sense.'

She taps these three words into the side of her head like Morse code.

'I just do not see why I should put myself out for a few wee smackhead part-timers who – and let's no mince words – wouldny give a flying fuck if the shoe were on the other foot.'

Claire tries a smile, for the first time.

'That is a very good question, and I'm very pleased you asked that.'

It's the first spontaneous thing she's said.

'I am here to say to you today that the Ways Out scheme is not just open to those women forced to engage in street prostitution. We're here for all of you. We want to get every woman in this city who is exploited out of the sex industry and into proper, dignified work. We're offering genuine, practical solutions. I'm going to leave some business cards here today, and anyone who wants to contact me about registering with the

Ways Out scheme is more than welcome to do so.'

An explosion of voices.

'You sayin ma work's no dignified, eh?'

'How does any of this make it actually safer for the girls on the street?'

'What about the men in this industry, Ms Buchanan? What about the men who used Sanctuary Base as a shelter? Sex workers aren't just women!'

'You sayin ma work's no *dignified*?'

Wide, flat, boring Claire. It's been so easy and amusing to dismiss her in my mean little head that I'm surprised to find myself actually feeling sorry for her now. Because I can see that she genuinely believes she's helping, however spectacularly she's misjudged her crowd, however bad a plan it is. The last time I saw her, she was tutting not at me but because she'd heard me using the word *hooker*. She must have thought it was derogatory.

She wants to make a difference in the world, Claire; must go to her work every day feeling that she's actually doing something. And it's not like I can say that.

Right now, though, she's just battling to be heard.

'At present, in its first, trial, form, the Ways Out scheme is just open to women –'

'Oh! So you're just going to give up on those teenage boys round the riverside, then?'

The woman called Helen is on her feet, suddenly, drowning out everyone else, twisting like a snake unleashed, going in for the kill.

'Aw, I know you, darlin. I know you. What ye've no realised is that we're ontae you. You dinnay think of us as real people, do ye? Oh, aye, ye'll say you do. But

167

what you're meaning is, we're aw poor wee victims. Intit? You dinnay think we're capable of living our lives properly. Too damaged. You canny admit that whit we do is work, or that mibbe, actually somewan might *choose* to do whit we do! So fuck off –'

'Helen, I'm going to ask you to sit down.' Paulette, from the front row.

'– with aw yer victim shite, yer sexual abuse survivor statistics –'

'Helen! SIT DOWN.'

'Helen, nobody's said anything about sexual abuse.'

'Aye, but they will. That's how they justify it, eh. They make oot like wur aw fuckin damaged, eh? No sane. Cos we couldnay be. Cos nobody sane wid be doin whit we do. No respectable wummin. No *dignified* wummin.'

She's marched up the aisle and is pointing at Claire now, chipped pink nail polish in her face.

'Now. You wanty talk tae me about workin the streets? Cos uh've worked the fuckin streets. I've been there. Huv you? Huv you got any experience of that, *Mizz* Buchanan? Or huv ye actually fuckin spoken to anyone who's actually fuckin done that joab? Cos mibbe we could tell you somethin about it, eh no? Mibbe you should give wan of us a nice fat consultant fee fer actually tellin you something useful, eh? I'll tell you this wan for free, sunshine. I might no be zactly sane, eh, but I'm a human fuckin bein daein ma best with whit I've goat. An see these lassies here? They fuckin know zactly whit thur daein.'

She breaks off, relaxes her arm, turns a beautiful smile on the chairwoman. 'Sorry, Paulette. Awfully sorrah abaht that, old fruit!' Her vowels stretched into caricatured Queen's English. 'One hud noat realised the sort of, scuse-ma-french, *scum* one would be associatahn with at this here meeting today! One prefers only to associate with ladies who do what one would call dignified joabs! Ta-ta, now!'

She saunters out, head high, one wrist limp, and the door crashes shut behind her. The room breathes. The girl beside me gets up.

'If that's everything for today, yeah? I just don't think this affects me, and I've got a lot on my –'

Anya , Sonja – whatever she is – stands, finally, turns round, a sharp half smile on her face, no mirth in it.

'Okay. Right. It *affects* you, Sabrina, because this is the first stage of a two-pronged attack. I am right, yes, Ms Buchanan? Ms Buchanan looks surprised that I know this,' she says, smoothly, playing the crowd for that small ripple of laughter, and it seems true; the back of Claire's bushy head has jerked, suddenly.

'The Ways Out scheme is only the start. I have it on very good authority that the council are about to start lobbying Parliament to criminalise the purchasing of sex. That means your clients and my clients. Because they think this will stop that nasty, wicked unspeakable thing they are calling the Sex Industry. Any woman –'

A cough from the audience.

'I'm sorry, Douglas. Any *sex worker* who wants to report a crime will have to first grass up their client list. They're basically going to war against us, whilst saying out loud that we are the victims in all this. Helen was on the right track, there.'

Claire has gathered up her things.

'I'm so sorry but I'm going to have to cut this session short. I'm not at liberty to discuss anything other than the trial stage of the Ways Out scheme today. For follow-up enquiries you'll need to go through my office. Thank you.'

The scuttle of an outraged, virtuous member of society.

I'm still riding all that pity for her, so I try and smile as she passes, realising only too late that she's staring, shocked, at me. Her face does goldfish mouth for what seems like a laughably long period. I wonder, almost idly, what sort of repercussions this is going to have.

Anya is shouting after her.

'You are not going to stop the girls going out there on the street! It's just going to mean they will not be so able to select their partners! Surely, you should look at complete decriminalisation and –'

Claire snaps back to life, turns, and flees.

The door slams, again. The girl beside me whispers to her friend.

'Well, that was a productive one, yeah?'

Anya is still in her seat, heaving with anger as they begin to file out. I hang around as the room empties, limp pockets of small talk not managing to cover the atmosphere. She looks up and smiles at me, still tense.

'So. Interesting meeting, huh?'

'A headfuck.'

'Ha! You should try it being on the inside. Let's introduce you to Suzanne. Suzanne! Suzy! Come here.'

Suzanne comes back into the room, stops short when she sees me.

'This is the one I told you of, yes? Do you remember her?'

That nice smile again. I can imagine it being very easy to relax around Suzanne.

'The girl who made us tea. Hello. Yes, I remember.'

Anya waits until the room is completely empty, until the older man, Douglas, picks up his clipboard. They make swift eye contact and he nods, seems to understand she needs the privacy, leaves us to it.

'So, Suzy. This is Fiona, and she thinks she can be of some use to us.'

'Maybe. Possibly. I'm not sure that there is anything. But I could try.'

Suzanne nods, looks me up and down.

'You're working in admin at RDJ Construction, is that right? So you're just in the office the whole time. Have you ever actually been to Sanctuary Base?'

I hadn't.

'Got time for a visit this evening?'

PUBLIC

Even though we're both traumatised people who you couldn't possibly call normal at this point in time; maybe because of that, Ally McKay and I run out of the wedding reception hand in hand, stifling what cascades into full-blown nervous cackles when we're out in the street. Saturday night screeches and flails around us, its sense of money let loose.

The bar we choose is quiet, though, smell of frying, ketchup still on the table, music turned so far down that it skips atmospheric and goes straight for insubstantial. The lights, we realise only after we have brought our first round to the table, are too invasively bright for us to pretend anything in.

Whisky, gin. Drinks strong enough to shoulder you through bad news and sad stories, but not likely to leave you with hope. And yet we pick them, and sit there, the closeness vanished. Ross's cousin: suit, baseball cap, eye bags, wrinkles. Probably, though I hadn't realised it under Heather and Ross's disco ball and heart-shaped spotlights, at least my age, maybe older. Rona's sister: playing-it-safe dress, pearls, hair frizzing back out, makeup melting. A failed first draft of the final product. That must be what he's thinking. Oh, what do I care what he's thinking.

'So.'

'So.'

We sip.

'Sorry for pulling you out like that. I'll not keep you away from your family long. It's just. I've – we've, my parents and me – we've not heard anything about her in so long. Anything you can remember is a clue. Sorry. God. I feel like I've ruined your night now.'

'Mate! Stop apologising, eh! It's no your fault. And, know what? Anything I can do. Anything I can tell you that would help you find her, eh. That's good stuff. Right?'

'Right.'

There's a fine gold chain round his neck, tucked under his collar, behind the bowtie. I like him for all of this, for not just renting a kilt. I like him, Ally McKay, for the baseball cap, and for his smile, and the ease he's trying to put me at. I like that he's called me *mate*.

'So. Begin at the beginning, eh? I used to be a, like, a sound and lighting engineer. In clubs, around Edinburgh. I did it at college, but I'd already learned the basics when I was about sixteen; one of my mates was a good DJ, eh, and because the club owners wanted him in, they'd let me in as well, as long as I didny drink anything. Sorry, man, eh. This is probably too much information!'

'No. No. You're setting the scene. It's good.'

'Yeah? That's what I'm doing? Magic. Right.' He catches himself in the act of displaying an inappropriate

173

amount of enthusiasm, given the subject matter, winds his face back down accordingly. I drink. I wish I'd ordered a double.

'Anyway. Long story short – I'd been doing it for years by the time I met your sister, eh. You'd see the various nights get popular, like, the DJs picking up followings with the crowds and either getting so big they'd pure loop –' he's waving his glass in a circle to illustrate, splashes the table '– it out of the circuit, out of there, or they'd stick, sink. Same thing with the promoters – see, because it's Edinburgh, most of the boys – an I'm no being sexist here, eh, it wis always boys – running the clubs were rich and at the uni, or at least had been. Fresh up from private school, coked off their tits instead of going to class, eh, that sort of hing. And I'd be socialising with them, because, after you finish work, you want to go for a wee bevy or something, man. And there were always after parties – the dressing rooms of the bigger clubs, or somebody's flat. Some of these posh dudes had amazing flats, eh? So. You get to know all the folk; all the ones who are hanging out with the promoters who are, eh, *in* at that point. An it's all cyclical, eh. Some of them stayed, but so many of them were students – like these kids only thought it was worth marketing their clubs to their own demographic, eh?'

He's too friendly for the bitterness of that laugh.

'Anyway. They'd move on. They'd all move on, eventually. And that's what I thought it was with. With Rona, when she went.'

'I think I'm going to need another drink for this bit. And so are you.'

When I come back, with doubles, he's looking seriously at me, like he's made use of his thinking time.

'Are you sure you want to hear this, man? I mean, I'm probably not going to be able to give you any definite, eh. Leads. *Leads*. Get me, on a case.'

'I want to hear this, Ally. Really. I just need to know something, anything concrete. Somebody else's idea of her. It's just been in my head too long.'

'Okay. This isn't going to be easy, eh. Rona was, was just another lassie hanging around this one guy, Jez, his parties. Now, Jez had been a student, but that was maybe five or six years earlier, like, back when I was starting out. So he was probably about twenty-six, twenty-sev– fuck. That's younger than me, now. At the time he seemed, you know, the Man. The big man. He'd been running clubs in the city for years, had all these London connections, so he could always get the guys, you know, like the guys you'd hear about four months later they'd be remixing Kylie? You'd seen them at one of Jez's clubs first, eh.'

I'm trying to look like I understand.

'No a big clubber?'

'Not really, no. Not even, really, before Bethan. Just, like, the indie disco or something.'

'Okay. I'm going to talk civilian speak for you. Stop me if I get too technical, eh. Rona. Rona had been working in a bar run by this pal of Jez's ... Actually, mate, I should write these things down for you, eh.'

We have an eyeliner pencil and a table-top dispenser full of shiny napkins.

'So, Rona was working in this bar called Dee-Lite on George Street, and I think it's now called The Grand or something, but it's under the same management. Somebody there would surely know who you were talking about. Anyway, as far as I could make out, eh, Jez had spotted her there and got her to do some modelling. Not like that! Although I widnay put anything past that fucker. But she was – she's a gorgeous lassie, Rona, eh. I mean, you know that.'

I know that.

'So he's got her, like, in this tight T-shirt with the club name stretched out on her – aye. She was on the flyers, and the posters – she became, like, the face of Jez's clubs for a while, eh. Part from anything else, it's good for business to have lassies that good-looking at your club. So, of course, she started coming back to whoever's house afterwards, when we all did. And that's how we got talking.'

'Was she doing drugs, Ally? I'm not going to, ah, judge you or anything. I'd just like to know.'

'Coke. We were all doing a couple of lines of coke; all that lot did. Pills, sometimes too, but it was mostly coke. Thing is, I know that sounds serious if you're – if you're not that experienced with it.'

'If you're a square like me.'

'Come on, man. You're fine. What I mean is it sounds like a lot, but actually Rona was always pretty restrained with it. You never saw her off her face or making a fool ay herself or anything. You never got the impression she was desperate for it. I dinnay think it was an addiction or anything. No like some of the others. Yeah. Some of those lassies.'

He drinks deep this time.

'Just to make it clear, man, this is a long time ago for

176

me. Coke is a fucking horrible drug, and the folk on it are even worse. The old Jack Daniels here is as hard as it gets now, and even then, only on special occasions, eh.' He raises his glass, gloomy. 'My wee cousin's wedding.'

'Oh god. Sorry.'

'Will you stop apologising!'

He's smiling, though.

'Anyway, so, me and Rona got friendly, at the parties and that. A lot of the time I couldny quite believe it, that a girl that pretty was actually hanging out with the sound engineer when there were full-on DJs and that in the room, eh. She was like that, though. She was the sort of person who'd always take the time to make you feel special. Like she cared.'

I swallow the splutter rising up in me again. I smile. I nod.

'She was maybe just that good with people, but I never felt she was snubbing me or anything, eh. Of course, a lot of the time at these parties we'd be the only ones there who hadn't gone to private school, likes, and that kindy bonds you a wee bit. We could have a private joke about some of the accents on the go in there or whatever – I mean, I always try never to stereotype anybody, eh, but a lot of the time it really was that sort of, *fwah fwah fwah fwah*! Ken?'

I'm wondering if I've ever actually met anybody from that sort of background, or if I'm thinking of comedy show caricatures.

'So maybe that's why we kind of ended up – eh. In bed together, a couple of times. Sorry, Fiona man. Your wee sister. Eh. Anyway. It was lovely. We'd maybe go and get a breakfast the next morning together, that sortay thing. Read the papers together, always a wee kiss on the cheek before she left me.'

He's smiling away at something beautiful in the corner.

'It was never anything serious, like. I mean, the lassie was out of my league for a start, and only eighteen. But we became friends, even out of the parties. I'd come and hang around her in the bar before my shift started, and maybe I was sort of there cos I was hoping for a bit more, but she never minded me trailing about after her. Lovesick fuckin poodle, man, but she'd always pour me a pint on the sly. I just wanted to see she was all right, eh. Then she started hanging about with this, this lassie, Camilla.' With gin on the brain, it takes me a while to sort this out, so he's started talking again.

'Camilla is my daught– is Bethan's middle name. Says so on the birth certificate.'

His eyebrows shoot up under the cap.

'Mate. Oh. Right.'

He drinks.

'Listen. I maybe shouldny –'

'You're going to need to tell me, Ally.'

'Okay. But I'm buying this round, first. Naw, your money's no good here, man.'

PRIVATE

Sanctuary Base is the bottom floor of a huge red-brick warehouse towards the bottom of the grid. The warehouses on either side are already covered in scaffolding and RDJ Construction signs: scaffolding that I'd put the purchase order through for. It was beginning to get dark.

Suzanne had tucked her arm in mine as we walked down the street together, making conversation: the age of my daughter, the ages of hers, recommendations for music tutors if Beth ever wanted to learn an instrument. She'd shown me pictures of them, made me show her mine. When we arrive, though, she disengages, becomes taller and more businesslike as she pulls a computerised fob out of her bag, swipes it at a small black box by a nondescript side door adjacent to the main entry with its friendly fonted sign. There's a people carrier with the same logo done small, on its flank, parked in at the kerb.

Anya had kept quiet and a couple of paces behind us: I'd needed to turn my head to make sure she was still there. I needed her still to be there.

Inside, squeaky lino floors and the institutional smell of bleach. From along the corridor I can hear conversation and a fuzzily tuned radio. Another swipe of Suzanne's fob brings us into a basic office, hung with peeling posters advertising sexual health. It felt rather like doctors' surgeries of my childhood. Not really what I'd expected. I should stop expecting, really.

'So, this is us. Coffee?'

Suzanne breezes through the room, her chunkily beaded necklace clacking as she moves. A thin, small woman in baggy clothes and a boy's haircut looks up from a phone conversation, smiles. Anya is right by me.

'An– and, Sonja. Do you work here too?'

She definitely notices what I was about to say, but I had to keep it up, this ridiculous fiction that I didn't know her real name.

'No. I have my own job. Suzanne is a friend, so I help her out with the campaign. I have done a volunteer shift for her once. It is fucking hard. I could not do Suzanne's job in real life – she's a magnificent woman.'

She forces her accent over the big word, then abruptly turns away to a poster above the desk. Suzanne returns, places a mug of milky Nescafe in my hands, and steers me through to a space with rows of squat padded chairs and pinboards. A kettle and some cups on top of a small fridge, and a sign printed in bright sugar paper beside a table: UGLY MUG BOOK. Two girls stretched out on the chairs, foam spilling out from a sharp rip underneath one of them, what looks like a photo album across their laps.

'We call this the rec room. Neutral space – there's a kettle and things for hot drinks. Sometimes that's as

180

far as it goes – you see these lassies just slink in here keeping their heads down, shoogle some coffee into a mug, take a couple of slurps once the kettle's boiled and when you look up, they've vanished, aren't seen again. We try and get them to at least take a look at the Ugly Mugs book before they go, note the most recent descriptions, but we're not here to insist that anyone do anything, you know. Not like that lot. It's just a safe space. But the majority of them, we have good relationships with them now. As good as you can have. We take it in turns to drive around during the night, help them feel safe, and they'll pop into the van for a wee while if they've got anything to tell us. These rooms,' she indicates three doors off the main space, 'these are for advocacy work. Legal advice. In case they need a voice, someone to shout for them. It starts in there.

'The other aspect of our service is outreach. We try – it's tricky, but we try – to get in touch with the girls who work out of flats or for agencies. Check there's no coercion there, that everyone's okay. Actually getting through to them, though. Pff. I mean, in here, the girls are all out for themselves. But those anonymous names, advertising. Keeping a track on them, even actually making contact. That's the bit that hits it home, you know, what it can be at this level –

'Sorry. I should be talking in the past tense, now. We've not got the staff any more. All our funding's been completely cut, and there's only so long you can power an organisation like this on the kindness of volunteers.'

She's brisk again, hand on a shoulder to take me to a side room, and I remember that this isn't just an excursion for either of us. The door shuts behind us and I'm not quite sitting as she explains that she wants the building plans. It's been an efficient solicitation, the music lessons, the coffee.

'You must have information on the history of the warehouse. It's Victorian. Leftover scraps of the Empire.' She laughs and I don't feel I'm allowed to. 'If there's not some history in here, worth saving, then I'm sure the Jackson Group will have passed through some sort of dodge to get their all-out permissions. There's something going on, and the records are the best place to look. We've got a week. Are you with us?'

PUBLIC

Camilla. Ally McKay is back from the bar, and he's telling me about Camilla.

'Camilla was just, always, like, around. I mean, she was about eight times as posh as the next of them, must have known Jez or Jules or one of that lot from, I don't know, school or something. Rich people club. London. But she was, was something else. I mean, another gorgeous-looking lassie, probably only about the same age as me, as you, about twenty-two when this was going on, but, eh. Just dead behind the eyes, man. Ken those hyenas you see on nature programmes, eh? Like that.'

'A scavenger.'

'Aye.'

She and Rona were well suited then, I don't say.

'But the thing about Camilla was, eh ... For a start, she tended to supply all the drugs to that lot. And there was no way this little flower was a full-time dealer, so I presume she was employed by somebody, somewhere, some, eh, Mr Big. Camilla was the contact, ken? But she also did, eh, favours. She was also the, eh, the entertainment. Sorry. But, eh, you know what I mean?'

'Less technical terms?'

'It was – you'd hear jokes about it. Jez and that lot. If they had a big guest, or a DJ or something, and they really wanted to impress him, like. Camilla would, eh. Well. She would keep him company that night. And as I understand it, she would –'

'Receive money for her services?'

'No always. Sometimes, like, *shoes* or something. One time, when I was working for Jez, he sent me out to pick up like this five hundred quid pair ay heels from one of they proper snobby boutiques, eh. That was the expenses code, *entertainment*, and I saw him handing them over to Camilla that night. Or coke. But she – eh – she didny do freebies.'

'And Rona?'

'Well, at first they were just pally, eh, couple of girls who liked to party. Good dancers, pretty, welcome everywhere they went. But after a while, I'd eh – I'd see Rona heading off, with Camilla and, eh, whatever visiting dignitary they were – Just in the taxi, and that. And then she just stopped turning up for her shifts at the bar. I'd go in to see her and the manager would say she hadn't turned up, she hadn't turned up, and then she was fired. But. Eh. She still had enough money to keep going out, to keep buying pretty dresses, eh. Shoes.'

We drink. The lights flash for last orders and I almost run to get there. Just to be doing something else, concentrating on something else. But he's there, now, still going when I come back.

'I'd tried to talk to her about it, but she just seemed

184

so happy, man. She said she was fine, could handle herself. And, to be honest, she didny look – no like Camilla. That lassie, you could see her shrivelling up. But Rona. Eh, they hung about together for maybe four months, five months, something like that, and then, one day, Rona just wasn't there any more. I was a bit freaked out about it, like. Well, you would be. I got hold of that Camilla at a club one night and I was just like, look, where the hell is she? And I swear to god, it was like the first time she'd ever actually lowered herself to acknowledge me, eh? And she just sort of bleated something about Rona having run away up north, couldn't handle it, something. Called her a silly little cow, so I had to, eh, remove myself from the area, man. But I just thought – I thought she'd be all right. Eh. Was that it, then?'

'Was what?'

Oh, I'm so, so drunk.

'Was that, it, the last – no. Wait. The baby. Fuckin hell.'

'She did go up north. She went to Aviemore. Stayed with a school friend who's a skiing instructor up there. Same story: got fired from a bar, made up the rent deficit by, ah ... Taking payment. For sex. It's just, it seems like she was advertising, this time.'

'Advertising. Mate.'

'She turned up here when I hadn't seen her for six months, dumped a baby I certainly hadn't heard of before on me, and ran away in the middle of the night. And that's it.'

He puts a damp hand over mine. It's the least sexual gesture I've ever felt.

'Last time I saw Camilla, it was about three years ago, eh. I'd been back, visiting the folks – I moved through here for my job. Ach. She was sitting up at the bar where I was meeting my brother. I recognised the voice, first, eh. She kept laughing too loudly and planting her hand on the knee of this old, fat dude. She looked fucked man, eh, snappable. Nothing left of her, inside. About to crumble into dust. Like a – like an Egyptian mummy or something. Death mask.'

And we drink, and we drink.

'Fucking hell. Tell me something good, eh. What about you, man? What do you do?'

'I do nothing. I just work in an office.'

'You're raising – her – kid, though. As your own. That's fuckin something, Fiona man. That's pure amazing-style, right there.'

For that, he gets a smile. Hear that, Samira?

'And you. Ally McKay. What about you, now?'

'Eh. I work with kids – I run a youth club out in the housing schemes in the east. Teaching them all how to be wee DJs! They like some pure terrible hardcore stuff, man.'

'Seriously? You're actually almost too good, aren't you?' And it is as close as we get to a joke.

When our bodies eventually flop together, you couldn't call it a seduction. The boozy inevitability of it all. We stand, across the table, as if accepting that it's now the time for it, and we press damp, sour mouths on each other. In the toilets I check that I'm wearing passable

186

underwear, buy condoms from a rusty machine, half worried he'll have run off while I'm in there, but he hasn't. He's there, acknowledging it. We kiss again and again on the fifteen-minute walk to my flat, as though we're trying to convince ourselves we're really into it.

My muscles creak out, remembering this sensation. I am not quite wet enough for entry, so there is some fumbling, some spit, a couple of sweet, whispered assurances that yes, I do want this. Because I really, really do, despite it all. Then the good, warm, filling, much missed. Then the gentle sound of something falling repeatedly onto wet sand. He doesn't come. I don't come. We just warm each other for a while, though, skin on anonymous skin. The being beside another person. Touching base for a while.

When I wake up again, it's fully light. Proper daytime. I can still feel that small kiss on my forehead. There's a note on the bedside table, beside the scribbled-on napkin and the torn condom wrapper.

She's still downstairs. Thought it best she didn't see you like this.
Please come and get her when you wake up.
Hope you had fun.
Mum.

I cried for five minutes. Just to get the gin out. Then I got in the shower, picked up a still-resentful Beth, smelling of clean wet hair. It was that night that I emailed Anya. Sonja. Whoever she is.

SPLIT PERSONALITIES

We are exceptionally good at duplicity, we persons
in the hussying trade. And I don't mean that we're
more likely to double-cross or betray you, despite
the number of movies I can think of which imply
call girls are not to be trusted (almost as many as
those where we're killed in the first act, to alert the
town to the presence of a murderer on the loose.
The canaries-down-a-mine-shaft of the serial killer
world, us). Actually, I've met few people as honest
as ladies of negotiable virtue. It's all out there, you
see. In one way.

What I mean, though, is that the vast majority
of escorts are, at any given time, keeping up a
complex series of appearances. We're all suffering
from split personalities.

Try and think of those casual acquaintances of
yours. The friends-of-friends. People you were at
school with, maybe, but don't keep regularly up

188

to date with. Your neighbours. The sort of people you'd wave to in the street or wish happy birthday to on Facebook, but don't trust enough to share the intimate parts of your life with. It's not that they're not to be trusted, either, it's just that you don't know them well enough.

Now, imagine every single one of those people in your life knew that you did a job like mine. A job everyone has an opinion on, without usually knowing very much about it. A job that many people presume you have to be damaged in some way to do; a job that the very doing of means people make serious, deep assumptions about you in ways they certainly don't do with dentists. Exactly. So that's your basic, entry-level secrecy right there: you need a convincing backstory to explain, as boringly as possible, your income, just in case these people take an interest. Now, perhaps certain members of your family and friends aren't as enlightened as you'd like them to be about the business. You either force all manner of uncomfortable discussions on them, or you up the secrecy even further. This amount of disclosure varies from person to person, depending on a whole host of variables conditioning your relationships with each one.

Even with those people who know, there's often something kept back. Perhaps you've reached a tacit understanding with them where they know, but don't want to be reminded of it, because in spite of you, they've never really got over their hang-ups about the profession, in which case you find a way round it, find a way to be more than half a person when you're with them. I know women who've been in relationships whilst playing this old game, with some exceptionally tolerant, loving men, and they've nearly always mentioned a keeping back of the details, as a way of making a distinction between work and non-work sex.

So, there's private face and there's hussy face, for starters. Then you get to the clients. Now, I'm fairly expensive, in this city and in this field, and as you'll know if you've read my FAQs, I'm also completely unrepentant about that. I'm worth it, and I know I am. And two of the reasons I'm worth it are I'll commit completely to your fantasy, and I'm as discreet as they get.

I'm not sure a lot of people understand discretion. It's not just a matter of not obviously looking like an escort when I turn up to an outcall. When I say discretion, I mean I've taken my own version of the Hippocratic oath. Client–hussy confidentiality is important. I hold a lot of very important secrets in my head, and most of them are not my own. I've often said MI6 should recruit former escorts to its staff. Not only can we keep track of multiple identities, we're experts in psychology; in gauging reactions, working out what people like, helping them connect. Providing a listening, counselling service is often as much a part of this job as the physical stuff. And clients can only feel free to be themselves with me if they know I'm not going to betray them.

Then there's the me I am with you, my little online perverts, and with my clients face to face. And I'm not going to pretend for one second that this is the 'real me' you're getting. This way I have of writing to you, this is just another personality. This voice comes from your fantasy girl, speaks from your fantasy body. I take her out of the cupboard and put her on when I'm going to work: I get into costume. And slowly, curling my eyelashes, painting my face, smoothing my skin and pulling up my stockings, I become her, for you.

And we both know that's what you'd rather have. You don't want a person who moans, farts and goes to the supermarket. You want arch and playful, with a great bottom. And you know you do.

Speaking of great bottoms . . .

It's a lot of balls to keep up in the air (baddoom tsch!), a lot of switches to be flicked on or off at any time, sure. But until the whole of society shifts on its axis to accommodate us a little more, or at least accept us, that we have always been

here, that's how it's going to be. And although
the obvious way for it to work would be for us all
to come out at once and say, here we are, this is
what we do, deal with it, this is an independent
business by its very definition. Dunno about you,
but the stakes are too high for me to be the first.

This week I went to see a talk by The Fallen
Woman herself, our great nation's most famous
former-prostitute-turned-writer. A huge hall-full
of people there to see her for one reason and
one reason only, and she knew it, had played
up the descriptions and her fame to get a bigger
audience for a presentation of the research project
she's been working on. She was working on a
book about identity, about the way we can hide
online; and she read from it, clicked through a
presentation of statistics, brisk, witty. She tricked
us, and she refused to be cowed by it, to allow
anything to touch her; controlling the crowd and
setting the agenda for the night so masterfully
that no one dared ask her about it, not the pervs
nor the anti-prostitution campaigners (and I
recognised a few of both in the crowd) . . .

Whole, she is. Whole and brainy and likeable and
bloody admirable. She wears great shoes. She
makes jokes about her great shoes. She makes
jokes. Saying, look at me. No, really. Look at *me*.

Tags: <u>celebrity</u> <u>stigma</u> <u>activism</u> <u>the business</u> | **Comments (32)**

FOUR

OFF

Once you've made that shift, interrupted the smooth line of day-to-day living with some sort of dissent, it's hard to go back. RDJ Construction had moved into sharp focus and I saw it all, its cold walls, hard carpets and the stale instant coffee on its breath, Elaine's old tattered magazines in the break room, the listless chatter about last night's telly. This grey place where we had to go, every day, none of us liking it, none of us able to change. I look around at Moira, Norman and Graeme, faces illuminated by their separate monitors but blank, all three powered-down humans at half-capacity.

This office had been just a thing that was, a condition of existence. Now everything about it, everything it asked of us enraged me. All the time and effort I'd taken to insure myself against feeling anything, all the careful barriers put up to avoid comparison with other possible worlds, all gone.

What if we all just said no? What would happen to RDJ Construction if Moira realised that the way they'd smiled and let her put Team Leader on her email signature after eleven years of service was appallingly patronising to any loyal worker, let alone one nearing fifty? Or if Norman worked out that his scrupulous insistence on double-checking the minute details of every task he was given, above and beyond his paid hours, meant the company got twice as much work out of him? What if Graeme just wanted to live a young person's life?

What if I did?

A soft metallic noise, and my 9.30 reminder list pops up.

Order sandwiches x13 for weekly review
Last week's minutes photocopy x14
Ian to call John McKenzie @ 11.15
File invoices

I stared and stared at the screen and couldn't find the energy to reach for the phone anywhere in me. The sandwiches were a matter of urgency: the order had to be in with the caterers by ten. The sandwiches were a matter of urgency. The sandwiches were a matter of urgency.

What if I just stood up and started walking. They wouldn't notice at first. I could be over in another department. They wouldn't notice unless a phone call came through and they realised I'd left Ian's desk unattended – Moira would reroute the calls through to her phone for a while, because it is assumed that that is what women do in this office. Questions would be asked at 11.25 when John McKenzie's PA called and Ian realised he hadn't been reminded. They would try my mobile number and I wouldn't answer it because I would be walking, because maybe I hadn't even taken my phone with me. There would be no sandwiches or copies of last week's minutes at the meeting, and big George would file a complaint because he's diabetic and the decision to keep everyone in over lunch for the weekly review was not taken lightly, and I would keep on walking, until I got to the edge of the city. Perhaps I could walk to Manchester. Perhaps I could walk to a village or a small town where the buildings didn't advance above two storeys. By the time I got there, the sandwich problem would have resolved itself somehow and I wouldn't be needed again until 5 p.m., when afterschool care would notice I hadn't come to pick up Beth. Again, though, they would phone Mum, and she'd cluck and fluster, but she and Dad would take Beth in, just like they'd always wanted to. It's not a rupture, a second daughter going missing. Not like the first. We're so numb now my absence would cause nothing more than an irritation of scar tissue. And Beth, and Beth, wouldn't her life be better with someone competent, someone experienced in parenting? Someone who didn't sometimes resent her presence? The invoices would be filed by a temp girl from the same agency I'd been with originally, who would gradually mould this chair to her back as her contract was extended due to her extreme adequacy.

That the sandwiches were once not got, that would be my legacy.

The four numbers in the corner of my screen advance towards 10.00, and Ian's face is there, above the monitor.

'Fiona, Jackson Group have decided to send an extra

representative to the meeting today. Can you make the sandwich order for fourteen? Thanks.'

And I pick up the phone because these are the things you do, because. And I begin to file the invoices, and I patch the phone call through to Ian at 11.15, and then I go to the photocopier and I photocopy the minutes, and I take fulsome, competent notes in the weekly review meeting where we discuss the very precise plans for how to deal with the irritating anti-progress protesters who want to stop these two rich companies from getting even richer, type them up briskly and print out two more copies than I need to, and at 4.30 I leave the building carrying the extra-large handbag I'd specially brought that day, the one that can hold A4 documents without creasing them, every colleague I pass in the corridors charged with the exciting possibility of discovery.

ON

A rapper is having sex on the sound system in the bar where Heather wants to meet. It's a Jackson Group bar, the biggest pub chain in the city. RDJ Construction's most valued, and valuable clients. Their bars spring up anywhere clusters of office workers or students can be found, named for babytalk, all of them. K-oko. Dada. BuU. Nuuba. Lol'lo. The same hard chairs on the floors, the same soft porn in the toilets. Straightening-ironed staff, squelchy RnB beats that bit too loud for conversation, that bit too rubbish to dance to.

I suppose it's handy – five minutes from both my breezeblock tower and the glass-fronted palace Heather works in – but it doesn't make you want to linger. The seats are primed to eject us, and the music's so loud, so doosh doosh pumping pumping that we're having to shout and it's only Tuesday evening.

'Hi doll. Hiya. How's you? How's my girl?'

Her hug is paper thin: I hardly feel it on me. She's got a white shirt on today and her honeymoon-ruddied skin pops against it. This will be deliberate – Heather would always wear white vests to show off her sunburn on the first days of autumn term. She is a constant, Heather. This is always what she was going to be, this married lady tilting her anxious head, eyes big and loaded. I have a fair idea of what's coming, so I head her off.

'Look at your tan! So. Tell me all about it. How was the honeymoon? Was it amazing?'

She relaxes, basks a little.

'Oh and look at *that*! I'm firing questions at you and we haven't even got the drinks in yet. What you having?'

Her sense of purpose returns.

'No, no hon. Let me. I'll get this. You don't have to. *You don't have to*. Wine? Glass of wine? My treat, hon.'

She swings up and off. Through the gloom a couple of nearby blokey necks swing to appraise her, the fleshy bounce of her, flick to me and then back to their pints. If Samira had been with us it would have been different, but Heather and I, despite the tightness of our work skirts and the height of our heels, do not merit second glances. We never really have done, it occurs to me. I goggle at the lumpen male shapes, trying to make them feel my hostility. They're laughing about something that isn't to do with us, already forgotten.

Heather tilts back from the bar, shouts my name. I teeter over, conscious of the catwalk I'm on. Perhaps I'm exaggerating the wiggle a bit, wanting to be noticed again. I have begun buying flimsy, silky knickers recently, the sort of wispy things I see in pictures. The sort of thing I used to assume would fall apart in the wash or give me thrush. I run my thumb over the line of them, through my skirt. Outer lines of vision, but I think the men are looking.

There are posters all over the bar.

MIDWEEK SPECIAL: BUY TWO GLASSES, GET THE REST OF THE BOTTLE FREE.

'They've got an offer on,' she explains.

'Really, I'm fine with just a glass.'

The young barman who has been salesman-flirting her smiles, familiar with this squabble.

'Ah, go on,' he says. 'Can't hurt.'

It's red, glowing blackish in those huge goldfish bowl glasses, even though I'd fancied white. There is really not very much in the bottle after the two glasses have been poured. We walk back past the men again. Hip, hip. Yes, they're looking at us. Good. I try a small, coy smile and look back to my feet. A Rona move. Just because I could. Heather's staring at me.

'Right. So. I want all the details. Talk me through every bit. Was the hotel wonderful? And you got lots of sunbathing in –?'

'We did. It was good, yeah. It was really good. How are you, though, Fi? It's been all me-me-me-wedding-wedding for so long. Looking forward to getting back to normality. What's going on in *your* life?'

She's been back four days. This is ample time for her to have met up with Claire, crusading Claire, save-the-women Claire. I try and imagine it, a family dinner, perhaps, and at some point Claire catches Heather's arm, takes her into the kitchen on a pretext. Your friend, she'll say, Fiona. I'm afraid I've got some bad news.

199

And Heather is shocked, of course she is. Perhaps she worries about it in bed that night, asks Ross for advice that he can't give. Perhaps he makes an inappropriate joke and they have a fight about it. This is my oldest friend that you're talking about here, she'll say. This is how their married life will be, now. The next day she'll phone Samira, who will be equally shocked, but less concerned because we are still not talking. I knew she was acting weirdly, Samira will say. Should we talk to her, Heather will ask, and Samira will find a way of getting Heather to do it without actually making Heather realise that we are not talking, because Samira is very clever like that. And that's why I get the text message.

Hi hon!!! Back from honeymoon and really want to have a catch-up with you!!! How's 2moro? After work? Xxxx

'Oh, everything's just the same with me. Had to buy Bethan a wedding dress, thanks to you! She's obsessed with brides now, makes a change from princesses!'

'Where's Bethan tonight?'

'My folks have got her.'

'Right. They're quite good about that, aren't they? I mean, they must have to take her quite a lot –'

Heather was never good at subtlety. I think about that long chain of worry and whispered conversations, decide to enjoy myself.

'Ha ha, yeah! All the overtime I'm having to do at work now, they're beginning to joke that I never see her! She practically doesn't recognise me. Still. Doing it for her future in the end, eh, and it's nice to have the extra money. Means we don't have to worry too much. Lot of late nights, though. Whew!'

Something diamond-hard is glinting away in me tonight. I laugh larger than usual, force it out, throw my head back and notice that we still have our audience. Heather has almost finished her first, huge glass, and tops herself up before speaking, her sympathy face on.

'I didn't know – I hadn't realised money was such a problem for you, hon. You should have told me. You know. You can talk to me. I'm so sorry I got pre-occupied with the wedding and everything, but I'm here for you now. Eh? Eh, Fi.'

'Aw, that's really sweet of you, honey. But I think we're doing fine.'

'No, really. If there's anything you want to tell me. Anything at all you need to get off your chest. I'm your pal, eh. I'm listening.'

It's a high, a sudden, powerful high. I flick one of Rona's smiles at the two men, topnote, playing everyone in this bar like a virtuoso pianist. My glass is empty too. It always comes down to getting drunk, I think.

'We drank those quickly, didn't we? There's the last of the bottle!'

'Fi. Talk to me.'

I put my neck to the same angle as hers, meet her eyes for the first time all night.

'What exactly do you want me to talk about, Heather.'

'About – about –'

Here it comes.

'Claire said she saw you. At a meeting. At a meeting of –'

'Of?'

'That meeting. You know what I'm talking about, Fiona. Stop pretending.'

She still can't bring herself to say it, though, the dirty word.

'Are you working as a ... As a –'

Right here and now, I could let it all out. Let Rona out. Heather, who I've known for more than half my life, would understand how to absorb her, help me soak her up. It's not just talking to a stranger at a wedding; it's actively taking control. Getting things back on track. I wouldn't have to bear the knowledge by myself any more; letting the air in on this private obsession, curbing it. Stopping it. I'd become normal again, and Heather would support me. She's offering to, right here; she just doesn't know she is.

It's not me. Ohmigod, you thought it was *me*? I'd say. No, no. It's Rona. And I'd tell her about what Christina had told me, about what Ally McKay had said. It would explain my strange behaviour on her hen weekend and since, which would go some way to bonding us back together again, and I'd feel less alone. She'd talk it through with me, help me straighten out all the tortured kinks of thought I've had in my head this past month. I might end up crying on her, if we stretch the talk into another buy-two-glasses-get-the-bottle-free and another, the barman winking at our drunkenness as barmen in this sort of bar do with office girls. Tomorrow she'll tell Samira, and Samira and I will have a tearful exchange on the phone where we both apologise and make up, and we'll be reunited, three fuckin muskahounds, and they'll help me through this,

202

this phase, and I'll be a better friend and mother for it. I can't believe you thought *I* was doing *that*, I'll say at the end of the night, and we'll laugh about it, one of those hearty, bittersweet shared laughs of friendship.

But I don't say anything.

What Heather thinks she's doing is bravely confronting a friend whose life has spiralled out of control, because we always seem to think that that sort of life must involve a spiral out of control. She might not have voiced it in these terms, but right now Heather thinks I'm a fallen woman, a desperate, shameful thing. Unclean. She's shocked and ashamed for me, of me, and she pities me. She keeps touching her wedding ring, worrying at it.

'You want to know if I'm working as an escort to make extra money?'

'I – Fi –'

'What would be the problem if I was?'

'What? Fi, come on –'

'I'm serious, Heather. What would be wrong with it, if I was?'

'It's . . . It's *prostitution*, Fiona.'

'It's not against the law. It doesn't hurt anyone.' This is marvellously clear to me, for the first time ever.

'You're hurting *yourself*.'

And here they come. I couldn't have scripted a better entrance point. English accents, bald patches.

'All right, girls? We noticed you was running a bit empty there, so we got you another bottle of vino. Mind if we join you?'

Heather says: 'No, sorry mate, we're having a private conversation here. Not a good time.'

203

I say: 'Thanks so much, guys! That's so sweet. Pull up a seat!'

We say these things at the same time and then she's shocked all over again, doesn't know what to do.

'Fi*ona*,' she's hissing over the noise of stools being dragged to our table.

'So, you ladies local, then?'

OFF

'This is good,' Anya says. 'This is really great stuff. So, we will need to get in there before them. It'll probably mean organising some sort of occupation, but we can use this, definitely.'

I could have dropped the minutes of the weekly review in to Suzanne directly, at Sanctuary Base, but that way lay danger, I'd explained. I could have been spotted by a co-worker. Much better to hand the info over to Anya, disguised as two friends meeting for coffee. Safer that way. Safer.

I'm trying to imagine what she's like on her university course, in a context where people knew her openly as 'Anya', where her body didn't matter, locked behind clothes. I'm trying to work out whether she's wearing makeup. Just a trace, I think.

'Well done. Thank you. I know this must have been difficult for you. I appreciate it and I'm sure Suzanne will too. You did not have to help us and you did.'

In her smile I get briefly bold.

'Can I ask something? Why does all this mean so much to you? Personally, you. I mean, you aren't affected by the new legislation or the closure. You don't volunteer there. And the risks of putting your head up, becoming known for this sort of thing. Aren't you worried they'll find you out?'

I keep expecting her to slap me down, that at some point I will have gone too far. Why on earth she continues to tolerate me I'm not entirely sure. There is nothing about me that could appeal, I'm sure. She's never seen the person I can pretend to be, the sparky one, inspired by her. Whenever we meet I fluster, make porridgy conversation at her.

Her smile gets tighter.

'Shall we just say that I like the fight? Things get boring otherwise.'

'Things get boring for *you*? Don't try living my life then.'

That clanks, so I try and add a laugh on, making a joke of it.

She nods.

'No.'

Nothing more to say on the issue. It glances off my cheek like a bruise, her honesty. Why would she want to live my life? Of course she wouldn't. Perhaps I am just tolerated because I can provide information. Only that. With white hot clarity I realise I don't really exist in either of her worlds, the academic or the other. This was always a transactional relationship. And I should ask for something back now.

'Listen. I've got you all this. And it's good. Could you – about my sister. I know some things. She was working with a girl called Camilla, in Edinburgh. An English girl, must be about my age. They, ah, they serviced – worked for – they did a lot of work for nightclub promoters, and I thought that this girl might, might know something, if I could find her. If you knew how to find her.'

She tips back in her chair and looks bored, blank.

'I cannot help you find your sister. We do not have a full, proper network – it is one of the unfortunate by-products of an unregulated industry, huh? The girls who really need the support, they sometimes just slip away. And you know, if she doesn't want to be found, it is not my place to betray another working girl's identity. That's something I can't do.'

'Okay. Sure. Of course. Even, the girl Camilla, I thought, maybe. But, sure. Sure. Okay.'

A tall man is knocking on the window we're sitting beside. T-shirt ripped at the sleeves, spiked, messed hair, and an absurdly beautiful face. Anya breaks into a smile at the sight of him.

'So. My ride is here.'

She reaches across the table and pats my arm, one, two.

'We appreciate this. Thank you.'

There is no mention of another meeting. 'See you later,' I call out, and she pretends not to hear me as she leaves, a move she must have had to practise, for persistent clients. I'm raw nothing, and they walk off together, down the street. She gets up on tiptoe to kiss him on the jaw as they go.

ON

I've always had problems making small talk; never been able to fully relax into the weightlessness you need, the gaiety. Tonight it's easy, though, pretending to be just as oblivious as these two lunkheads, Andy and Dave, in town for work for the one night, staying at a Travel Inn round the corner and thick-skinned enough to butt into what is clearly a very serious conversation between two women on the merest sniff of sex. I giggle and chatter to compensate for Heather saying nothing, and her mounting disbelief gets me badder and bolder. I'm only able to be this thing because she thinks I already am, but it's a pure, lovely high of the sort I haven't felt in years. She and Claire will commiserate over me, and Claire will feed her statistics; perhaps they will work out how to rescue me from myself. The men are smiling, unfurling, telling rough-edged jokes. Dave strokes an enquiring finger up the outside of my thigh, almost accidentally. Andy goes to top up Heather's glass, and she puts a firm hand on top.

'No. Thanks guys, but no. It's getting late and both Fiona and I have work in the morning.'

'Oh, go on Hedge, have another drink! Heather just got married,' I tell Andy and Dave, 'but she's not an old married lady yet. She used to be wild at school, didn't you?'

'Did you girls go to school together?' Andy asks.

'That must have been about a year ago, right?' says Dave, and I preen for him.

'Fiona. Can I talk to you for a minute, please?'

Heather has pushed her stool back and is clutching her coat.

She steps away, towards the door. 'What the hell are you doing?'

'Just having fun. We didn't all get married this month, Hedge.'

'I was trying to have a very serious conversation with you. Can we go somewhere else, get this sorted out. I'm worried about you, Fi. I want to help.'

'What about the Travel Inn bar round the corner? I'm sure Dave and Andy would get us a residents' discount.'

'What are you doing? What are you – this isn't you, Fi. This isn't you. Come on, let's go. Not with them. Come on.'

This isn't you. I said that to Samira less than two weeks ago. How would you know, she said. This *isn't* me, though. Poor Heather. She's just trying to care. Her eyes are huge and hurt; for a second it flashes through my head that I must be a very hard person to love.

'I'm going to stick around for a bit,' not-me tells her, bright smile. 'Seeing as I arranged Mum to babysit and everything. Might as well make the most of it, eh?'

'I really think you should come home with me, Fiona. It's not safe. It's not.'

'Heather. I'm a big girl. Come on. Thanks for the wine, and it was lovely to see you. You're looking great. We should do this again sometime soon.'

I've hugged her off and out of the door before she knows what's happening, and somehow, she absolves me, takes all the worry with her. This isn't me. Not me who strides back up to the table and says, sorry about that boys, she's just had a wee bit too much to drink. You two don't mind if I stay around for a little while? Not me who likes the genuine relief on Dave's big red face when he says hey, gorgeous, thought we'd lost you there; not me who likes being called gorgeous, who laps it up, who shares her attention out equally between the two of them when she senses Andy getting bored. It doesn't have to be me, not tonight, not even when we move to the shamingly bright lights of the hotel bar, and the jokes get uglier, the speech slurs and both of their hands fondle my kneebones with almost anthropological interest.

And it's not me that makes a decision to go back to their shared room, flouncy green valances on its twin beds, to actually feel myself getting off on having two big, drunken men trying to explore my body at once, beer breath on my coat collar, fingers in my knickers and my blouse unbuttoned to let a mouth get at my nipple. They're not really attractive at all, either of them; there's very little to tell them apart. It's not about them being attractive, though.

Two guys, in a Travel Inn.

I watch her in the mirror, being felt up and kissed,

clothes still on, and feeling that surge again, I wonder if it's possible to stop all of this, to just say, no, that's enough now.

'Boys. Boys. Have either of you got protection?'

Neither of them do.

'Well, I would very much like to fuck both of you, hmm?' Kiss, kiss. 'There was a machine in the little girls' room by the bar – it'll take me two minutes. Will there be two big hard cocks waiting for me when I come back?'

'Andy can go, can't you mate?' Dave is a little irritated. Andy takes a couple of seconds to work out what's going on.

'Why can't you go, *mate*?'

'No, no, I'll do it. Really. This is a fantasy of mine, yeah?' I kiss them both again. 'And I need you to make it come true. Hard cocks, okay?'

And I've slipped out, just like that, into the air-conditioning. Leaning up against the lift, breathless from running the length of the corridor, I contemplate actually going back up there, actually doing it. I'm horny. I could. It might feel good.

It feels even better to have been able to stop it, though. To know that that was possible. I sneak quickly past the receptionist, convinced I can feel his disapproval, out into the night. There's a taxi rank just round the corner with only two cabs at it, the drivers both reading their papers, and I'm sure they think they know what I am too, a girl by herself in this area, leaving a hotel at this time of night. My driver says nothing, though, just takes me home.

In my bathroom mirror I come back to my body,

inky wine stains on my lips and crazy eyes, and I don't mind at all.

Heather spends the next morning on Facebook, changing her surname to Buchanan and posting a flood of honeymoon photos. Ross, grinning, lobster pink in his trunks. The two of them by the pool with their arms round each other.

OFF

Just the hush and hum of computers. If anyone calls from the papers I am to say RDJ Construction are unable to comment at this time, and take a number for a callback that won't happen. There have been three already this morning, bloodhounds blindly following scents.

Norman, bristling with the importance of himself, was in the office to brief me.

'It's like they'd anticipated our every move,' he said. 'Bunch of lunatics. They've been in there since god-knows-when, and they've barricaded themselves in. Some people. Some people.'

Norman doesn't understand that people could care this much, I thought, cruel, hard to him on the inside. And then I looked at him properly, his genuinely baffled face, and I realise I've hit it exactly. He's been forced up against a whole way of being that simply doesn't make sense to him, the company man, doing his time in the Territorials, driving home to the family every night and earning his World's Best Dad mug. He'd never expected to encounter *these sorts of people* beyond scare stories in his favourite newspapers. And in a way, it was me that did this to him. I'd enabled the sit-in; I'd enumerated every possible tactic for them. Hell, I'd even given them the names of the RDJ staff most likely to be involved in any break-ins.

I felt a bit sorry for the poor fucker. Just for a second. He sensed it.

'Just because we're all out, that's no excuse for you to be prancing about on the internet all day, remember. We're a steady ship and it's staying that way. There's work to be done. Ian says to carry on as planned – he'll still need the blue files couriered there this afternoon.'

It must be comforting to be Norman. To have everything you'll ever say or think already scripted for you. That's why he's struggling to cope just now. I did the finger at his retreating back, pulled up my browser almost as a reflex. The words were already forming around my fingers.

HOLLY'S BLOG

OMG, bad day today. A lot of shouting in my head and I feel like I can't breathe

New tab.

SCANDI SONJA

This weekend, the Jackson Group will begin demolition and reconstruction on a Victorian warehouse space in the so-called International Finance District. Their plans are for a huge leisure complex: bowling alleys, three bars, chain restaurants. The council spokesperson commenting on this transfer of property – oh yes, this was a council property – said that they felt the development would 'bring new leisure investment into the area and open it up for regeneration'.

Now, as I am sure a number of my regular readers are more than aware, there is already a considerable amount of leisure activity in the area. It's not really the sort that the council want to encourage these days, of course. And that particular Victorian warehouse currently houses the Sanctuary, which is a shelter for street-based sex workers of all genders, run by a team of people who are basically volunteers at this stage. The Sanctuary team have been served a notification of eviction for tomorrow. The council claims to be replacing the Sanctuary with a 'mobile unit' (a bus, in case you don't speak bureaucrat. Maybe a people carrier) from which they will practise their new Ways Out scheme. Ways Out, right now, is only available to female sex workers.

But, Sonja, I hear you saying. This is all very well but you've been talking about this Sanctuary for a while now. How does this affect you, as an independent escort, or me, as one of your clients/a fellow independent escort or parlour sex worker/an interested bystander?

Well, Ways Out will eventually affect all of us.

It's the first stage in legislation to criminalise the purchasing of sex between consenting adults – which, as I don't have to remind anyone who reads this, is perfectly legal at the moment. It's also the first stage in a city-wide scheme to infantilise and further stigmatise sex workers. I've written at length about this in the past: see here and here.

Which is why I invite you to join me in occupational action. They can't knock down the Sanctuary and take that first step as long as there are people inside, demonstrating its use. We could use as many bodies as possible down here: there will be filming, so bring any sort of disguises you feel are necessary. Gathering point available if you leave your email address in a comment.

Comments (6)

PunterJohn

Go on yersel Sonja! If anyone can teach these bastards a lesson it's my favourite domme . . . er, Mistress. ;-p

19.06 on 03/07/08

Mr Enigma

I don't really see what business it is of the council's. This is persecution and it's outrageous. I bet you girls could get together and mount a legal defence (I can think of some other things I'd like you to mount!!) that this is an enfringement of basic human rights. Typical of the nanny state – surely there's a better use of council time than interfering in what goes on between two consenting adults???

21.45 on 03/07/08

JustAnotherClient

Sex workers perform an invaluable service in society that is not appreciated. Sex workers have been there for me at my lowest points, providing companionship when no one else would help me. They are there for lonely and desperate people. They should be treated like queens. I salute you Sonja and the work you are doing.

02.28 on 04/07/08

Merry Marie

Well said, love. Can't make it down today but with you in spirit. Solidarity with all my ladies down there. Sharing this on my blog. xxx

06.32 on 04/07/08

Albert

Can I enquire as to whether you have an upper and lower age limit for the clients you are willing to see?

07.11 on 04/07/08

> **Scandi Sonja**
> Hello Albert. I usually only see clients over the age of 21. No upper limit! Sx

09.36 on 04/07/08

Staring at the words on the screen was all I could manage. Cold heat pulsing. She'd shared the plans. The plans were on her blog. Bowling alley, three bars. Not that RDJ Construction was the only place that information could have come from, but questions would be asked. So much for your fucking discretion. And then she just gets back to business as normal.

I ran possible scenarios for what was happening at the Sanctuary Base site. Strange that I could cause this sort of situation – well, okay, not cause, but I helped,

I did – and not be part of it. My colleagues put into action their containment strategies, the management and sustaining of a project I have typed minutes, couriered files and organised meetings for but had no real involvement in. And Anya and Suzanne and their helpers and supporters, yes, they're using my information, but the protest would have happened anyway, the fight to save something that doesn't touch me, at all.

Anya's face, closed off, shutting me very deliberately out once I'd served my purpose. With distaste, almost, I began to think. Like she'd seen the shame of me, had worked out something in the heat of my body, my nervousness around her. Norman's officious kiss-off. Both sides letting me know exactly how little I count for. Again, it all comes back to Rona, her fault. Her selfish fault I'm in this job that I could be about to lose, in these cheap nothingy office clothes. Her fault I even began investigating escorting, her fault about Anya. Her fault I feel like this and her fault I'm still, now, doing what I always do, peering at the action from a distance, through a computer screen and other people's second-hand accounts.

A shovel. One good crack.

I hurl the nearest heavy thing – the mug on my desk – at the door Norman's just left through, and I scream sounds, wordless angry sounds as it breaks. Fuck them all. Really. The phone rings – I assume it's Elaine, the nosy bitch, fidgeting around any sort of deviation, wanting to know what on earth that noise was, Fiona – but the light is beeping for an outside line. I take three breaths in and pick it up, and I try to remember what I'm supposed to tell any journalists, muckrakers.

'Good morning RDJ Construction surveying department how can I help you.'

My mouth just spills it out, like I've been bent this way now. And I haven't.

'Hello darling. It's Malcolm from the *Express* here. Just wanted to ask you a couple of questions...'

His voice is supplicant, wheedling. I take a deep breath in and realise I already know what I'm about to do.

ON

'No. Absolutely not.'

Beth's school had been closed due to a problem in the kitchens. Exasperated parents were clustering at the gates when we got there.

'Well, what the bloody hell do you expect me to do with him, then?' A man in a suit was shouting at one of the teachers, nodding down at an inconvenient piece of luggage in a Spider-Man coat.

'Your dad just swore.'

Over the heads I'd seen the other 'Fiona', staring at her son, worried eyes, before nodding, decisive, turning, pulling him down the road.

I had taken the day off specially. Okay, I'd called in sick, doing pathetic tones down the line, thankful it was credulous Moira I'd got.

'Aw darlin. You just tuck yourself right up in bed, okay, and get lots of rest. I'll get Elaine to cover the phones today. It'll be fine.'

I was going to go through to Edinburgh and follow up every name, every half-remembered bar and manager that Ally McKay had been able to scrawl drunkenly down for me. I was going to take some action for myself, stop bothering with other people's business. The point was to find Rona, that's what, and I intended to retrace her steps until I did. Or found something. This girl Camilla, maybe, or their pimp or whatever he was, Jez. I just needed to be there, in the city, keep feeling her around me. It would be the key. I knew it.

'Your mother and I have both got jobs to go to, Fiona. We are not a twenty-four-hour babysitting service and we're getting tired of you treating us as such. You already have a day off.'

'I have things to do today. A lot of walking about. She'd slow me down.'

Mum pats my hand.

'Be good for the two of you to spend some proper time together, love.'

And they're gone.

There are two schoolgirls draped over the sinks at the bus station toilets when we come in. They can't be more than fourteen; in fact, they're probably younger, but my synapses have snapped back fifteen years, recognised the hard kids and prepared for flight. They peer up at us for a second through faces toughened by layers of makeup, then decide I'm not worth the bother.

'The lighting is barry in here. Come on, take a couple pictures of me.'

I usher Beth into the mother-and-baby cubicle, the one with more room. She cranes her head back over her neck to look at them, in love again. Their conversation filters over the sound of her pee.

'Awright. You ready? Naw, naw, you need to look way sexier than that. Right, I'm gonny take it from above, and you should look up at me.'

'Like this?'

'Aye, that's good.'

'Let's see – ohmigod that's minging. I look so fat. Take another wan.'

'Mibbe if you showed your tits a bit more. Think ae that picture ae Jemma whatsherface from the fourth year that did the rounds. Okay. Cheese!'

'I wisnay rea-dy – oh here, actually that's quite nice . . .'

'Sex-*ay*. Okay, pull your shirt down a bit more.'

Beth has been silent throughout the procedure, eyes fixed on the door, alert to every sound and nuance. We come out, and one of them is standing on the sinks, training the lens of a pink mobile phone down. The other, sucking her cheeks to the pouted bone, shirt unbuttoned to the waist, is manhandling the lace-trimmed puppy fat where her breasts will be in a couple of years into a make-believe cleavage.

'Aye aye aye! Like that! Bet you could get it on that Jailbait site. Make a fortune.'

I wash Beth's hands for her, as she's fascinated, unmoving. I pull her out through the turnstile, and she's still silent.

On the bus, after staring determinedly at her hands for a while, she turns a small face up to mine.

'Mummy, what were those big girls doing?'

'The ones in the toilets?'

'Those ones. The ones with the pink phone.'

'Well.' Fuck. 'They were playing, sweetheart. They

222

were just playing dressing. Up. Dressing up. They were very bad girls, honey.'

Very bad girls. I wonder if this is where it comes from. That early. The understanding of all the things that good girls don't do. I think about the stigma that Anya and the others talk about and I wonder if I've just infected my daughter with it.

She nods, seriously, and I look at her, how very, very small she is, toggled up in her little red coat.

'Well. They weren't actually bad girls, darling. It was wrong of Mummy to say that. They were just a wee bit confused, and they were trying out things. But those things that they were trying out could hurt them.'

Was that even worse? The enormity of it all, the responsibility for filtering and probably warping this child's idea of the world is hitting me, fast as grey towns rush past the window.

'Were they playing Sexy Ladies?'

'What? Where did you get that one from?'

'Sexy Ladies. It's a game we do in the playground.'

'Okay. How does Sexy Ladies go, sweetheart?'

She wriggles up onto her knees, and I reach to keep the seatbelt round her.

'You go: duh duh duh duh de neh deh! Sexy! Ladies!'

Her little bum waggles aimlessly and she flails her arms into a child's approximation of a cheesecake pose, wheeling round to me at the last minute with the same dull fish pout the girl in the toilets had done. Across the aisle a grey-haired man begins giggling, innocently enough, but I stare him out for a second. 'Sometimes we get the boys to pretend to take photos, but they get bored quite quickly and they just want to run about. Sometimes they want to blow us up.'

'I don't know how happy I am about you pretending to be a, eh, a sexy lady.'

'It's nice to be a sexy lady! They're pretty, and everyone looks at them!'

'Hoo! She's got a point there!' the man across the aisle says, snorting out coffee. I ignore him.

'Bethan. What do you want to be when you grow up?' I know what the answer will be. We've asked her this over and over, since she was old enough to understand what it meant, giggled each time at the answer, Mum, Dad and me.

'A princess.' She lowers her gaze a bit, flicks out a glance, a little smirk wrestling at her lips. 'Or a Sexy Lady.' She's giggling, but not sure if she's going to get away with this.

All this time. I come home from work, and it's late, and I put her in front of the television or a DVD and the stories tell her the same things. And because she was little, the point at which it stopped being colours and fairy stories and started being something tangible as concrete, the foundation she builds the world on, has slipped by me.

'Mmhm. Do you know that ladies can be other things, as well as sexy?'

Her face suspects a lesson coming.

'They can be teachers –'

'Like Miss Armstrong.'

'Just like Miss Armstrong. And they can be, ehm. Doctors. And – and bus drivers, and estate agents, like Granny.'

And administration and data entry officers. She's picking quietly at the buckle of her shoe, as bored as if I'd actually said that.

The day I'd planned ahead of us. Walking around a city, in and out of beer-soaked rooms, asking coded questions of hungover staff who aren't old enough to have been there seven years ago. Beth straining my wrist, whining, pulling us into toyshops. Me snapping, taking her home early or buying her some pink tat to shut her up. The bus coughing its way into the city by increments, the route it takes to get there. The five photos of teenaged Rona in my bag, sneering, pouting. The route the bus takes.

'Do you know what else ladies can be?' She's not even pretending to listen any more. 'Beth. They can be zookeepers. Do you remember that time Grandad took you to the zoo? To see all the animals? You were quite little. You were only four.'

'Four! That's tiny!' She is very amused, animated again, giggling.

'Do you remember seeing the animals, honey? Grandad said you liked the stripy tigers.'

Her face furrows.

'I had strawberry ice cream.'

'Probably. Probably you did.'

The bus drops us off just across the road. I use my body to shield her a bit from the velocity and force of the cars going by, grip her hand tight. We wait for a quiet moment, run across. The sign is huge and she stares up at it, impressed into silence again.

This time round, she likes the red pandas, and the poisonous tree frogs, and the way the penguins swim, and the rainbow-winged parrots that flock to you if you have bird seed, perch on your shoulders, and I'm so proud of her for not flinching or crying like the few tourist kids there.

'Look! There's one, Beth. A zookeeper who's a lady.'

A girl in a polo shirt, pleasant face, wearing gloves, throwing fish to the seals.

'Is there a dance for that, do you think? Duh duh duh duh de neh deh! Zookeeper! Ladies!'

'No. Duh.'

She says it with such scorn, full force of her Rona-face, that I feel winded for a second.

'That one goes like this. Der der, duh DAH! Zookeeper! Ladies!'

It's exactly the same dance, but I don't point that out. Instead, I pick her up and swing her round, there on the path, till her shoes brush the foliage and we're both laughing.

OFF

One lovely day's respite, then back to it. Screaming protests over brushing her hair. Gritting my teeth as the train just stalled, stayed stalled, vibrating, overheating. Everyone inside, their frustration mounting with the driver and the signals and each other. Didn't even manage to get a copy of the paper, either; the last one swiped by the woman ahead of me who fumbled for an age in her purse for change while I tensed and tensed and tensed my fists. I decide to tell Ian there seems to have been an accident in the motorway tunnel. In fact, I could come into the office asking about it. Has anyone else heard about it on the news this morning? I imagine Moira shaking her head and worrying about smashes and the people trapped inside them all day, checking the news websites, holding out for the afternoon paper to come round. I imagine that the seriousness of it would put Ian off from having to have the time management talk with me again.

The office is empty. Particles of old skin and paper dust dancing, tiny, in the blind-slatted sunbeams. None of the computers seem to be on. I cough, and Ian opens his door.

'Ah. Fiona. Could you come in here a minute, please?'

'Look, I'm really sorry, Ian,' I'm saying before I even get through the door, but he's just holding up a hand. Sitting back in his chair, holding up a hand and looking older than I'd ever seen him before.

'Fiona. Graeme and Norman were called down to the Jackson site yesterday evening. After the, ah, public demonstration at the site yesterday afternoon, once we'd finally got them out of there, our partners in the Jackson Group asked me to make sure that the protestors hadn't, ah, caused any structural damage.'

My brain flickers over it. He's telling me this because someone left my notes down there. Anya. Anya did it. Maybe she did it deliberately, maybe she just didn't think, or care, what it meant for me. She just didn't care. Shit. Shit.

Ian is still talking.

'While they were at the site there was, there was an incident, Fiona. One of the ceilings of the hall collapsed, and they were underneath it.'

'Oh. Oh god.' Words are coming out of my mouth. 'What, where. Are they –'

'Graeme was relatively unscathed. He's been treated for shock and a few minor cuts and bruises. He acted with considerable bravery and foresight at the time, you know. It was Graeme who contacted the emergency services. It was Graeme who managed to pull Norman out.'

'Ian,' I say. 'Ian, how's Norman?'

It's taking him a gigantic effort of will even to make his mouth shape the words.

'Norman was caught underneath a great deal of

falling masonry. His legs were trapped. It's not certain he'll ever have the use of them again. He, ah, he hasn't yet regained consciousness, but his family are with him, and the doctors have described his condition as stable.'

'Stable,' I repeat. Stupidly.

'Fiona, I had to tell Moira this morning. Myself. As you know, they're, ah, very close, and she is – naturally – very upset. She hasn't really been herself today.'

'Surely you sent her home, though,' I say.

'Moira, ah, Moira may be in shock too. I believe she's still in the building – she seems to have, ah, locked herself in a stall in the ladies' bathroom. I didn't feel it was appropriate – I've been waiting for another female member of staff to come in.'

'Of course,' I say. 'Of course.'

The Ladies is so quiet I wonder if Ian is mistaken. One of the two cubicle doors was bolted, though, and when I stand very still I can hear faint scrabblings of tissue from behind the door.

'Moira?' I'm using her own soft voice back to her. 'Moira, it's Fiona. Do you want to open the door to me?'

Silence. I imagine Moira perched on the lid, staring at nothing, maybe not even hearing me. But then the lock clanks back, its noise a shock in the still.

'Oh hen,' Moira is saying. 'Oh Fiona, hen. Oh.'

I put my arms around her strange flat body. She still has her fleece jacket on, handbag strapped across her torso. She collapses onto me and I lean against the cubicle wall to hold the two of us up.

'Come on,' I say. 'Let's get you out of here, just for now. Come on. We'll get you home, Moira. I'll call

229

your husband, eh? Have him come and pick you up?'

'Nobody told me, but,' she says. 'Nobody called me last night to tell me. Well, why would they, really, eh? Why would they, hen? I'm not his family. I'm not his wife.'

I take it all in again, their fourteen years of working at the same desks beside each other, the quiet ways they looked out for each other, the reverence in their voices. That it would never occur to them.

You give people in shock sweet tea, usually, so I guide her through to the one decent armchair in the staff kitchen and fold her into it. I pull down her outsize teacup with its stupid wispily sketched design and we wait, in silence, for the kettle to boil. Moira looks at the cup on the counter and moans, flops forward in her seat.

It's only after she's come back round that I realise I'd automatically set out Norman's World's Best Dad! mug too. Stupid. Stupid.

ON

Anya hadn't answered her phone all day. I'd even risked calling from the work line after a while, in case she was deliberately avoiding my mobile. Nothing.

Actually, she might not have even been at the Base, now I thought about it. It could have been any one of Suzanne's volunteers who'd done it. It could have been Suzanne herself.

Suzanne answers the third time I ring.

'What? Oh yes, I heard about that, yes. Your colleague. The poor man.'

'Suzanne, I'd like to come and talk to you about it. Today, please. Anya too.'

'Today isn't a very good day. Not for either of us really. What with everything. You know. I take it you've seen the papers?'

SLEAZY STUDENT'S DOUBLE LIFE
AS £500-A-NIGHT VICE GIRL

By day she's a boffin . . . by night she's a-bonkin'!
Brainy blonde Anya Sobtka thought she'd found the
perfect way of raising money for her PhD – by working
as a vice girl.

231

We can exclusively reveal that the Polish exchange student, 27, who has been living in Scotland for four years, has been buffing up her income as a high-class hooker.

By day, she works as a PhD researcher in Strathallan University's Politics Department.

By night, the only politics she studies are sexual.

The sleazy swot's actions in the recent disturbances against the Jackson Group's new city-centre development brought her to public notice.

A spokesperson for the police has confirmed that Sobtka has been twice cautioned in recent weeks for disturbance of the peace and making a public nuisance of herself.

Our reporter endured the filthy language and obscene images on Sobtka's website, where she poses as 'Sonja, a sexy Swedish girl who's up for anything' and claims to 'specialise' in 'fetish fun'.

He arranged a 'date' with her in a luxury city-centre pad – a far cry from the stories of starving student bedsits.

On arrival, he was greeted by the blonde, who has several piercings, in a negligee.

In our exclusive recording, which can be heard on our website, the curvy Pole asks our reporter 'what do you like?' before going on to list a range of sordid, kinky practices, and confirming that the minimum charge for the night is £500.

At this point our brave reporter made his excuses and left, but not before obtaining a photograph of Sobtka in action at great personal risk to himself.

We later confirmed that the flat is rented in the name

of Anya Sobtka. A spokesperson for the letting agency said: 'We had absolutely no idea that the flat was being used for sordid purposes. We are absolutely shocked.'

A spokeswoman for the Jackson Group said: 'It comes as no surprise to us that an individual who has been so outspoken about the restructuring of a base for prostitutes should turn out to have been acting from self-interest.'

The Jackson Group is a Scottish-run company, who have been operating for fifteen years, and have made a large number of charitable contributions to the city.

A spokesman for Strathallan University said: 'The University has no comment on this matter at this time.'

PAGE 4: PROSTITUTE PROTESTS LEAVE LOCAL MAN FIGHTING FOR LIFE
PAGE 7: CITY'S VICE GIRL SHAME: IS IMMIGRATION TO BLAME?

The second photograph was captioned, rather unnecessarily: PIERCED: Polish vice girl Sobtka.

'It's like a poem, isn't it? Like blank verse,' Anya says, from Suzanne's kitchen table.

'Are you okay?'

'Sure. Sure. There were maybe ten people waiting outside my door this morning, with cameras, and the head of my department has suddenly taken a personal interest in my career, as we have a meeting first thing tomorrow morning. But physically, no scars! At least I got a good look at the little fuck, huh?'

'They won't – they won't throw you off your course?'

'I don't think they can. I haven't actually broken any

law or done anything illegal, and I do not think they want to lose my nice big foreign student tuition fees.' Her smile. 'But it will not be pleasant, no. I imagine I will be told I have brought the department into disrepute. Certainly, there will be no job for me, no nice reference, now. I expect they will, ah, restrict my student contact time, too. This is not a loss. My students are mostly assholes. Luckily, they did not get a picture of Dan, so his job is safe.'

I must be staring blankly.

'My boyfriend who looks after the incalls? Although I wonder if we may have to have an uncomfortable conversation with his parents some time.'

'I'm amazed you're being so, eh, strong about it.'

'It is like I told you,' she says, shrugging. 'I have had a feeling that this was coming. I am an immigrant and I am a working girl, and I am not quiet and I do not let them pretend I do not exist, so they will punish me. They do not like it when you stick your head above the, ah . . .'

'The parapet,' says Suzanne.

'So. It is not as though I am a celebrity. It is not Britney Spears who charges five hundred pounds a night. This will be gone by next week. For now, Suzanne is being very lovely and Dan and I can sleep on her sofa.'

'Oh, I've got a spare room! You can come and stay with me,' I say, the words spilling out too quickly.

She looks at me for a fraction of a second longer than is easy.

'No, it's okay. You have your daughter.'

'She won't mind!'

'Fiona. You have not seen the scrum outside my flat. These people are animals. You do not want them to know

234

your face, or your daughter's face. Trust me. You are safer staying out of it. Although, thank you for your offer.'

'It's nice you've come, really,' says Suzanne, 'but I think you might need to be careful. You could lose your job if you're pictured with us. Think.'

They are managing me as though prearranged, encoded meaning flickering between the two of them. I can feel it.

'Well. Not really much of a job, is it? Working for them.'

Suzanne's face sets, because she hasn't caught the sarcasm. 'Everybody needs a job. Especially with that lovely wee girl.' The judgement in that nips the air for a couple of seconds.

'Right. So, what you're saying is, I *shouldn't* have jeopardised my livelihood to help your campaign out with some inside information? Because right now, I'm feeling exactly the same way.'

Anya has turned away, so she doesn't see that I'm saying this right at her.

'You volunteered to help us,' she says, with a shrug.

'And it was the right thing to do, dear.' Suzanne has switched back to mothering.

'No, it wasn't. Because what seems to me to have happened is that I gave you information which you have used to cause structural damage – maliciously – to the building once you'd conceded defeat. That damage has left a man who I have worked beside for three years hospitalised and possibly unable to work again. As you can imagine, I'm not feeling very good about this.'

'You think we did that? You're swallowing the line those murderous bastards at Jackson Group have fed the press, huh? This is what you think of us? We are not the ones who disregard human lives, Fiona.'

She's flicking through the paper, rustling it angrily. The story of Norman's accident is thrust in my face, the word 'HOOKER' in the screaming headline accidentally right above his photograph, and I have to swallow an impulse to burst out laughing at Norman's own personal hell. Anya's furious face is up close, her spit on my cheek as she talks, her accent stronger than usual.

'So, either your buddies in Jackson Group have this fantastic, sharp PR team, or they have perhaps been expecting something like this to happen?'

A finger with chipped black polish directs me to the final paragraph.

A spokeswoman for the Jackson Group said: 'We are deeply saddened by this incident, and our thoughts and prayers are with Mr Black and his family at this time. We are also working with our partners RDJ Construction to examine whether this might have been the result of deliberate structural damage occurring during yesterday's protest. Mr Jackson urges parties involved with the ongoing campaign against the development who might have any information about this incident to come forward immediately.'

'They got that into an edition of the newspaper that came out last night.'

'That doesn't mean anything. That doesn't mean it wasn't you. Maybe you didn't do it deliberately, but you still might have done something.'

'Fiona, you need to remember that you weren't there,'

says Suzanne, in a purposefully reasonable voice. 'We spent most of the time in our own main space, absolutely not touching the walls or beams. We didn't want to give them an excuse to arrest or sue us.'

'We made a film of us in there, to put up on the campaign page,' Anya says. 'We will be able to prove this if it ever comes up. You know what I think? I think your good friends Jackson Group maybe wanted out of this altogether, hey? Maybe they discover the investment won't work, set this up, have it pulled down for scrap, save their fingers from being dirty, huh? Maybe your Norman Black is just collateral damage for them. For them, not for us.'

'We've no proof of that,' Suzanne says, quickly. 'They're a corporation; of course they will have a PR team who move fast. Who knows what they do. Don't get paranoid.'

The meetings I take minutes at with the Jackson Group representatives, their expensive aftershaves choking the air conditioning. Norman nodding seriously along with everything they say.

'Whatever has happened, they are capitalising on it pretty nicely, hey?'

'Anyway, it's been a rough one, Fiona. I think both Anya and I could do with a nap. Remember, we've had it pretty hard today too. Anya especially.'

As I wonder whether Suzanne knows she's being quite so patronising, the secret understanding between the two of them crystallises in the air around me, begins to escort me out. I just need to check.

'Do you know who it was, the person who tipped the paper off about you, Anya?'

'Oh, we've got ideas.' Suzanne's lips are set tight.

'This information, I think, could have come from someone at Jackson Group,' Anya says, 'or maybe from our lovely friend on the council, Ms Claire Buchanan: she certainly was not happy with me the other day, was she?'

'Oh no: Claire is an idiot, but she's not –' I'm saying before I've thought it through. Shut up, I'm urging myself. Why are you standing up for *her*?

'So you do know her. We thought so.' Anya is staring me down, one eyebrow raised, her nostrils flared again.

'We just met at a hen party. She's not a friend. We don't get on.'

'What is she, an old girlfriend? You are angry with her so you try to help us, make up some story about a missing sister to get in? Then, maybe she takes you back, or you make up after you see each other at our meeting, after your eyes meet, and suddenly you want to help her again? So you tell a journalist who I am? Is that how it worked?'

'Anya,' Suzanne says, flashing a warning. 'You maybe just need some sleep now.'

It's rising in me.

'Sure. Sure. That's what you think of me? Sure.'

'Well, you know that I am at the university, don't you? You seem to have worked out my real name somehow although I have only ever referred to myself as Sonja around you. And it would not have been difficult for you to contact a journalist – I would bet many of them are calling your office at the moment, hey?'

Her face is red with it, red and sharp with scorn for me,

scorn that I realise has always been there. Anya thinks I'm a weed, something flimsy and disposable, and she's right. I don't stay and stand up for myself. I run mimsily out, take my anger out in tuts and forceful elbows on other bodies in the bus queue. I grip Bethan's hand too tightly pulling her up the hill away from afterschool, and when we get in I put a bowl of cereal and a carton of milk in front of the television for her, then go straight to the computer and spend three hours composing a long and nasty email to Anya. In it, I point out that

– my sister is very real

– Claire is not my ex-girlfriend, and I am not a lesbian

– her real name was in the paper after the first report on the protests and it couldn't have just been me who made the connection

– she is disgustingly ungrateful given that I risked my job to help her

Because that is how we do things, we cowards. By stealth, behind backs.

I have a look at the copy of the paper, after I've hit send, after I've fizzed, after I've noticed that Bethan has fallen asleep on the sofa and felt, again, like a terrible mother. Norman and Anya, Anya and Norman. The two people I'd been most angry at, on pages one and four.

I scoop Bethan up in a move I've practised over the years, so gently that she doesn't wake. I tuck her in and decide to curl myself around her, as though tonight she needs an extra layer of protection.

ANGER

All right. It's going to get political. And angry. I am very, very angry. So those of you who just come here for the pictures of my bum, be warned, there's going to be precious little in this one for you.

On Tuesday I was on my way to a booking with a new client. I sat in the back of the taxi, checking my phone, idling away the time, when the news filtered through, as it does. A woman who I knew, as we all know each other, by her pseudonym Ravishing Rosa, was dead.

I never met Rosa, but we'd been in touch online, and I knew her work. I admired her for her keen anger, her sense of justice, her humanity. She was a mother, a great writer, a passionate campaigner and a sex worker, and she was murdered. Not, as you've immediately assumed, by a client or a pimp. Like the vast majority of murder victims the

240

world over, Rosa was murdered by someone she knew very well indeed.

Rosa was murdered by her ex-husband, who had made a number of threats against her, but who she was forced into contact with three times a week by the legal system in her country in order to have access to her children. Rosa lived under a legislative system which has criminalised the purchasing of sex, leading to a rise in rapes and attacks on sex workers as they're forced into the shadows to carry on living, and which proclaims loudly that sex workers, or 'people who have been prostituted', as it would rather have us called, are victims. Victims of the wicked male demand for sex on tap, and victims of their own bad choices. A legal system which looked at a woman who has fled an abusive husband, and ordered him sole custody of the children because she, as a 'person who had been prostituted', was suffering from 'diminished responsibility'. They didn't conduct any sort of mental health assessment, the people who declared this (although they work for a state which sanctions sexual assault – in the form of forced genital swabs – on sex workers when collecting evidence to pursue their cases). They simply looked at her occupation and declared her not sane. Unable to care for her children. So, when she reported that her husband was making threats upon her life, these threats were not taken seriously. Rosa was told by the legal system that could have stopped this that sex work was a form of self-harm, and as she refused to accept this, she was mentally unstable. There are no other circumstances where a man with a conviction of violence could have been granted sole custody, and no other circumstances where a woman who claimed this man was making threats against her would be forced into continual contact with him.

Rosa was twenty-six years old.

And now.

This is the same system, the same way of looking at sex workers, that certain politicians are trying to introduce in this country today. This month. Despite it not having led to any convictions in the ten years it's been part of legislation in Rosa's home nation. This is the way that a certain percentage of the population of our country – our friends, perhaps, our neighbours, the people we sit beside on the bus – think of us. As babies. Damaged children, incapable of making our own decisions.

They say they want to bring this legislation in because they want to send a clear message to the men who purchase sex. That message is 'women are not for sale'. They say that they're doing this out of concern for us. That this is about equality. That this is about feminism.

What they've forgotten, in their excitement to spread their message, is the day-to-day lives of

242

their poor little victims. Our right to safe working conditions and being treated like the adults we are. Our equality, with every other human being.

If there's one thing that Rosa's case shows, it's that sex workers need, above all else, to be able to trust and confide in the police. It's very difficult to do that when even just admitting what your job is makes you immediately an accessory and uncooperative witness to a crime; it's even harder to do that when it means immediate erosion of your basic rights as an adult.

The Scottish Union of Sex Workers will be taking part in worldwide protests this Saturday to remember Rosa and make it clear that her death, and the attitudes leading to it, will not be allowed to stand in this country. There's a complete list of the protest sites across the country here. We expect there to be some photographers there, so please do bring a wig and mask or some sort of disguise if you're attending. And a red umbrella. Bring a red umbrella.

Tags: anger activism the business rosa | **Comments (279)**

FIVE

MIND

We're snacking on small-person food tonight. Half-sized white and orange sandwiches with the crust cut off, squares of cheese and tomato pizza, dry slices of cake. The bland things that children are taught to like. Most of the decorations are down now, but the plain grownupness of the room is broken up by scraps of wrapping (pink) and shards of burst balloon (also pink). It's been a long, loud day – at one point all three of us winced as one at the volume of noise bouncing off the ceiling – but it's been good. The planned garden treasure hunt was rained off, but we managed to keep them entertained even as they were caged up. Bethan and Amy, her current best friend, loaned out for the treat of a sleepover, have finally collapsed into sleep after performing speeded-up versions of all the songs from *Mary Poppins* for us in a state of near hysteria. We'd clapped, applauded, overseen toothbrushing and pyjamas together, like a three-headed parenting machine. Then we sank into companionship in the sofa, me, my dad, my mum. I hadn't felt as close to them for a long time.

Dad had gone downstairs for another bottle, and his bringing it back, uncorking and pouring me a glass seems to have been a prearranged signal between the two of them, because the air in the room tilts and they breathe in as one.

'So, we've been thinking, lovey.'

'It has occurred to your mother and me that this is a significant – a, well. Yes. Anniversary.'

Tripping over each other's sentences like they've rehearsed it.

'Seven years, Fi. Beth's birthday means it's been seven years now.'

'That's the time, you know. The period of time they need.'

'Need for what?'

'Well, do you remember that the policewoman told us that when we first reported her? No, no, maybe, no. Of course you wouldn't. None of us were really . . .'

I cough, cut through her.

'Are we talking about Rona? Are we? Could you come out and say it if so? And then, could we just drop the subject again? We've had a great day today. It's been one of the first times I can think of that all three – four – of us have properly enjoyed ourselves. As a family. Let's not let her intrude. Just this once. Come on.'

Mum is backing down before I've finished, ever-conciliatory.

'You're right, you're right. Of course, darling. Not today –'

'Why not today?' says Dad, suddenly, my quiet befuddled dad, rubbing his eyes. 'Why not, and for all the reasons you've just said, Fiona. It's been seven years, and your mother and I were discussing that that means we can have your sister declared legally dead. What do you think?'

'What?'

It's not just what he's saying. It's the force of it.

'Have her declared legally dead. And then we get on with our lives. Perhaps we move house. She doesn't seem to want to come back to us: why should we wait around for her for the rest of our lives? This isn't healthy for us, especially for you and for Bethan. The two of you need to live in a new place, away from here. Too many memories here: I'm sure you feel it every time you come downstairs: imagine how it feels for us living in it. You're still young. You should be able to have a proper life, not one your sister dumped on you. What do you think?'

The effort seems to have exhausted him. He doesn't like to speak for this long, with this sort of force. Mum is staring as though she's never really seen him before. She actually looks a little bit turned on.

'She's not dead, though,' I say, finally.

'Well, none of us know that really, lovey –'

'Yeah, I think we do. She's not dead, she's just deliberately dragging it out. She wants us to do this. We're not giving her what she wants. Not again. We carry on, and when she comes back, we force all the pain she's given us back on her. Twenty times and much more if it makes us feel better. But that's what we do.'

I storm off to bed, shaking, leaving them to finish the bottle on my sofa. I put my head under the covers, and try to work out why I'd said all that. Because really, it made sense. Kill her off. Finish her. Let it go. Perhaps it's just hearing my parents voice it, that they could cut her off. No, I really just don't want to let her get away with it.

She can't feel as present to them. She left me, not them. The wound's not as fresh. Not like the way she lives with me, seeping through into my life, sticking angry fingers into her curls, jabbing and fuzzing them higher till the light glows through them.

'It says here that your hair should always have volume and lift in it, so that's what I'm doing. So shut up, flathead.'

And she closed the door to our mutual bedroom on me, pop static flaring out from her radio.

'Will you both be quiet,' our father howled, from the room he insisted on calling a study. He only communicated in cries of pain and frustration over this period; it was a long time before we got sentences addressed to our individual selves, by name. He would be in there by the time we came home from school, typing, typing, swearing, moaning. At the weekends he would leave in the morning, switching on the telly for us, come home in the evening with shopping bags full of tins. In the period after our mother left him, during which point Rona and I shuttled between our old flat in the city and this wobbly-walled semi, he was Writing. If we'd listened, perhaps we would have heard him tell a story of child and wife and work-thwarted ambitions; but we were thrawn, hurt teenagers, so we mocked him for it.

'Mr Shakespeare, is that you?'

'Watch out, Rona, there's Very Important Writing happening in here today.'

We were never closer, Rona and I, than when we were making our father feel small and bad about the breakdown of his marriage.

Back. Mum's red face, a head below his, screaming.

'You arsehole, you weak, ineffectual little man, stabbing away at that self-indulgent crap while I raise the fucking children you foisted on me.'

We'd sat at the top of the stairs, just out of sight, scared to breathe in case they heard us, and Rona had curled her thin pyjamed limbs into me.

Forward. Mum, slightly boozy over the Moses basket I'd found at the charity shop, on the third night, when we'd pulled our three shell-shocked selves together in the same place, whispering.

'Fiona, I should take her. It should be me. It's my fault, it's all my fault. I let her think this was acceptable. She's just copying what I did to you. Let me take the baby.'

No, I'd said. No. And I'd ushered her away from the room where Beth was sleeping, let the shame sit on her. This is just how we communicate, in a lazy slick of unsaid resentments, and I think it's suited us all, ever since, to live in our own guilt, stay mucky with it. Imagine we actually did it, declared her dead, drew a line under it and began to live again. The shock of such a psychologically healthy action could actually kill us.

The next day, I dropped in on them at breakfast: they'd promised to take Beth and Amy to the park. I held the girls in front of me, human shield against conversation.

'Let me think about it, okay? Just give me some time.'

BODY

Ask, and ye shall receive, right?

'Thanks for coming in, Fiona. Have a seat.'

'That's okay. I wasn't. I wasn't too busy or anything. Thanks. Thanks.'

There's something about his manner worrying me. He sighs.

'As you might have heard, we lost the Jackson Group contract. The development won't be going ahead. In fact, there won't be any more contracts with them: they've decided to sever all ties with RDJ.'

Norman was still in hospital, a week afterwards. He probably wouldn't be able to walk again. The enquiry had already 'discovered' that the site was certainly not suitable for the planned developments, meaning that the Jackson Group could whisk away from the investment. The office had been a silent terrible place where no one met anyone else's eye. It wasn't just that we missed Norman's forced, terrible jokes against the air con whirr: we all had a sense that when blame came, it would lie with the surveying department. Probably

249

even with Norman himself: in the last few days something almost imperceptible had shifted, and it was only Moira who could bring herself to mention his name. Without being told, the staff had somehow picked up who the pariah would be.

All the many meticulous surveys Norman had completed, to the letter, always to the letter, the teeth-grinding irritation of his checks and double-checks. Anya's conspiracy theories about Jackson Group came right into focus there, in my boss's office.

Ian is frayed at the edges, one hand gripping his desk to make sure it is still there.

'The thing is, Fiona, that relationship meant a great deal to this company, and especially this branch. An awful lot. Our finances have not been, ah, excellent. Not for some time. There was a lot resting on this project, and I admit it was a big risk to take. We took that risk, and it hasn't paid off. And now we're going to have to look at ways of economising, ah.'

'Starting with my job,' I finished for him.

He sighed again.

'I'm sorry, Fiona. I really, really am. This has come from above me – this "credit crunch" thing they're all talking about –'

He did quote fingers, not trusting the idiom to carry.

'We'll give you at least a month's salary, just to get you back on your feet. It's just, your position is the most – expendable. Elaine can do a few extra hours to manage my calendar, and I think we'll be putting the databasing project on hold for a few months, at least. It's not a priority any more. And there are people who've been here longer.'

'Is this just because of the circumstances?'

Another pause, another sigh.

'I have always been very happy with your work, Fiona. Very happy. I'll be giving you a satisfactory reference, certainly, and let there be no doubt that the only reason we're having to let any staff go at all is because of our current financial situation. But I'd be lying if I said that your, ah, two years here have been entirely without incident. There have been complaints, about your loyalty to the company, and about your use of computers.'

'Elaine,' I say. Clenched jaw. No point hiding what I feel, I think. No point, now. At the same time, I've realised, they have not found me out.

'And your efficiency. Look, I know you're a clever girl. I'm well aware that you've just been doing this job because you need the money, because you need to support your daughter. I know that organising my meetings, basic data entry and making sure Norman gets his tea in the mornings – I know you've always felt like this was a temporary stop, that it's not the sort of work you thought you'd end up doing. But management doesn't see it like that. Those employees to whom this company has meant a career, has become their life. They don't necessarily see it like that.'

'I've always worked hard here,' I say. One of those comforting little lies you tell people and yourself, sometimes.

'Fiona. You were seen taking cups of tea – cups of tea made with *company teabags* – to those idiots who chained themselves to the railings last month. Those idiots who had, not half an hour before, committed criminal damage on my car. Those idiots whose actions contributed to

RDJ Construction not only getting some very unwelcome publicity, but also losing one of the biggest contracts in our history. You made them tea, Fiona!'

Company teabags. Oh, he suspects. He does. But he can't prove it was me. Everyone at that meeting had access to those minutes, and he doesn't know for definite that they were leaked to the protesters. I decide to keep bluffing it out, keep angry and innocent. Keep my reference and my redundancy pay.

'Look, I know Elaine's always had a problem with me, but to be quite honest she's not –'

'It was Norman who showed me the footage,' Ian says. 'The police wanted the CCTV tapes of the day of the protest, and I'd asked Norman to go over them for me. Tea. Cups of tea. On a tray.'

Norman, his checks and double-checks. The petty little jobsworth soul of him. I thought of the denouncement that would probably come to him, his prone body, and he'd be unable to deny it, build a defence as two big companies hung him out to dry. I don't know if that makes it better, to be me just now.

'It was a cold day,' I said, helpless.

XXX

'Can we take you out for a wee drink, hen?'

Moira, her hand smoothing the back of my shirt, perhaps not even aware it was there.

'Just me and Graeme. Maybe Elaine? Maybe big George? After work on your last day? We can pop down the road to the pub, get a wee bit of food? Just thought you'd maybe like a wee send-off.'

252

'Och no, Moira. I wouldn't want to put anyone out.'

'Ah, go on,' she says. She smiles and her features dissolve in it. 'We'll miss you here. You've been a good girl, and it's a shame, so it is. Go on. You deserve it. We'll put a kitty together. God knows we could do with a wee bit fun, eh?'

Features gone entirely now, just the smile. It's the first time I've seen her do that faceless smile since the accident. Even the news last week that Norman had come round, had gone through the first round of surgery successfully, would be able to have visitors, hadn't shaken the fat grey silence hanging over Moira's desk.

'I'll lay a wee bit of a guilt trip on Ian, eh. Get him to pay for it.'

There's a bit of me that's looking forward to walking right out of RDJ Construction, wiping my feet, climbing the hill and never having to come back. That's not the bit of me that nods at Moira, says, okay, and gets on the phone to beg yet another favour from my mum. A good girl. No, Moira, I'm not. But out of everyone in that office, it's important to me that she thinks that.

Red velvet seats and framed adverts for cheap wine. Everyone buys me drinks. We sit round a table where conversation needs to be jump-started every ten minutes, Elaine and big George and Graeme and Moira and me. Ian had stopped off 'just for twenty minutes' to put £50 behind the bar and kiss my cheek drily, awkwardly, wish me luck. He stayed, though, talking work and avoiding my eye, burying himself in conversations

253

about the local council and the motorway works, about taxes rising, and big George saying I know, I know, you're right there man.

Elaine. Why is Elaine here? Because it's correct, I suppose, the company represented correctly at every work social gathering. Elaine talks mostly to Moira, sometimes to me. Sometimes she talks to the table, and when she talks to the table she is mostly addressing Graeme, and her voice is lacquered.

'So, what do you think you're going to do now, Fiona?'

Elaine has no problems with me any more. There is patronage in her voice. I am no longer a problem in the work place, a discredit to the company. I've become a formality, and Elaine understands formalities.

'Well, I don't know, Elaine. Think of all the possibilities, eh! Two months' salary and the whole world spread out in front of me. Certainly no need to go back to the old nine-to-five right off – it's not as though I've got any ties, now, is it? I think the first thing I'll do is buy myself a really nice handbag. Maybe get my nails done. Where do you go? Who does yours?'

Her face shuts down. She understands that something isn't correct here.

I am bright. I fizz with the drink in me, talking too loudly and laughing hard, brittle at everyone's jokes. I am made of exclamation marks. I'm dazzling.

I'm playing Rona, shellac-glossed. I am too good for these people, that job, this bar.

'Anyway,' Elaine's saying. 'Anyway. I'm going to have to get going. Moira, you wanting to share a taxi? George? Any takers?'

She's done her duty, has Elaine. She doesn't have to stay here any longer.

'Aw, come on!' I'm shouting. 'It's my leaving night! Who's up for staying out? Graeme? Ian, you going to stay out and see me off?'

'I think I'll go with Elaine, hen,' Moira's saying. 'It's just making me. You know. Norman would have loved this, all his colleagues out tonight.'

Norman would have hated this, I think. Too much frivolity. Too much me.

She hugs me again, kisses my cheek.

'Bye, love. Thanks for everything, eh.'

'I'll just get these girls home, I think, Fiona,' Ian says, a hand on the small of Elaine's back to usher her away from the table, the shameful sight of me.

She leans in to him with surprising familiarity. I wait until Moira and big George are out of earshot at the door.

'Are you two sleeping together, then?' I say, cheerily. 'Gosh! Just think of the blackmail opportunities there! If only I'd known, eh?'

'What?' Elaine turns round on me. 'You watch your –'

'Just leave her, Elaine. Just.' Ian holds onto his dignity. 'Fiona, I know you're upset but that's a very wild accusation. I suggest you go home and get some sleep.'

'Right, Graeme,' I'm saying, volume up as we watch their backs leaving, their stupid boring coats, their self-righteousness. 'Right, Graeme. Looks like it's just you and me, kiddo.'

Graeme just looks at me with his stupid face, giggling.

'I can't believe you said that to Ian and Elaine! Did I

laugh? Shit, you don't think I'll get into trouble for it? Hah! They totally are, aren't they! Can't believe you said that, eh!'

There's an approximation of a smile, and the weight of alcohol swimming behind his eyes. Doesn't matter. I've made my decision for the evening. Mortal fucked, we used to say at school, meaning drunk, that crazy drunk where you've no responsibilities. I am getting mortal fucked tonight.

Last orders comes and goes. I ask him a couple of times how he's feeling, and he shrugs, says the bruises are healing, says he doesn't want to talk about it. We talk instead about films we've seen, lurch out of the pub with our arms round each other like a cartoon of drunks. We stand there for a bit and there's that long moment that seems to go on forever, his head and his smile hovering over mine. The bit before it happens, where men look down on you.

He puts a hand on my cheek. I stroke a finger down his neck and he shivers, and I wonder who touches Graeme, really, with his acne scars and his mumbling. Who lays hands on the single people? Why shouldn't we have touch too, if we can, take pleasure in this close-ness? I think of the cold-bodied quick hugs I've had from friends and parents, a perfunctory rub of arms through jumpers or coats as greeting.

'We need this,' I'm maybe whispering, and he nods and kisses me.

Who touches the ugly people, the shy people? Who touches the ill people, the disabled, the ones who don't win? I think of Anya, imagine her performing this sort of service with the professionalism of a nurse. Graeme's cold hand flutters around my waistband, timidly reaching down.

'God, you've got the most gorgeous arse,' he says, heavy boozy breath. 'I've always thought that.'

Something in me freezes there, turns off, just for a second. Cover it, cover it.

'Want to share a taxi, then?' I'm saying, gesturing to the empty road.

He's laughing. He's holding me with a revolving grip, like it's a dance, like we're at school, and I turn under his arm too hard, and we stumble, and we begin to sing.

Step we gaily, on we go. Heel for heel and toe for toe.

Old songs.

Arm in arm and row on row, all for Mairi's wedding! Graeme's rented flat in a new-build block, just on the edge of the Drag. He shares with other boys. Tiny hallway clogged with nothing but bin bags, air full of the crackle of electrical static. The noise of computer game guns and male competition coming from behind a door.

'Zat you, Gayboy?' someone's shouting.

Graeme opens a door for me and ushers me in.

'I'll just be a second,' he whispers.

He bends in for another kiss and misses my mouth before leaving me in the dark.

From next door, deep voices muttering. I put the light on and look at the very featurelessness of what must be Graeme's room. Hard blue carpet, the same sort of thing we have in the office. Cream walls. No posters. Piles of clothes on the floor, double bed shoved in one corner, telly in the other and a tiny strip of floor space between that and the mirrored fitted wardrobe

257

taking up one wall. I sit on the bed, on its plasticky-feeling sheets, rumpled. There is nothing to say about this room at all. There are no books, no CDs, nothing. Through the wall come grunts and cheers, and someone shouts Get in there, my son! Go on yourself, Gayboy!

The boys. Always with the boys.

Graeme's feet coming back down the hall. Too late to run for it. Not that I was going to run for it. The light is too bright, dead, so I fumble for an anglepoise, check myself out in shade in the mirror, all the gravity of the drink in me.

Graeme, it seems, has had a very different idea about how this evening is going to go. He comes towards me all eager clumsy hands and muttered gasps into my neck.

'You're so sexy,' he's saying, and I'm thinking yeah, actually. Yes, I am. I am sexy. For tonight, anyway. Not like Graeme, who isn't sexy at all. Graeme with his wet boozy mouth. I'm leading.

'Hey, hey,' he's saying. 'Take it easy, eh? We've got all night.'

I push him down on the bed and rub my hand over his crotch, thin Topman smarts left over from work. I probably say things like I know what you want. You bad, bad man, maybe. I straddle him, conscious of the weight of me pressing his legs apart and down. Crushing him, feeling him get hard underneath me. Gripping his wrists in my hand and doing violence with my mouth on his, just because I can. Because this is the sort of thing he likes, this bland man I've shared an office with for two years.

He's unzipped and still not quite hard in my fist now,

so I'm forcing my hand up and down, pinning his arms above his head.

'Come on. Come on, you bastard. Yeah. Yeah,' I can hear myself muttering.

There is no erection. There is even less erection.

'Look. Fiona. Look. Can we stop? Can we just –'

These things my hands are doing. These things my mouth is doing.

We lie there for a while. He says comforting things about it probably being the drink, and I realise that my skirt has ridden up around my waist in front of Graeme from my work and hustle to pull it down.

'God. Sorry. Sorry. M'drunk, eh. I should go. Sorry.'

He puts an arm over me, reaches round and tucks some hair behind my ear. He kisses my face, Graeme-from-my-work does. 'Hey. Hey. It's okay, Fiona. It's okay. You're just upset. It's been a hard week for you. Listen. Listen. Why don't I do something nice for you, mm? Let me.'

He kisses my neck and gently tugs my skirt up again, fumbles over my new-bought knickers and struggles a little to untie them at the sides. There is very little hair there any more – I've been experimenting with my razor. This is Anya's – Sonja's – look, and my favourite so far: everything gone bar a small dark triangle, its point blunted just above my slit. He runs a thumb over it clumsily, gasps, lunges.

Then the sudden wetness of tongue, spreading over me, broken uncomfortably by his cold sharp breath. A feeble lapping around all the wrong bits; the sharp sting of the booze from his mouth on the thinner skin. Graeme has absolutely no idea what he's doing here, but I'm touched. He's trying to make me feel better.

I wind fingers into his hair and begin to rock and stiffen against his mouth. I moan a little, just to encourage him, feeling absolutely nothing. The ceiling has been artificially lowered, has crusty Artex sworls and tufts all over. Why did anyone ever think that was attractive?

'Mmm. Mmm. Oh god, Graeme. That's so good.'

I raise my voice a bit, and through the wall 'the boys' whoop and laugh. Graeme, encouraged, laps harder.

I shuffle sexy images. Anya, her clitoral piercing exposed. Those two men in that hotel, their hands and mouths on me. Holly on all fours, looking back over her shoulder, mouthing fuckyoulookinat. I imagine getting my own photo shoot done, revealing myself slowly to a cameraman, showing more and more, and I find I'm rubbing myself, my neck and breasts, through my top. I imagine going to a hotel room with a stranger, that it just becomes about a cock, about a fuck, that it's anonymous. Behind the camera, the man has taken his cock out and is stroking it because I'm so fucking hot –

The pillow is between my teeth. From the living room, the sound of cheering. Perhaps I did that out loud. Graeme is sitting up, looking pleased with himself.

The sort of man who wants to make a recently fired woman come. The sort of man who will pull his co-worker out from under fallen bricks. All that time I'd idly dismissed him as nothing much, and there was all this depth and goodness in him. I want to do more for him. I sit up and kiss my own taste off his mouth.

'Right,' I tell him. I cup his face. 'I want you to tell me exactly what you'd like me to do for you.'

260

Remembering his emails, I let my hand slap him, just a little this time.

'Bad boy. What do you like? Tell me. We're going to do what you want. My little pervert.' It's a command, whispered, but with affection and through a smile, and he responds. This. This is how you do it, I think.

I wake up as dawn is beginning to prickle through his curtains. His cheeks are pink and fat, and one of his thumbs is lodged in his mouth. There's a decision to be made here. I can either curl into his arms, ride the hangover out when we wake together, let him see me lurching and ill, and make arrangements to go to the cinema some time, maybe get a pizza. He's nice. He's caring. You could do a lot worse, girl.

But. But but but.

People fuck for lots of different reasons: the taking or providing of comfort is just one. Out of gratefulness can be another. It doesn't all have to stem from actual lust: sometimes the simulation of it will do just as well. I might have been pretending half of that last night, but it doesn't change the connection we made, or the things we trusted each other to do.

Gently, so as not to wake him, I unknot the plain work tie still attaching his other wrist to the bed frame before I leave.

Outside, the Saturday morning streets are sleepy. In the distance, industrial drones from the motorised road cleaners scooping up payday-Friday debris; the abandoned fish suppers, the condoms. Not my job any more. I smile up at the sunrise and feel like something's changed in me.

MIND

Beth had been building something on the floor, her back straight up against the sofa, her hair streaming over my knee. I was making tiny plaits in it, stroking her furzy curls smooth as TV flowed over us.

This calm, after school, before dinner, time just to enjoy my girl. Space where we're quiet together, resting easily against each other. It happens in time that previously belonged to the office, had been held for me by afterschool minders. I'd been quiet around the house during the day while she was at school. I'd cleaned, shopped, organised games and surprises, bought treats, new books, new toys, waited for her coming home like a moony new lover. The computer, that hard little portal connecting me to the outside world, to all the mess and fuss I'd created for myself, stayed closed. If you don't allow yourself to think about any of it, don't allow it in, it can't touch you. That was a revelation, actually, that if you just pull away, opt out, the world will carry on quite happily without you. Graeme called me, once. I let it go to voicemail, and didn't listen to the message, and then I didn't have to think about that, either.

Beth had been opening out under this new sun-lamp of attention I could give her, telling me more about her day, creating jokes with me. She's louder, laughs more, asks more questions. I don't – the other thing I was trying not to think of is that it would have to stop, and soon. My redundancy money would only last us so long, especially at the rate I was spending, and Mum and Dad can't support the two of us. There will have to be another job, chosen as arbitrarily as the last one and as dull as the last one, because what else can I do, now? I'm twenty-nine years old with a limp CV of low-order admin jobs and temping, and four months as an intern at a publishing company before all of this. I have no particular talents or transferable skills, or if I do I've never had a chance to discover them –

– Beth wheeled her head round, hissing, 'Ow! You're hurting me.' I'd been pulling her hair too tightly without realising. Now, I've played this scene back in my head, over and over, and I think it started here, meaning the fault was ultimately mine: her scornful mouth and the knit of her eyebrows channelled Rona, again. This had been happening more and more. The resemblance has always been there, yes, but it was just the markings of the tribe, denoting her as ours, of our family. Now, as her features shift out of babyhood, Rona's there, almost all of the time. It smarts, if I think about it. That's the hardest one not to think about.

'Don't be cheeky,' I'd said, irritated with all three of us.

'It's not being cheeky to say you're hurting me.'

'Bethan Cam– Bethan Leonard. What have I told you about answering back?'

'What have I told you about answering back?'

And she was so exactly Rona then, right down to the high-pitched sneery voice that used to drive me impotently angry when the tired old repetition trick was played on me as an older sibling. So exactly Rona that I struggled for breath. Bethan shrunk small again, and neither of us really knew what to say.

'Apologise for that. Now.'

The dance across her face, as she decided to push it further. This was new ground for us, so her 'no' didn't really have the courage of its convictions. It was enough, though. Had I been spoiling her, these last couple of weeks? Had she stopped respecting me? Was that it?

'You go to your room. You go to your room immediately. And you sit there, and you don't even think about playing with anything, any of your toys. You will sit on the chair and you won't come out until you can tell me why that was wrong and that you're sorry.'

She didn't move.

'Did you hear me? I said now.'

Her arms and legs flounced, the strop exaggerated, but she turned and left the room. There was something still to come, though.

'Fine. Fine. You're not my real mum, anyway.'

Oh, you'd known this was coming, hadn't you? Admit it. Always somewhere there, at the back of your head, the anticipation of this moment. No matter how needily I court her affection, you knew she'd always really known the truth, was just waiting to grow into it. I'm not her real mum. You are –

I'd tuned in to myself screaming at her back.

264

'What did you say? What did you say? What did you say?'

Then I was sitting on the floor, pulling my knees in on myself.

Then I'd started shouting, through her closed door.

'Maybe you'd better go off and live with your real mum then, Bethan. I'm sure she'd love that. On you go. She really wants you to. That's why you're here, with me.'

Who told her? Did she overhear some conversation between Mum and Dad? Was it someone from the school – ideas flicking, a flash-fast shuffle, all the ways they could have found out. Someone with a grudge against me, someone in on it, like Samira? Was it something I'd said? Had she found something? Who told her?

And she shouted back, through the door.

'My real mum's a princess! My real mum is a Barbie Princess!'

I think the silence scared her, in the end. The door clicked open, anyway, and even from the place on the floor I'd curled up on, even with my eyes closed I could feel the soft flutter of her panicky movements.

'Mum. Mummy. I'm sorry. Mum, wake up. Mum. I was being bad. I didn't mean it. You are my real mum. Mummy. Mummy!'

Eventually, she'd lain down beside me on the floor, pulled my arm over her, sobbed in time with me, and I'd scooped her in and held her tight.

BODY

The skirt is tight and short and bright and she's right, it
fits beautifully. I just stare and stare, fascinated by the
curve and shape of my own backside reflected back to
me across three mirrored cubicle walls. It's a betrayal,
though, and I know it. It's a betrayal of principles I'd
held to myself for some time.

Her hair smooth and her makeup thick and lovely,
the assistant calls through the curtain, coaxing me in
the faux-intimate language of girly bonding.

'Well, come on out and let me see you, then! Aw, that
is so totally you! You've got such a great figure! You
need to show it off a bit more, eh? Look at your bum
in this! Here, hang on.'

I can smell her perfume and hairspray as she pulls a
scarf from the rack in the Personal Shopping Boudoir
and knots it round my neck; more of the strange close-
ness of strange women that I'm getting used to this
week. The last time I felt it was in the beautification
scrum at Heather's hen party, the cottage with its four
mirrors to fifteen women, cans and tubs and tubes and
sprays and pots rammed onto every flat surface, the

266

chemical-sweet air hanging heavy on us. Heather's friend Kelly was the furthest gone, up an hour before the rest of us and setting about her own face with the precision of a surgeon, twice a day, swabbing, plucking, squeezing, a different lotion to be applied to every contour. I'd watched her from my sleeping bag on the first day, woken by the faint hum of her straightening irons. The fascinating foreign ritual, smooth, practised movements as she bent to open and then close each tub in turn. The silliness of it all.

Heather had bullied and pouted Samira and me into a sad semblance of glamour at school, coaxed us into keeping watch in Boots while she slipped kohl and bruise-purple lipstick up her sleeves for us, although really our places in the social order had already been allotted and neither Samira's natural beauty nor my enthusiastic use of blusher would bust us out of that. Our jobs were to get good exam results, which we both did.

Two years after we'd all left school, Samira sent word up from Durham that she had no intention of being a doctor and had decided to move into public relations. She'd hit some sort of restart button whilst down there, discovered the uses of being appreciated only on the surface level, just as a pretty face. Or that's how I saw it, entrenching myself further in a self-righteous belief in my cleverness, even though I was struggling with my courses. Samira, from the centre of a bubbling, popping social life, began to resent her wasted teens, and the way I still personified them. We would sit together, grouped around a table at occasional Christmasses when we were all home, privately disapproving of each other, Heather (ever constant Heather, unchanged in her small vanity) our only conduit to conversation, and a decade's worth of rot set itself about us from then.

So it became a deliberate choice for me, not to dolly up. It became one of the only things I was really sure of: that I could see through the beauty myths fed to other women, that I had no need to waste my money and time on these rituals and potions. Back at home for the holidays, I'd cultivated it as a way to annoy my sister, my preternaturally wise sister, her breasts stretching the word **b a b e** on her T-shirt.

'God. Don't you ever pluck your eyebrows? You look like a yeti.'

'I'd rather look like a yeti than a vapid tart.'

'Fuck you.'

'No, fuck you.'

In my final year of university, I found a boyfriend who agreed with me. Brian was a member of the Socialist Party, and the first man I'd ever met who called himself a feminist. He felt things far more intensely than me; while I had always been content to understand the theory, Brian liked practical elements: he organised demonstrations and was earnestly committed to the principles of the female orgasm. He encouraged me to throw away the few sops I'd made to 'conventional femininity': my razors, face powder, mascara, deodorant. There was nothing wrong with my smell, or the way my hair sat naturally, he said. The girl in his politics class he dumped me for had beautifully sculpted eyebrows, and wore L'Air du Temps.

If I really believed any of this, of course, that wouldn't have been a turning point. Eight years on, I would have become Claire, sensible and defiantly hairy while henz around me clucked and pouted. Instead, I wear enough makeup to pass in the world, at work, even out dancing at a hen night; just enough to be ignored, overlooked as neither beautiful nor freakishly insubordinate. Last place in the pecking order round the mirror, but still being seen to do it. I shave my legs for nobody in the shower every day, and I have done since I was fourteen, hacking chunks of accidental skin with my father's razor.

As the woman in the beautician's rips the strip off my face (and I notice a couple of the pores above my eye prick with blood before the tears start, and she coos to comfort me, don't worry darlin, it only really stings the first time) it occurs that at least I'm feeling something.

For some reason, this needs more justification than the underwear, than shaving my pubes. The haircut; the free session with the personal shopper; the makeover at the beauty counter, me grown and freakish in a line of teenagers. Perhaps it's because I'm finally altering the outside of me, and it feels like a declaration to the world, not just a secret to hold close to my skin. I have allotted a certain amount of my redundancy pay to it.

Perhaps it's because, when I walk into my parents' kitchen that evening, my dad scalds himself with the pasta water and my mother bites her lip, hard, before they tell me how lovely I look.

I know what, and who, I look like. I also know what I'm doing.

There's not that much to all this, Rona, not really. Is this what you did? You just drew the person you wanted to be on top and then became it?

269

MIND

'Oh wow, I totally didn't know you were there! Hi! Can I speak to Dad?'

'No, you can't. He's out.'

'...'

'You didn't come to my graduation.'

'No ... I got your messages though. Couldn't get the time off work, yeah?'

'Jesus, Rona, I could really have done with the support. Dad was being ... Dad, Mum was carrying on as though he wasn't, and it was fucking awful.'

'I'm sorry. I'm really sorry, Fi. I'm sorry.' Sigh. Pause.

'How are you, anyway?'

'Oh great, great. Working, like, all the time, but great. This city's amazing, and the social life after hours is intense! Amazing clubbing. I love it here, yeah? So beautiful. Nothing like a fresh start, right! Amazing, seriously.'

'Great.'

'Great. How's. How's, ah – the boyfriend?'

'We split up.'

'Right. Sorry. Oh well, plenty –'

'Look, Rona, I'm going to have to go. Please give Dad a phone sometime. I think he'd really appreciate it. He's not so well at the moment.'

Pause. Sigh.

'And he misses you. She does too, you know that.'

'Yeah, I will. Totally. Couple of days or so. It's just been so busy. You know. New place, you want to live it to the full.'

'Rona? I'm moving back home properly next month. Got a flatshare in the West End, it's nice. Nice. You'll have to come through and see me? Or maybe I could. To you. Show me all the good bars. We can have a wee drink, talk properly? If that's okay. I'd like that.'

'Me too. Totally. Yeah, that'd be good. Great. I'll be back for Christmas so maybe then, yeah? Anyway, gotta go! Running late!'

BODY

Our clanging non-connection echoes off the past and the haughty architecture of this place that Rona once lived in and I could not. Basslines and saccharine-high vocals thumping, screeching from doorways tonight, the street pulsing with wealth. Gorgeous bodies spotlit through windows, clinking glasses, laughing, and I realise I am always looking for my sister on these sorts of streets: streets commandeered for pleasure, for the loosening of ties, the booze-buzz, the suggestion of sex. Whether you're in a winter sports hub or a capital city, the motivation's still the same. I watch a blonde woman in a black dress let a fake laugh warp her face, throwing back her head, patting a suited forearm. She's creased, skeletal, aristocratic cheekbones then a hollow. The stupid spark of a thought that I might have found the mysterious Camilla, first time, dissolves as my arm is bumped, gently, by a near identical blonde being escorted along the pavement.

'Oh my god, darling. Too funny. Too funny. And Tasha really believed him?'

The first woman clocks me staring, autopilot, curls a tiny lip and turns her back. On another street, in another city, I would have merited a fuckyoulookinat warface. I check the outside of the bar. Yes, this is The Grand, the sort of name I imagine gentlemen would have given to their clubs in Edwardian London, formerly Dee-Lite and, for four months, workplace of my sister.

Were my mistake not already obvious from the curl of that woman's lip, it clicks in as I open the door. I simply do not do this often enough to understand how to be here. With no pack of henz to belong to I do not make sense. Also, I have come in on a Friday night, as the various brokers and lawyers I presume I'm seeing around me are releasing a week of work all over the fast-paced all-female bar staff, who flick and turn within their enclosure like a ballet. Big eyes, short skirts, pretty hair, skinny legs. Red, bloated faces flirt with them, earn dutiful smiles. I add my body to the scrum, four-deep, press against other people's sweat and work, the rising rising noise of three hundred shouting voices. Rona's world, one of them. She knew this stuff like breathing.

I'd actually told my parents I had a date. I'd said it shyly. Asked it as a favour. Someone from my old job. Yes, he's very nice. I'd really appreciate it. There'd been so much genuine delight on Mum's face, as she teased me for answers, the recent makeover suddenly making sense to her in a world of logic that we all stopped operating within a long time ago. And was it the man from a couple of weeks ago? And how tall was he? And what was his position in the company?

I began to feel genuinely bad for lying.

It takes almost twenty minutes for me to work out how to get one of the girls' attention. They're lured by taller eyes, subtle gestures and the professional flick of banknotes. I have already missed chances – burrowing for the photos in my bag, pulling back in a crisis of confidence when I realised that none of the bar staff would have been old enough to have worked here seven years ago, simply not paying attention. The business of getting a drink is serious, competitive.

'May I speak to the manager?'

She doesn't hear me, frowns, mouths 'Sorry?'

'Gin. And. Tonic,' lips stretched, for show, because I've chickened out again. When she leans in close to take my money, I haul my torso half across the bar to get her ear.

'The manager. I need to speak to the manager.'

She shakes her head. Not a good time.

'Please. Please.'

She points to a corner of the bar, mouths 'Wait. There,' flicks off, ponytail swishing with the self-righteous weariness of someone who owns her corner of the world, works it, knows it. I find my place, tucked under a large pot plant, back to the wall, hide.

Streets full of bars and their beery insides. I'm conscious again of that other world out there, the one where people understand the language of the music and the codes of the night. That world I missed out on whilst living someone else's middle age. I'm not sure though that the people here know it. They are all a good decade older than the bar staff, a good few years older than me, even, and there's a smell or a pulse striking through them, thronging the air. It's desperation of a sort, a grabby panic that turns them on to each other, underscores all the flirtations and forced group interactions. This idea of the fun that we are supposed to be having, that we have all been sold. We are not so different, you and I, I think in the direction of my sneering blonde, now turning a sun-lamp smile on her partner. The bar girls are high-stepping queens, thin and lovely and impervious to our stench.

A man is coming towards me, all hair gel and official assurance.

'Hello, darling,' he says, in tones that even I can tell mean he does not fancy me a jot. 'I'm Carl, the duty manager here. As you can see, it's a bit of a busy time for us. What can I do for you?'

Deflated, I do not give good account. I mumble, repeat myself, apologise a lot. His eyes keep drifting off me to his work, his girls: I have to tug his sleeve to get him to look at the photos of Rona.

'Yeah, she's a bit familiar. When did she work here?'

I tell him for the third time.

'Sorry, I wasn't here then. To be honest, we've got a pretty high turnover of staff. A lot of young girls. I think the best thing to do would be to speak to Frank, he's the owner. Maybe come during the daytime. Phone first. Okay, I'm going to have to get back to work, dear. All right?'

The 'dear' a cursory sop to a much older woman, one who has lost her sex. Like a pat on the head. We are very probably the same age. He may even be older than me.

All this for that. All this. I still have most of my expensive drink left, and I decide not to waste it. There's a small table over in the window, near my blonde, my

Camilla-manque. A lone chair at it, the rest cannibalised to accommodate packs of cheering office-mates.

So, what would I say to this Frank, really? What would he say to me? Yes, she worked here for a while, years ago. No, we don't exchange Christmas cards. I wonder how quickly a job like this wears them out, the bar girls, when their bodies start refusing another and another late night. This is not a job you could do for years on end; it suits only young people in need of quick cash.

What did I really expect to get out of being here? Camilla's home phone number? For these people to capitulate and explain they'd been hiding Rona in the cellar the whole time? Behind the bar, Carl oils his way through the ballet, urging them on, mush, mush. One of them turns to face the till, blows air through rounded lips, counts three and slaps her smile back on for the next customer. No one stops.

Why would they remember Rona, really. High turnover of staff. The girls' value is all in their bodies, their youth and the stores of their energy. When they finally have enough and quit it's probably pretty easy to replace them. And all I get is another name, Frank, another road of possibility to set off down. And he'll just give me another name, and that name will give me another, and none of them will ever really get me anywhere.

There's a shadow over my drink.

'Well, you look like you're lost in thought.'

Yorkshire accent. Not from around here. He's large, this man who has placed himself in my eyeline. Not that he's fat, not exactly, although it's looming there, in his future. But for now, he's just large, in that fleshy way. Round face. Curved shapes under his shirt and a bit of a foolish smile on. I wonder if he's already regretting it: if he doesn't find me attractive up close, or if he's just playing that line back on itself in his head. I give him a smile and decide to see what can happen.

'I was thinking I'd like to get out of here. Want to come with me?'

'Sorry, didn't mean to bother you. Quite right.'

He's already turning off. I catch his forearm, make a gentle movement on it, bring him back round to me.

'Did you hear what I just said?'

He replays it in his head. Ding.

'Would this be a good time for me to say "I'll get me coat"?'

I can't tell whether he's more excited about the pull or the joke. He kisses fast and sloppily in the street and the taxi, ushering me up the stairs and past the sleepy-eyed concierge in his fairly expensive-looking apartment building. His breath is sour, his hands move steadily and his cock has a nice heft in my fist. Warm bodies moving together, and what moves and stirs me on is that I was able to conjure this. I wanted and I got.

There is nothing like the sweetness of my still-recent encounter with Graeme, but it's a thing in and of itself, this physical connection. He comes with his face clenched somewhere in the pillow over my shoulder and his fingers locked round mine, and freezes there for a second, making tiny noises on my skin. We disengage, and he smiles, strokes my face.

'Mm. Nice.'

'Nice.'

I use even, slow movements, because I don't want to

trivialise anything: I bend to check the condom – yes, still intact – then smooth hands on his chest and kiss him on the cheek. My clothes are tangled round the foot of the bed, and I reach for them.

'You're going already?'

He's still buried in the softness, and I'm in danger of snapping him out of it.

'Yeah. I've got a train to catch. But that was great. Thank you.'

'Wait. Are you – you're not a. Er. Is there a charge for this? Sorry. I hadn't – oh.'

'Hey, hey. No, I'm not. It's okay. I have to go, but I mean it, that was great. It was very nice to meet you.'

He sees that I'm biting back a giggle at the formality, meets me in it, and just like that, we're easy again.

'Would you let me see you, for a second? Just, before you get dressed? You're so lovely. Would you do that for me?'

Yes, I would do that for him.

Three hours after I arrived, I'm back at the station in time for the last train home, and I keep sniggering out loud in the empty carriage, dizzy with the ridiculous ease of this game.

Mum is sitting up at my kitchen table when I get back in, all that new glee still switched on.

'So. Tell me everything. Where did he take you?'

'Big bar, full of people. He was nice, but a little dull, really. Not sure we had very much in common.' It's not a lie.

'You had fun, though?'

My mother does seem to want me to have fun.

'Yeah. Yeah, it was good.'

Not a lie either.

'It's just great you're getting out there again, lovey.'

She wraps unaccustomed arms round me and her thumb brushes back and forth across my temple.

THE MEANING OF CONTROL

A well-meaning person once told me that she
worries about me, because I habitually put myself
in danger, because I do it daily. I told her I'd never
been in danger, and she wouldn't believe me. You
spend so much time alone with men who hate
women, she said. Your daily existence is a series
of situations you can't control. There is no way you
haven't encountered some sort of threat to your life.

Like I said, she means well. But she's also firmly
on the side of the angels; and by angels, you
know I mean the righteous ones, the campaigners,
the people who want to rescue me from myself.
She's earnest, and hard working. I like her. We
probably could have been friends, if she hadn't
suggested that I chose my job because I had been
sexually abused as a child, and I suggested in
return that she chose her job because she'd never
got over the trauma of losing her hamster to the
neighbour's cat when she was eight.

She's wrong about a number of things, my well-meaning almost-friend. Shall we bust some myths, my little perverts?

MYTH NUMBER ONE:
ALL MEN WHO USE THE SERVICES OF A SEX WORKER HATE WOMEN.

Of course, every one of my clients would say that they love women. In the moment, at least. Mostly, what they mean is they love women's bodies, and of course they do. Who doesn't love women's bodies (apart from the women themselves, ha ha)?

I might dress up as the big bad domme in my pictures, but the vast majority of my clients come to me for the girlfriend experience. They want a nice, affectionate fuck for fifteen minutes, then they want someone to hold them and listen to their worries until the hour's up. This might be because they're recently divorced or widowed, badly missing that companionship they've always had and not ready to try and find someone else. Or maybe because they're too shy or inexperienced to interact with potential partners. I have a number of disabled clients who just want to be treated like any other human for an hour.

When it comes down to it, we're just two people, alone in a room together. And who knows what's going on in their heads, but when actually con-fronted with a strange woman, the men I see are

overwhelmingly courteous, a little shy at first. It's
my role, in that room, to tease the sex out of them.

This isn't to say I haven't experienced misogyny.
Or the odd idiot who's there to act out a porno on
me. Most of the time, it comes from the ones for
whom a woman's right to say no has become a
personal insult. It can crystallise into hate, that sort
of frustration. You learn the tricks of them, though.
It's a challenge, making them see you as a person,
whilst still keeping them happy, but there are ways.

This is what my almost-friend is getting at, when
she says, with no practical experience of what
I do, but don't they just look at you as a female
body that's already been degraded?

And what I want to say to her, but don't, is that
this is the condition of earning money in this
world: sometimes, you do have to put yourself
out, in some way. There are people who work for
construction companies, who do manual labour
every working hour of the day, whose bodies
are used and used up by a system that never
adequately compensates them. Me, I can live
well off fourteen hours' work a week, and that's
including the time it takes to manage bookings and
keep myself in shape. And these idiots make up
maybe a twentieth of my total clients. Sometimes I
can go six months without so much as a sniff of it.

The reason I don't say any of this to her is because

it's really her who looks at me as a female body degraded, poor thing. She can't get past it.

MYTH NUMBER TWO:
AS THE CLIENT IS PAYING, THEY HAVE CONTROL OF THE ENCOUNTER

Oh no they don't. Do you call a plumber out and then sit there telling him exactly how to fiddle with your pipes (Ithangyew)? My services, my body, my rules.

I never, ever take risks. I don't accept last minute or late night bookings. I always insist on a landline number or registered, non-webmail email address as verification. My incall flat is security equipped, and if I'm going on outcalls, someone always knows where I am.

I control every aspect of my life, from the way a situation will unfold with a client, on a booking, to the people who can or can't be trusted to know what I really do, to the hours I do, or do not, decide to work. I don't drink any more, because I don't like the feeling of being out of control, not even for a second. Before I did this, I worked for companies who seemed to believe that they were buying a lot more than my services with their piffling salaries. As an employee, I was directionless, half my brain just shut down, marking time. I'm fully engaged now: with control comes self-respect. Funny that, isn't it? That it took working as a prostitute to get me to respect myself? And if you don't understand that, you won't. Ever.

MYTH NUMBER THREE:
ALL SEX WORKERS SECRETLY HATE THEIR CLIENTS

There is no such thing as 'all sex workers'. The reasons people decide to do this job are as varied as the people doing this job. (Although, we're all in it for the money, right? LOL.)

Personally, I think if you can't empathise with the client, see them as just another human being, you're not doing the job right. I've seen the bitching on the boards, girls sniggering about overweight or ugly clients. Well, fine, do what you need to do. In order to have a good working experience, I've found it's important to connect with the client, match yourself to them, whether they want to confess their secrets to you or just fancy a quick impersonal blowjob. And I seem to get a lot of repeat business . . .

Of course, there are the aforementioned idiots. The ones who start with a smirk, a glint, the hint of a fight. There are ways.

I begin by looking them in the eye now. I take the full force of me out on them. Here are the ground rules, I say.

You wear a condom for everything. You don't do anything without asking.

You need to take a shower first.

You must show me your fingernails before they go anywhere near my pussy.

After this, after this telling, often they're erect already, stiffening at the strength of me. Either because it's hitting some primal sweet spot, some small early fantasy of a teacher or a childhood friend's mother, or because they want to break me. And this is when I sugar it, smile and curve myself, look down and up again into them and let it come out all honey and husk, *And then we'll have a lovely time, hmm?*

Because that's the transaction. That's what we're going for really; that point of exchange where I can intimidate them into respecting me, but still leave them feeling manly, moved, protective. Because one sour bastard leaving a bad review could hurt my business worse than an over-long fingernail can tear, and that's the deal I've made. And there are worse deals you can make –

Oh, stop. Stop the show. This one isn't going out there. You don't get to see this. It's just for me.

Tags: private| **Comments (-)**

SIX

US

The hard stone of the Drag, again, as grey and nothing as today's flat, void sky. I stumble a bit on the concrete pitched slope I used to walk down every day, because my body doesn't recognise the balance needed any more. I'm out of the way of it.

Closed doors everywhere: the geographic heart of a city shut down at weekends. There's more to it, though: every third or fourth business is boarded up, the vacancy advertised in fading yellow, a jolt against the quiet streets.

TO LET

A number to call.

The long-faded warning signs that a crash was coming.

I'm early, deliberately. Not being nostalgic: I've no intention of sticking a wistful nose between the bars of what used to be the RDJ Construction car park gate. I just wanted to feel it around me, this area. I wanted to feel my own smallness under these buildings again, remind myself why I got out, why it was good that I got out. Instead, the whole of the Drag spreads out underneath me, coming closer as I begin to speed up, hunching my new leather jacket tighter around me, splashing coffee from a still-scorching cardboard cup. Through the grey there's a hard-edged beauty about it, the many storeys of steel and glass.

Tiny movement in the corner of my eye: something in one of the lanes ahead, a rustling in the shadow. I keep on down the hill, holding my legs back from breaking into a run, taking the time to use the proffered windows into empty call centre stations, vacated offices. All those jobs, one for every desk or computer monitor, precarious or already outsourced. A leopard-print thong draped on a parking meter. I give into the run for the last block, because no one can see me, using the pace to take me round the corner on to the flat.

Almost four years on from the plans, the protests, the building collapse, and they haven't even touched the site. There's a notice up proclaiming it unsafe, and splintering chipboard where the blue-painted Sanctuary Base door used to be, but no sign that anyone's taken an interest in it. It's just been left there, to go back to nature, weeds springing out of cracks on the upper floors. Still, it all looks complete, sturdy even, from out here. I wonder which bit of it fell in on Norman.

The girls, these days, have mostly been moved on. Gates wedge up most of the lanes, council iron, strong. They've drifted down to the river, hidden themselves away online. It's harder to reach them.

Footsteps. I'm pretty sure it's her, but I continue looking up at the building, throwing my neck so far back I'm at right angles. I let her come right up to me, take in the warmth of having a person beside me for a moment, an idea of height and weight in the air.

YOU

Camilla has one of those faces. One of those faces that used to be beautiful and hasn't yet realised it isn't, quite, any more; sour etchings around her mouth, a forehead that may have been repackaged, eyes with not enough spark in them to pull you past it. And she's thin, so, so thin. The well-cut dress, the heels and the huge head of styled, expensively streaked tawny gold waves would have intimidated me straight off if I hadn't noticed all this. Camilla the destroyer. Camilla the cause, the tempter. I'd made her into such a huge symbol in my head. Just a person. Just a strained, thin person.

She clocks me, comes over to the table, doesn't bother to introduce herself.

'Christ. You really do look like her.' Her laugh is one mirthless note. 'I mean, there are differences, sure, but, gosh. Family resemblance much?'

I don't really feel that she's earned this informality. There's an edge to it, a contempt. I'm remembering what Ally McKay said, that she'd laughed about my sister, called her a silly little cow. Sure, I've called Rona worse. But I've got reason, and besides, I'm related.

288

I stand up to shake her hand, letting her know the expected protocol. These investigations, from here on, will be conducted professionally, and will proceed as I want them to.

'I'm Fiona. Thank you for coming to meet with me.'

She takes my hand, resets her face to serious, and we both sit back down.

'Now, I'm not sure whether you know this, but my sister has been missing for seven years. She left Edinburgh, I understand, in some distress, after a period of close acquaintance with you; while we know that she then spent some time living up north, I'd like you to tell me about the period that led up to that. As I said, I'm happy to buy lunch for you in return. Perhaps you'd like a glass of wine?'

'That would be lovely, thank you.'

She modulates her tones to mine almost exactly, with a mocking aftertaste.

'I should let you know in advance that I was given your name by a man called Ally McKay, who filled me in on how you and Rona spent some of your time together. I also know that following her acquaintance with you, she earned money as a sex worker. Mr McKay told me that you were the person who introduced her to this profession.'

'Mr McKay.' Something like a smirk works her mouth. 'Lovely. Glass of Viognier and a green salad, please. No dressing.'

I've put so much concentration into my performance I haven't noticed the waiter standing by.

'Tell you what, darling,' she says, after he's gone. 'I'm happy to help however I can, but you really are going to have to be a little more discreet than that. So. Not a peep from her in seven years, then?'

'No. And my parents have raised the possibility we could have her declared legally dead now. So I'm – we're making one final attempt to look for her.'

'Gotcha. Urgency is the thing, yeah? May I ask, why only now?'

'We spent a considerable amount of time, patience and money looking for her. There was nothing for years, but suddenly, just in the last few months, there's been a new burst of information.'

She's right, though, and she knows she's rattled me. Running into Ally might have been a coincidence, but I could have gone and spoken to Christina again any time over the past few years. And I didn't.

'It's not leading us anywhere conclusive, though. Now, I'm aware that things between you and Rona didn't end well, but for a while you seem to have been her close friend, and so I'd really appreciate it if you can think of anything, any clue as to where she might have gone.'

And again, deflected.

'Wouldn't it be easier on your family just to have her declared dead? I mean, you'd think after seven years, if she'd wanted to be found – must be hard on you, mm?'

Camilla dropped her head, smoothed out a cuticle. God, she really didn't care. The words had all been said in the right order, but there was absolutely no concern here, none at all. Was this how she worked, this woman – cutting a thin blade through life, through other people's lives, stepping through, moving on? Could you be happy in a life lived like that?

Not that I was any expert in attachments myself, or happiness. The callousness though, the dismissing of my family, our worries, all contained in that one little gesture. The attraction she and Rona must have felt for each other, two beautiful sociopaths.

'I understand this isn't an issue you're particularly invested in, Camilla. I'm sure there are far more important things you could be doing right now. I'm sure my family's pain is of absolutely no consequence to you. On that note, is there any point in us sitting through lunch? If you're not interested in telling me anything, I don't really see that I'm interested in being around you.'

And like that, her face sparked awake. Joints slow and liquid, she leaned across the table, rested a hand around her face, sucked idly at a fingertip for a second.

Game played, game won: *coup de grâce.*

'So. How's my goddaughter?'

XXX

How had I found her? Camilla, the gatekeeper, the final clue, always out of reach. She certainly didn't advertise in the usual way. She wasn't google-able – god, no, darling – didn't run an outspoken blog or cheeky pay-per-view peep show website. Camilla, who worked for the most exclusive escort agency in the country, only saw very, very rich men. Politicians. CEOs. Visiting dignitaries. Her agent's phone number was locked in the BlackBerries of the concierges of five star hotels and country clubs, passed from gentleman's gentleman to gentleman's gentleman, and even managing to get the number didn't necessarily guarantee you a date with her.

It wasn't so much that she was ravishingly lovely, she would admit very honestly to me later, or that she had any particularly unusual talents ('although I am a great fack, darling. Obviously'). It was the very exclusivity of it.

'Oh, they rather go for it, yeah? The fact that hardly anyone can afford me. These chaps just like to think they're getting the best of the best, you know? And, obv, the accent helps. I mean, they can meet me and know straight away that I understand their world, lovely: I'm not some little street-girl faker who'll tell tales to the tabloids. Or worse, one of those bloody Eastern Euros, you know?'

As I was very much indebted to 'one of those bloody Eastern Euros', and had absolutely no frame of reference whatsoever for anything else she was saying, I kept quiet.

ME

It had been my newly proactive dad who'd forced the issue, eventually. Just the very fact of it having been seven years seemed to have jolted him out of our comfortable mutual torpor: that the law considered it an appropriate mourning period was good enough for him, and he had every intention of bringing the rest of the family with him. He was happy to respect my need to think over actually having her declared dead, but was giving absolutely no ground in any other part of his life. Physically, you could see the change in him too: he was standing taller, his beard was trimmed and neat and there was colour in his cheeks. I was also fairly sure I'd overheard sex noises coming from downstairs.

'Right. Fiona. Have you had a look at that email I sent you, with the new careers website details?'

'Sorry, Dad. I haven't really been looking at my emails.'

'Why not? What if you're missing job offers? Interviews?'

'Well, I haven't really been applying for anything recently.'

'How recently? What do you mean?'

'At all. I haven't really seen anything appropriate.'

He walked over to my computer, which was still shut where I'd left it, brushed a layer of dust off it.

'You won't see anything appropriate if you don't look, will you? Come on. Your mother and I have been very patient with you in this period, but we simply can't provide for you indefinitely.'

He pulled himself straight, formal, and I saw the teacher in him. He hadn't always been feeble and a laughing stock, my dad.

'I would also remind you that you argued for a long time that you, and not your mother or I, would be Bethan's chief carer. While I'm happy to support my grandchild in any way I can, you undertook a very significant responsibility to your d–. To your daughter.'

It may be the first time he's directly referred to Beth as mine. The moment takes us both by surprise, but he recovers first, still steely.

'To your daughter. And, quite simply, you need to be employed in order to fulfil that responsibility. If you have no other plans for the rest of the afternoon, I suggest you spend the afternoon searching for jobs.'

He taps the computer, and the dust brings him near to a sneeze, snaps him out of it.

'Anyway, love. I brought you this thing. It's an info sheet – a sort of template, you see? We've been doing CVs with the fourth year. I thought it would help you lay yours out properly.'

And he's shy suddenly, almost cringing as he hands me a dog-eared sheet of A4 with wrenched-out staples, scurries to the door calling over his shoulder.

'I'd be happy to help you, Fiona. I could have a look at it for you, if you want?'

I'm shamed more by his sweetness than the lecture, and switch the computer on for the first time in almost a month. It connects to the internet automatically, reloading all my bookmarks for me, all the websites and blogs I used to sit refreshing obsessively, all the punters' forums and call girl search engines with the details already filled in. Ping, ping, ping, ping, my other life, revving back up around me, its codes and colours, flashing GIFs and nipple shots.

It's like pressing a bruise, this feeling. It smarts, but you can't stop. I had reasoned with myself – just five minutes. Just until half past, then I'm going to go and look at this job search site of Dad's.

None of the searches returned any new Ronas, just as they never had.

On 'Scandi Sonja', Anya's fingers were still frozen across her piercing. The blog part of her site had been locked, though; there was only a short note informing me I did not have the authority to look at this page.

Holly's blog wasn't there either. In fact, her website had been taken down. I looked for her on the 'field report' section of the punters forum, where someone had removed her profile. The last review was dated seven weeks ago.

A session with Holly is always worth it, boys.
Everything about her is delicate: her slender figure, her kissing, the way she gives head, her little cunt. Truly a special pleasure – treat yourself to a night of it!!!

And that was it. There was no way of finding out what had happened to this girl, no matter how worried I was about her, no matter how real she felt to me. I could have said something, that day when I saw her in town; I could have contacted her, made an appointment, just checked that she was all right. Instead I just carried on reading her blogs and reviews, like they were there for my entertainment.

Enough. This was just not my world: my world was my daughter, and the only thing there was for me to do was look at the careers website my dad had sent me.

My email inbox wasn't exactly overflowing.

SENDER	SUBJECT
Gus Leonard	Jobs
Heather Buchanan	Answer your phone Fi!!!!
Scandi Sonja	Apology

YOU

Camilla passes me a napkin as I choke on nothing.

'I'm sorry?'

'My goddaughter. Bethan Camilla Leonard. I mean, we didn't ever bother with a christening, but you can see the intention's there. Left in your custody, I believe. How is she? Must be ... just turned seven. Oh. I see.'

She smiles, and it's sweet, almost caring. Of all the things I don't understand, in that second the sweetness seems most important.

'First off, darling; let's not assume that Mr Ally McKay is the greatest authority on either my life, or your sister's. Secondly, can we not come over all Spanish Inquisition about this, yeah? Won't be any fun for either of us.'

I take a huge gulp of wine.

'And thirdly, shall we order a bottle? Might help?'

'You need to explain things to me. Now. You saw my sister after she left Beth with me?'

'That does appear to be what I'm saying, yeah.'

It takes a huge effort not to claw at her face, jump over the table and snap her skinny bones. Fists around the metal poles of my chair, the new fingernails gouging skin. She does that laugh again.

'I'm sorry, lovely. Really. This isn't fair of me at all, and you must be feeling the shock.'

'Are you still in touch with her? Is she still alive?'

'Ah, you see, your information is partially correct. We did have a bit of a falling out in the end. Five years ago. Haven't heard from her since. Sorry – that rather facks with the whole "legally dead" thing, doesn't it? May we have a bottle of this, please? Thank you so much.'

Again, she doesn't break breath, turning her head and entire manner to the waiter, then shifting back to me again.

'Your sister left Edinburgh because everything, and I very much include your Mr Ally McKay in that, had got a bit too heavy for her. She needed a change of scene, one where she wasn't being facking stalked by a chippy little Glaswegian.'

'Ally is from Edinburgh.'

'Really? Gosh, doesn't sound like it. Anyway, he was, like, obsessed with her. Weirdly. Always turning up at her work, and when she left the job, he started coming round to her flat. I moved her in with me, but even then, he'd always be there at the clubs, you know, mooning about. Always trying to take her to the side for a private chat, bit playground, I thought? He seemed to think she was some helpless little innocent being corrupted by the big bad yadda yadda – I mean, it was her own fault, partly. She'd encouraged him at first, you know? And she would keep on falling into bed with him. I rather think she did it to annoy me, at first, but he did get all these ridiculous ideas that it was true love. Like they do. Anyway, it had gone beyond boring into, like, stabby psycho territory. He was just always, always there. So, we came up with a plan where she'd run off for a bit – hide out with the old school chum, you know, suss out a new market for us. Then I was going to go and rescue her, and we'd go travelling for a while. Of course, we hadn't planned for her to get preggers, little idiot. And she didn't even bloody notice it until she was five months gone! I mean, I thought she was putting on a bit of weight, but I assumed it was, you know, country air or whatevs.'

She talks so, so fast it's almost too much for me. I'm grabbing at syllables, trying to worry meaning out of them, not quite able to take it all in.

'So, you were visiting her when she was up north? Christina was fairly sure she hadn't had any other friends.'

'Christina's the drabby school chum, yeah? Oh, fack her, darling. By all accounts – well, by your sister's – she had not a clue. Besides, I wasn't about to spend the night at the Mansion du Drab when there was a perfectly okay hotel nearby. Your sister had a particular genius for finding us work – you mentioned you knew what we were up to, lovely, yeah? Well, that was mostly her. Oh look, you're empty again. Anyway, one thing to, ah, help out the boys in the band, as I'm sure your Mr McKay told you; quite another to move to a new place and suss out a market, in less than a month. It would never have occurred to me to advertise in the local rag, darling, and then once she'd built up a client base, well, some of them were interested in seeing me as well, you know. She was phenom at it, honestly. Yes, I'm finished, but I think my friend might like a little longer.'

And I realise there's a fork in my hand and two small incursions in my lasagne, that we're three-quarters of a bottle of wine down, and that the plate of salad Camilla has been shuffling is being removed practically untouched, and she's saying, 'Need a break, lovely? I must just pop to the loo, anyway,' and my head is very full of the wine and her chatter.

That's what it is, chatter. She's recounting these things as though they're weightless. As though she's catching me up on the latest gossip, as though her words aren't hitting like rocks. There's some sort of disconnect, somewhere in the middle of this table, a barrier between the method of delivery and the way it's being received.

She leaves me for what seems like a very long time. I finish the wine and wave away the plate the next time the waiter comes, filleting dizzily through her story. For all the talking she's done, very little of it is actually new – beyond the crucial revelation that Rona was still alive five years ago, she has filled the air with empty calories. As the shock passes and the lunchtime bustle begins to empty out, it occurs that she may have run out on me. I'm steeling myself to deal with that when there's a light touch on my back, a thumb passed softly over my shoulder blade.

'Hello, darling. Sorry about that. Now, where were we?'

Her face is fresh with new makeup and she's sniffing ostentatiously, almost as though she wants me to ask.

'Have you been taking drugs?'

She pulls a face.

'Oh no, not drugs! Honestly, lovely, how do you expect me to get through this otherwise? Ta–Rona's sister comes to town and suddenly I have to deal with an awful lot of heavy stuff I've been very merrily burying away for years. I'm not off my face or anything. Just keeping it together. Sorry, darling. I must seem utterly callous to you, mm? I promise, I'm just dealing. Just like you, in a way.'

Her voice has got louder, and our waiter, embarrassed, brings the bill unasked.

'Oops. I expect that's a hint then,' she's saying, provoking a harder blush as I hand him my card. 'Nice little cocktail bar two doors down, lovely. Shall we? Why don't you tell me about the kid now, mm?'

Her arm tucked into mine, steering me.

ME

FROM: scandi_sonja@hot...
Wednesday June 30th, 20.40

Dear Fiona,

I have wanted to write to you for a while now,
or get in touch with you in some way. Firstly, and
mainly, because I wanted to say sorry for the
way I behaved to you. While I am sure that you
understand that I was under a lot of pressure on
that day, it was not in any way fair of me to place
the blame for what happened to me on you. If
I am late in getting this apology to you, it is only
because after my outing to the newspapers I have
had to hide for a while, and I was not at first sure
my email was not being monitored. I am now
almost entirely sure that I know the person who
has done this to me, and I am very ashamed that I
have accused you.

I also wanted to wait until I had something I could

give you, in return, to say thank you for the very valuable information you were able to give us. As I am sure you know now, we lost that fight. However, as Suzanne made me realise, you took a very great risk in helping us. It is easy to be cavalier about someone else's life, I think, if you are not really living it.

I was very sad to hear that you had lost your job: I had wanted to give you this apology in person, and I visited your office (please do not worry – I was dressed like a very polite politics student and they did not recognise me!). A kind older woman said that you had left three weeks ago, and she was perhaps a little worried about you as you had not been in touch with your friends there. I can only hope this was not because of what you did for us, and if it was, well, I am even more apologetic for this. Because I suspected that this might be the case, I have worked very hard to get this for you, in the hope you may feel better for your involvement with us.

I have been asking about your sister's friend Camilla. I have asked every one of my contacts who have been based in Edinburgh, and I have told them it is a matter of urgency: we do not usually break our silences on the other girls like this. The first possibility, I have attached the contact details of – she is an English girl living there and I have her name from a mutual client. She may be too young though, to have been your sister's friend – I do not know if she was working seven years ago. Clients never really know our ages, they only guess.

Below this one, you see an email from a woman who is working for a very exclusive agency in Edinburgh. I hope you do not mind that I have removed her email address and name from the message – this was her request. She is a friend of a friend and I do not know her directly. Anyway, she was booked recently for a session with a fellow escort who I think fits your bill too. It is her personal number we have managed to get for you, and the woman has specifically asked that you do not say, at all, how you got hold of it.

This is so far all I have found. However, I have sent out many little contacts to let people know I am looking, and should there be anything else for you I will of course let you know.

I hope that, despite your recent trouble, your life will be a happy one.

My apologies again.
Your friend,
Anya.

And all those small sparks in me seemed to be firing up again. The nearness of her, the fact that she had sought me out, her tone. Your friend. Your friend. The possibility of having her in my life, of making Anya my friend, learning the sex and confidence of her.

Not only am I a coward, though, I don't know that I could ever be anything else around her. I felt suppliant and dusty even just in electronic proximity. And no matter how bad she felt about having accused me now, I would always keep coming back to that look on her face, in the café, something closing down as she realised some of the truth of my feeling for her. There's no way out of something like that: a relationship can't be reset on an equal footing. The boredom in her eyes, disgust, even. Seeing it, realising it for what it was, I'd pitched into that white hot anger, had thrown things and screamed, had given her name to the first journalist who'd phoned the office. Anya Sobtka, I'd said. Look it up. Try cross-referencing Swedish Sonja. I'd hung up then, hating myself. But I'd done it. I'd earned that disgust, and I certainly hadn't earned the right to her friendship, her apology, or these women's names and numbers.

I'd use them, though.

YOU

Camilla knows what she's doing, of course, throwing out enough clues to take us on to the next round, and then the next. At some point I'm going to have to stop buying: her choice of both cocktails and bar are well out of my unemployed price range. I don't want to tell her that, though. I don't want to let anything else go. And in spite of the concentration it takes to play her game, in spite of subject matter and the fact I'm clearly being taken for a fool, I want to stay around her, just for a little longer.

Some of the things Camilla tells me:

'So-o, by the time we realised she was up the spout, it was too bloody late. It was a client who asked about it, actually. We laughed it off, but I made her sit and actually pee on the facking stick in front of me later, and sure enough, bing. Idiot. She bleated something about her periods never having been that regular or something, but I think she'd known all along, been, like, in denial, yeah? I think it's why she left Edinburgh. Anyway, it put a stopper on our plans to go travelling. And she was just, you know, utterly panicky at first.

All the docs telling her it was too late for an abo. Got to say, I was pretty worried about what she might try and do, so after the dull old school chum chucked her out I moved up to the bloody sticks for a while, rented us a cottage, and we saw out the rest of the preg like a splendid couple of bucolic facking dykes!

'Oh yeah, pretty sure the daddy was someone from Edinburgh. Honestly, sweets, it's better for the kid's sake that it is: some of the darts-playing chubbos we dealt with up north ... There's even a slim chance it could be your Mr McKay, you know. Still got his number? Make the bastard stand you seven years of child support! Ha. Joking. You'd never get rid of him, even with a negative test, and I did say only a slim chance. Course, he probably would have tried to marry her anyway, yeah? The wanker.

'Oh, it was lovely, in our little cottage. Just taking time out. Of course, the natives were pretty shitty to me whenever I went on a grocery run and they caught the accent – and neither of us could bloody drive, so it was always taxis in and out of town, and the one taxi driver had picked up on our particular means of income a couple of months earlier. Seriously, awkward, darling. Mostly, we stayed put. She's good company, your sister. Was. Ha. That's not a clue, honestly. I mean it: haven't seen her for five years. Another one? Don't you love it here?'

'Well, I'd said adoption, and honestly, I was convinced she was going to go through with it, you know. I mean, we were getting it organised and everything. But then the bloody thing – sorry, the kid. You know I didn't mean that, lovely? – was, like, three weeks prem. And that rather facked everything – by the time we'd got her out of the hospo, Ta– your sister had only gone and got bloody attached to her. And I was like, seriously darling, we were going travelling. This has been planned. And you are nineteen. And she was like, look, can we just give this a chance, just try it? And I said, okay, but bad for business, for a start. Anyway, we didn't quite last a fortnight. Babe was a bit of a whinger, mm? And your sister wasn't really coping, not with the crying thing, and I said, listen darling, what are we going to do? We are too young for this, and she was seriously getting worse, you know, the full post-natal, and I could see it wasn't doing the little darling any good, being stuck with two stressed-out fackers who couldn't look after her properly, and that's when we thought of you.'

I got up, at that point. I got up without saying anything and I went to the bathroom and I rested my forehead against cold porcelain and I counted to twenty. Then I stood by the mirror and splashed my stupid painted, plucked Rona-face with water and the expensive mascara didn't run, and I wondered how one person could so casually tell another person these things, and then I went back to our table. Camilla had kicked off her shoes and curled her feet up under her, and ordered another two drinks.

'I was being insensitive again, wasn't I, lovely? God, sorry. I'm running on numb just now, you know? Need to watch my whorish mouth!'

She reached out a lazy arm to me, pulled me down onto the sofa with her, ran her thumb gently over my hand. Then she told me something.

Then she told me something.

Then.

Anyway, after that, these are some of the things that I said:

'And so – no. No. I'm fine, really – you went to Manchester, or was that just her?'

'I hadn't even considered she might have left the country. We checked – her passport hadn't been –'

'But you're here now. What happened?'

These are some of the other things she said:

'No, we were never in Manchester. God, why the fack would we go to Manchester, lovely? I was in Carlisle to meet her off the train, after she left you, hotel room already sorted and all. We got the next London train in the morning. Figured that was the best way, you know. And god, I wanted to show my girl London. Best cure for anything, London. Just to get her out dancing again, you know, skin on skin. Bring her back to life. We had, ah, contacts, you know? On the club scene. Promoter chums, DJs we'd met when we were – well, when we were in Edinburgh. And this was how we'd planned it. This one guy, I don't know if you'd have heard of him. I mean, he was super huge for a while, on the scene, you know. DJ Fleidermaus, he called himself. Except it was spelled flee-da-mouse. He thought that was really funny, god, I never got it. Anyway, he was off to take up a residency in Strasse in Berlin – that's like, techno mecca, darling. Or it was in 2001, you know? So. We went with him, moved into his flat. He called us his two girlfriends, but well, he paid the full whack for it. We were basically supposed to laze about and be in his pad if he threw parties; put on a little show for his friends, sometimes. We weren't to tell anyone about the paying, yeah? It was all supposed to be like we were two girls who genuinely wanted to share our lives with him, you know, because he was, like, so phenom. And from there, we made more contacts. I mean, neither of us really spoke German, but they loved us anyway, you know. T–Rona just bloomed out there, darling. It was like she had found her calling, yeah?'

'Pff. Passport? It was pre-9/11. Nobody checked! We'd borrowed one off some girl we knew in London who had hair a bit like yours. Like your sister's. Told her we were just going for the weekend! And we went, took the train. Great big rail jaunt across Europe, no serious border checks. Ah yeah, we were facking happy out there. For a while. I mean, obviously our gentleman friend got a tad much to take after a bit, but we'd already cosied up to another couple of promoters then. We had far bigger fish to fry, you know? And it was phenom. I mean, we'd spend our nights dancing until dawn, then running these amazing, immense sex parties darling, I mean you really can't imagine. It was like we were the hub. I mean, it put turning tricks for facking shoes back here into some perspective.

'What happened was, she got bored of me, darling. We had a fight, one of those that had been brewing for a while, you know, and then the next morning I found she'd just gone. Facked off in the night. Ha. I'm

310

sure you know the feeling. And the place just wasn't the same without her. I mean, she wasn't quite as good at covering her tracks with me, you know. I had a pretty good idea where she'd gone and who she was with, which is more than you ever did, isn't it, lovely? But fack it. The whole point was that it was the two of us, and besides, Berlin was always more her scene than mine. So facking grungy, god. So, yah, I ended up back here. There's only one job I'm really any good at, darling, and London's a bit of a saturated market, you know.'

She was bruised with her own failure, with having to admit it to me even as she spread clues about more worlds I wouldn't ever understand. And then we were both quiet, the sort of quiet that buzzed the air.

I said: 'She's been using another name, hasn't she? You keep wanting to call her something else. I've noticed.'

She said: 'Astutely deduced.'

I said: 'Are you going to tell me what it is?'

She said: 'Not unless you want me to. And I'm not sure you do, darling.'

I didn't say anything.

She said: 'She's got no facking online profile with it, though. I've checked, obv. She's too good. God, she may have even changed it again for all I know, yeah?'

I still didn't say anything.

She said: 'But I could give you leads, though. If you want them. I know people who could get her scent, mm?'

I said: 'Sure. For a price.'

She said: 'Of course for a price. But it would be a good price.'

I didn't say anything, because she was suddenly leaning right in to me, her hand cupping my face. And she was kissing me, and I was being kissed, and the loud group of men at the table beside us got even louder. And I don't think I kissed her back. I don't think, but everything was slow, and smelled sweet and boozy, slightly of vomit. And she pulled away again.

'Sorry, darling. That was tacky of me. You want to know, I'll tell you. Just. I just couldn't resist. You just look so facking much like her, yeah? Lost loves and all that.'

And she laughed at my face, and broke the slow spell with what she said:

'Yes, yes. Lost loves. Come on, darling. Our speciality was girl-on-girl. I mean, we're not lesbos, not for anyone else, but honestly. You don't lick someone's muff that often and not come to feel something for them, you know?'

XXX

It's still early, on this train full of drunks. Sun finally setting, condensation on the windows, and the elephant stamps of football fans trying to tip their carriage over.

Camilla had been apologetic, charming, expressed a vague idea of walking me to the station that she hadn't meant me to take seriously so I didn't. She'd said:

'Listen, go away and think about it. I'm not going to tell you now even if you beg me. Even if you kiss me, baby. Ha. Ha. Go away and sober up, and tell your parents if you want, mm? Come back to me after a week, if you're really sure. And god, if you decide

312

to go ahead and declare her dead, don't worry about me popping up to chuck a spanner in the works, you know? I might be a money-grabbing slattern, darling, but I'm honest with it.'

And then she'd called me back, and she'd said:

'Ooh, by the way. You wouldn't happen to have twenty for a taxi, would you? I've only got bloody plat cards, and they don't take them.' But before that, and before that, when she'd pulled me down to her and held my hand, this is what she said:

'I mean the thing is, lovely, I assume she didn't tell you why she left the bub with you? I suppose she couldn't really. She said it had to be done that way, you know. She said if you got any sort of wind of what was up, you'd stop her. Well, of course you would. Anyway. We were trying to work out what to do, and she was like, I can't give her away. What if I want her back again? And I was like – because I was being bloody honest with her at that point, only way to get through to her – listen babe, you're doing a facking shit job of being a mother right now. Give the kid a chance, you know? I mean, I have to say, I was fearing for its life at this point. So I said look, why not stick her with your mum or something? And my god she went mental at that. I mean, I knew your parents were a bit of a touchy subject with her, but god. She said, god, my dad can't even look after himself, and my mum would only fack off on her – sorry, I need to watch my mouth, your parents, sorry. Anyway, the point is –'

Her thumb went back and forth, back and forth over my hand.

'– the point is, the next time the bub woke us up, she

313

said, I've been thinking. Do you think I could leave her with my sister? And I asked, like, are you sure, and she said, and I still remember this: "I think right now, my sister is the only person in the world I trust apart from you, Cam. And you're doing just as shit a job as me." And that's when it was decided.

'And I was surprised, when you said there'd been no word from her, of course I was, but, you know, at her lowest she was utterly worried she would do some sort of damage to that baby, and you were the only person she was sure wouldn't. Maybe all the dark, facked up bits of her kept her away, you know? Maybe she feels like she can't come back now, like she hasn't earned it. But I rather think she ought to have let you know that one thing, lovely. So. Now you know it. Message passed along, yeah?'

And I'd said another thing. 'Christ,' I'd said. 'I don't know how I ever came to deserve that.'

The train pulls away, like it seems to do a lot recently, taking me away from this place, back to where I'm supposed to be. And I make it home, and I'm still held together by skin, even if I can feel something else underneath, something breaking and turning.

I creep into the flat with the lurch and guilt of a teenager trying to pretend she isn't drunk. I'm not sure I fool my parents.

'She's just gone to sleep, about an hour ago,' Dad says, like a soldier reporting mission accomplished.

'Thanks. Thank you.'

I'm trying to stand up straight, trying to cope with all of it and still seem normal.

314

'I think I need a nap, now. Can I pop down and see you both tomorrow? I want to have a chat with you about a few things. To do with Rona.'

And then it's just me and my daughter. I stand perfectly still so that her breathing is the only sound in the flat and I think about that. About my sister is the only person in the world I trust.

Bethan stirs a little when I push the door, but she doesn't wake, and it's enough just to stand there and watch her. Fat little pink thing. Asleep, she doesn't resemble anyone at all, just herself.

Camilla's job is to make people feel this way about themselves. Give them release: work out where they need to be touched and peel back till she gets there. I could carry on investigating that moment in my head, play it back and back on itself, weigh out every nuance, until I conclude that it was very probably a lie.

Or I could let it go.

ME

The taxi cranked its old brakes to a stop.

'There you go, ma dear. Six pounds twenty,' the driver said.

White hair. Grandfatherly. Familiar. He needed to be reminded about the receipt and I hit a white note of panic, right off. Was it a giveaway, asking for a receipt? Should I tell him I was here to interview someone? Or for a business meeting? Would that make it look more suspicious, covering myself with excuses? Fumbling for a pound coin stuck in my purse, I heard myself apologising over and over again. This was no good. I couldn't be like this.

The first trick was just to walk smoothly past reception, wasn't it? Not even to acknowledge them, or that you might not know where you were going. Even if you didn't. Especially not to acknowledge the tightness in your stomach or that high-pitched flush of adrenaline flooding you.

The second trick was Paulette's. Look for the toilet near the lobby bar, she said. There's always one. Get in there, and just you take a look at your gorgeous self there in the mirror. Drink yourself in, lovey. Drink her in.

There she is. My fancy new frock of an other self, put on for the occasion. She winks like a corny cheesecake pin-up, dabs at her lipstick with gestures too delicate to be mine, and is completely in control again. Her heels ring out on the tiles, loud and teacherly.

In the lift on the way up, I thumb out a text to Paulette, on the new slim mobile that slots into my new slim handbag.

In the lift. On the way up.

She's got the grandchildren today, but she's there for me anyway, at this appointed time.

Will phone u in 3 min. Ur beautiful honey!

I'm sure it will prove to be a fairly solitary life, but over the last couple of months, ever since all the pieces fell into place and I began to make mousy enquiries about buddying, I've been surrounded by concern, advice, affection. A new sort of sisterhood, one I've never really been involved in before. They don't get paid for it, Paulette, Jo, or any of the other women I've met through the buddying system; they're just there because they know that someone has to be.

More than once, one of them has asked if I was sure. Did I completely understand. More than one person has told me that it won't be all wine and roses. In the end, though, there was no great ethical struggle. No threshold. Just a very logical click.

Here's the room. The mad jolt through my veins as I raise my hand to knock. I could run away, right now, another half-crazed dash down an air-conditioned corridor. This, now, is the threshold. Is everything really, really going to change after this? Is everything about me going to change, my cells begin a slow death, shift to not-person?

I don't think I could be here if I still thought that, could I?

Too late. The door's opening, on a skinny man, shabby, in his early forties.

'Hi,' he said.

'Hi,' I said.

'I'm Jimmy.'

Irish accent.

XXX

Noise of cooking and conversation steamed through from the kitchen next door. I thought I could hear Helen's harsh, raggedy laugh, like a bassline. Music was playing – Dolly Parton, something corny like that. Shania Twain.

Suzanne's living room was cosy and unfashionable. Slightly shabby grey three-piece suite, perked up with flowery cushions. She'd put out a plate with jammy dodgers and iced fancies in an interlinking display on the coffee table – no one had taken one. Paulette and another woman were sitting in the corner talking. I had tried to tune out what they were saying, just to be polite. Paulette's intonation was high, calming, lilting up.

It was very warm. My fingernails badly needed filing. I was wondering what I was doing.

XXX

These are the buddying system open sessions – open groups for people who have contacted the SUSW or any of the forums because they're considering becoming an escort. There will always be experienced independent workers there, offering advice. They're held every couple of months, in different people's houses. This one was Suzanne's first time hosting, since the closure of the Base. When I arrived, she hugged me to her hard on the doorstep, pulled back to look in my face with strong eyes, and hugged me again.

I knew in advance that Anya wouldn't be there – she'd been put on forced sabbatical by her university and gone travelling with her boyfriend. I say boyfriend, but I had just learned they got married in Lisbon two weeks earlier. His family weren't happy. Suzanne updated me as she led me through and I breathed in warm savoury smells from the kitchen – just a couple of pizzas, some snacks, just to keep us all going, Suzanne said. Lisbon suits their temperaments, apparently – they were thinking of staying for a while, possibly taking on some teaching. A change can be a great thing, you know, she said. Even if you weren't expecting it.

Suzanne spilled all this in a rush of warmth. She was trying to make it all up to me – all this solicitousness an apology for our last encounter, when Anya accused me of betraying her to the press. You're one of us, Suzanne's soft hand on my back was telling me. I know you wouldn't do that. I'm sorry.

So I sat there, everything about me a great big fat deceitful lie. Across the room, a small thin woman in her forties was pulling her knees to herself, eyes moving quickly, back and forth.

Paulette came over to me, perched on the arm of my chair, graceful. She smelled wonderful and expensive, smoothed a flick of hair around her ear.

'Hello, my darling. How are you today?'

I'm not sure she recognised me from the meeting. It was a long time ago. I think this is how she is with everyone. With all of the new girls.

Look, I had tried other things. I had. Camilla, for the price of a meal she barely touched, a bottle of wine and enough spirits to tranquilise a shire horse, had managed to provide me with something real and peaceful. I had some lovely unbroken sleeps. I felt whole. I felt bold. I tried to pick up the threads of my life where I'd left them, and applied for three jobs related to books and editing. I added my ex-boyfriend Simon as a friend on Facebook.

Two of the jobs didn't even send me a rejection. Simon lives in England and has been married for the past two years; it seemed to have been one of those very lavish weddings, that happen in a marquee, with no discernible personality.

I applied for administrative jobs. Data entry. There were precious few – the jobs section of the local paper has got much slimmer since the credit crunch – all of them on even smaller wages than I'd had at RDJ. I signed up with a temping agency. I report to an oily-voiced man in his mid-twenties called Dan, who occasionally rings me up to tell me that he hasn't found anything for me yet, babes, but I'm still his best girl, eh? Last week: two days stuffing envelopes on minimum wage in the sort of glassy office Samira works in. I'd been given a desk in the corner by a woman who eyed me

320

suspiciously and told me not to touch the espresso machine.

I think I'd already made my decision, though. This particular switch had been flicked a long time ago, without my even realising it.

Paulette stood up in front of Suzanne's gas fire, fake coal glowing behind her. Her voice was beautiful. Musical.

'We're here to make sure you feel totally supported as you enter this phase of your life. If in fact you decide this is what you want to do. We've been there, remember, and we don't want any of you to be taking this decision lightly. Use this afternoon to find out whatever you want to. Ask whatever you need to. There's no judgement here – no question is too stupid. Helen, Suzanne and I have had very different experiences of working in this industry, and we feel it's very important that you can benefit from that before making your final decision.'

'At's right,' Helen called out from her seat, all jagged edges and smoker's husk. 'An youse dinnae want tae go the route ah did, ah'll tell youse that for nothing, eh!'

The thin, nervy woman had stood up.

'I'm really sorry – I can't do this. I've made a mistake. Sorry. Sorry.'

She jerked towards the door, knocking the plate of biscuits off the coffee table. Suzanne followed her out.

Paulette smiled.

'That's absolutely fine. And a completely natural response, you know. If anyone else' – here she'd looked around at those of us remaining – 'feels similarly, at any point today, just feel free to walk out. Make a complete break. We'll understand. We won't be in touch again.'

The three of us left nodded. We didn't make eye contact. A busty girl with flicked eyeliner, big skirts and rolls of red hair. A clever-looking woman, possibly Chinese, late forties, long hair, leather boots. And me. A liar and deceiver with no prospects and no money.

Camilla, her brittle bones, the coked-up car crash of her.

Little Holly, fucked up and acting out.

Helen, raw, burnt and surviving.

The other Fiona: pragmatic, defensive, always there at the school gates.

Anya, beating the fire and anger of her brain against it, righteous and strong.

Rona. What would my sister think about all of this? About what I'm intending to do?

I couldn't even begin to answer that one, because I don't know how my sister thinks. I've never known. And it didn't and doesn't matter, because I realised there, in that living room, that I was surer of this than I had been about anything in a long time.

US

We crash back down together after the second time, his fingers still clenched in mine.

'Oof. Oof. Bloody hell. Bloody hell, babe.'

His thighs are heavy over me, and I twist round to give him a little peck on the cheek.

'Oof. Did you like that? Did you?'

'I did. Yeah, I really did!'

We laugh together, and I pull back a bit to let him wrap around me.

'Mm. Mm, this is nice.'

He plants a couple of kisses on my arm, and we lie there for a while, smiling, until I feel his muscles begin to slacken into something like sleep.

'All right now, I'd better go.'

I unpeel myself from his arms, slick with a faint sheen of his sweat. Aftershave and sex. He's sleepy, moans a little.

'No. No, you should stay here.'

I sound out a couple of notes of a laugh. Faint limb ache. Slightly raw upper thighs. 'Is that right, Jeremy?'

'Yes. That's right. You should stay here for ever. We should stay here. We should run away.'

I'm already out and on the floor, easing into my pants. I swat his foot with a stocking.

'Oh, I don't think you can afford to keep me forever, can you?'

He beams out contentedly, a fat mass of bedding and loose skin.

'You're probably right.'

Bathroom. The door closed, a breath. Wipes. One for face, to sort out the smudged mascara, one for under the arms and a third to catch the excess lube. From through the door a fuzz of static as he switches the telly on, then soothing bland afternoon chat. I don't want to shower here, eke out the time. Not with this one. Powder. Deodorant. Hair clipped back up on top of my head. Bag on my shoulder, a quick kiss for Jeremy as I'm walking out the door. I don't break stride.

'I'll be back this way in November. I'll be in touch, babe.'

'Sure thing, darling. I'll look forward to it.'

Kiss off on my fingers, one, two. From bed to hallway in two minutes. I have this bit down now. Into the box of the lift with the warm animal smell of myself as I pull my flats out of my bag, swap shoes. Straight through the lobby, not looking, and on to the street. My fourth and my last of the week.

Flat grey Scottish day, the sky just void, doing nothing. I take my place in the press of pedestrians, and even if you looked specially, you wouldn't be able to pick me out. Two crossings and a slight slope down to the station, quick, fluid. Up escalators where I let myself rest behind suitcases, stride through the concourse, people lost, smell of baking pies, and down the grubby glass staircase. It's thirty pence entrance to the ladies and another £4 for a shower; the coins are counted and waiting in my coat pocket.

Not ideal, but I've come to like it. Undressing in a tiny private space, knowing that a city's worth of people are still zooming about just through that door. The blue plasticky soap squeezed from a wall-mounted dispenser, the quick hard scrub, and discard the smell of complacent rich-man aftershave with the throwaway towel. Jumper, knickers and leggings from one corner of my bag, not too creased, still-new leather jacket back on and I'm a completely different person by the time I come out. I queue up with everyone else to buy myself coffee, smile at the puffed-out lady behind the counter, scorch my palms slightly through the cardboard. Like every day.

Passing through the ticket barriers at this station, coming or going, is my secret doorway. I leave at different exits depending on whether I'm going to the college, a hotel or the incall flat, pull myself up smart, beat time with the click of my heels. Early in the morning I'm a social policy student, folders under my arm, sitting keenly up the front with the other mature students, asking all the questions and irritating the younger ones. Lunchtimes, I usually have a client: lipstick and lube in my locker, all washed off immediately afterwards. In late afternoons I turn myself into a mother again, soft flat footfalls, drift to a window seat and watch the city turn slowly to hay bales, shimmering water and big melting sky as we get closer to the village, the grass, the neighbours, the crabbit cat and the cottage that Beth and I call home these days. My work phone buzzes occasionally with bookings and the sort of time-wasting idiots who want me to send them pictures for free, with the daily anonymous abuse I had to grow elephant skin to cope with. It doesn't matter as long as I'm heading home, as long as the city and all its wants are slowly receding behind me.

Beth doesn't want me to pick her up from school any more, and that's all right. I'm there when she comes home, and she can wrap her arms around me as soon as she gets in, my girl.

But I've got a different mission today. A different route – back up the hill, bearing to the left. The hard stone of the Drag, again, as grey and nothing as today's flat, void sky.

XXX

We stand there for a while, outside the Sanctuary Base. Me, with my head tipped back, her silently at my side, height and weight.

She breaks it by putting a gentle hand on my sleeve. 'Hi.'

Claire has not changed. Not in the least. Her hair's slightly longer, and she's wearing quite a smart coat, but that's all. There's a plain wedding band on the hand touching me, but I knew about that from Heather, who had two weeks of hard rage that she wasn't asked to be a bridesmaid. Perhaps the touching is new: I don't remember her being one for physical contact, for the softness of social affection. But we didn't really know each other at all, back then.

I can still smell the station soap on myself.

'It's good to see you. Really. Thanks for coming.'

'I take it you wanted to rub my nose in it?'

A half laugh, but she's on the defensive.

'In what?'

'Your choice of place.'

It had been deliberate, and my earlier pettiness is making me anxious now. I don't want her hurt.

'Not very subtle of me, was it?'

'Shall we go and get a coffee?'

'Actually Claire, can we stay here? I honestly don't mean to be rubbing your nose in it.'

She snorts at me, but she's friendly.

'Okay, I don't mean to rub your nose in it much. But can we just stay down here, walk around? It feels like an appropriate setting, and I like it, a bit. The quiet. It's never usually quiet, this area. Only weekend mornings.'

And we walk the block.

'I probably deserve some nose rubbing,' she says.

It would be childish to quibble about that 'probably' right now, when we're on friendly terms. This conversation will soon end exactly the way that all of our email exchanges have, with the statement and re-statement of two completely entrenched points of view and a slightly huffy sign off. There's no point pre-empting it.

We don't want to fight, Claire and I. We've danced this dance over the past couple of years, back and forth, always reengaging, because we actually seem to like each other. Can you like someone without respecting their views? We can't understand each other, but we do like each other.

'I'm really glad we're doing this,' she says. 'I'm really glad you said you'd come. It took me a long time to work up to asking you.'

'I'm glad that I'm here.' We've never groped this awkwardly for conversation online, but then it's always easier when you don't have to look someone in the eye. She seems pleased by that, though. Patronising, bossy Claire with a shy smile on her.

'So. Why did you ask me to come?'

She clears her throat and stares around her for a bit.

'Well, I wanted to offer you a job, actually.'

'Oh. I didn't think I was your type.'

That's too far for her, and I should have known it – she can take some teasing these days, but she always backs down when confronted with it.

'Not – don't. No. A prop – a different kind of job. I wondered if you would consider coming to work on a new project with me. As a liaison officer. Liaison coordinator, in fact. Between the women and, well, and us. I think you know about the new steering group I'm heading. Mentioned it a bit in the last email? I've been taking on board what you said, about not being able to help people if we aren't, well, in conversation with them. I know you don't agree with – with what we're trying to do, but there's a discussion to be had that we're not having. And you're the right person to start it.'

When we began this, we were stilted by profession-alism, and by the disconnect of our first encounters. Claire was heading up a group who were lobbying

328

parliament to have the Ways Out scheme enforced across the country, and trying to build support for criminalising the purchase of sex, criminalising our clients. She is a Big Deal now, is Claire. She writes op eds in the local paper; she has a byline photo. She is the enemy, and I am fraternising with her.

Ways Out isn't working, though. They've kept it quiet, but we know. Any of the girls still in the Drag prefer to go to the needle exchange or one of the homeless shelters for their mid-shift cup of tea. Most of them have retreated indoors, online, and with no bond of trust between them and the Ways Out team, it's very difficult to reach them, check that everything's all right.

My blog about Ways Out – basically an interview with Suzanne – got a lot of hits, and the Scottish Union of Sex Workers asked if I would write a press release for them. Claire figured out my identity pretty quickly, which meant I had to change my working name, redo my website. I'd only just started out then, and hating Claire for her bustle and the hassle that came with her was a sturdy, familiar totem to take with me as I crossed over into the djinn world.

Then we met, at Heather and Ross's housewarming; were forced face to face with each other at the buffet. It's easier to rage and storm at an idea of a person; when your eyes meet over a sausage roll platter, sustaining that anger becomes near impossible. A philosophy I was still learning three years ago, when this happened; I live by it now. Maybe not specifically the bit about the sausage rolls.

Because this is the other part of what I do, now. I agitate. I write press releases and tip off journalists, from behind yet another pseudonym. I organise protests and petitions and online campaigns, curled up round my daughter, in front of our new fire, as she blips and bleeps at her friends and the cat shunts his head at our legs. My blogs are being read, not just by potential clients and online pervs after a wank.

Thanks to social networking, we are a collective stretching around the world – we don't work alone any more. We have a voice and we're not going to be silenced. Your local government wants to raid the brothels it winked at last year, to make itself look active? We'll make sure you have a quote from the women who work there, about how this affects them. A tabloid newspaper outs an escort? We're condemning it. Loudly. Vocally. The internet has given us the space to talk and the ability to be heard, without outing ourselves. Sex workers' voices, and the things they have to say, gradually, eventually being taken seriously. I thought if I could study it, study the way that laws are made and council policies are decided, I'd be much better placed to help. This, I think, is what I want to do, in the long term. Sex work has got me there.

And yet, if you pushed me on it, pushed me not that hard at all, I'd admit that I'm doing penance for Anya. I'm trying to make things right with her, wanting her, somewhere, wherever she is, to see all the good I'm doing without my having to tell her, thank you, and I'm so sorry. Trying to deserve it.

I think about Anya quite a lot. The strength of her, over that lunch we had. Her absolute conviction that this job was just like any other. That you could stay sane and whole and still do this. I wonder how much

330

of that was bravado, a front for a nosy stranger. I think about that whenever I wrap my legs round a client who hasn't engaged with me as a person, as I'm tuning my brain off while they're pumping away into their whore fantasy. But that's the trade I've made. And let's be honest: I wasn't really whole to begin with.

'The thing is,' I say to Claire, 'I have a job. I know you don't understand this and you probably won't, ever, but it's a job I actually enjoy. It's not something I'm going to do forever, but right now it suits me. It supports my study and allows me to spend proper time with my daughter. I appreciate the offer, but –'

'What I'm offering is a *good* job, Fi.'

She doesn't even notice that her emphasis makes me wince.

'It's full time, though?'

'Yes. I mean, I'm sure you could job-share, if you'd rather.'

'I have college. I'd have to. On a pro-rata salary of?'

'Entry at this level is £18,500 full time.'

'Claire. I make almost twice that a year for far fewer hours.'

And she touched my arm again.

'I know we've had our fights, Fiona, but I've come to care a lot about you. And I know what you'll say, but it terrifies me that you put yourself in danger like this, all the time.'

And there we are, back at the entry point, this thing she's said so many times to me and thought about even more. This is why we can't be friends, Claire, I want to say. Because you'll never, ever get past the things you think you know.

331

I understand the pain that the people who love me are in when they think about my life. I can't give them the same sort of assurances of my security that they'd have if I still worked in an office, and I know that's selfish.

'You can't promise me that,' my mum said, shrill, after I'd told her, after I'd said 'I'm safe'. We were unpacking boxes in the sunny kitchen of my new little house, just the two of us. Dad had taken Bethan down to the loch, to stop her getting underfoot. I'd been deliberately trying not to spend time with Mum by myself, and six months' worth of unspoken questions – about my 'management consultancy' job, about how I was really affording the rent – filled the room as we moved around in silence.

There are various schools of thought about coming out to loved ones. I didn't sit her down, prepare the ground, suggest she read certain books; I didn't know I was going to say it at all until it came out, in a rush.

'Mum, I'm working as an escort.'

She nodded, slowly. 'I wondered. I did wonder.'

She didn't cry, although I could tell she was close. We sat down in the garden, in the autumn sunlight. I'd poured us both a whisky, with a half smile, trying to make a joke she didn't want to get. The things I had to say, over and over, were:

Nobody is forcing me.

I'm not on drugs.

I always take precautions.

It's temporary: it's just to make enough money while I'm studying, to give us a good foundation for whatever comes next.

I'm safe. I'm safe.

'We shouldn't tell your father,' she said.

'No, I don't think we should.'

For the rest of the afternoon, once they'd come back, she was jumpy and sharp with Dad, too fussy with Beth, didn't really look at me and made him leave early.

She worries about me. All the time. I know she does. But a few weeks later, she sent me this.

I don't know whether this is a generational thing. We thought of prostitution as something that fundamentally harms all women, darling. I marched for equality with you in a sling, in the eighties. I don't see how I reconcile that with this, and maybe I never will. But then maybe I gave up the right to sit in moral judgement on anyone else some time ago.

I know you, though. I know that you think things through; I know that you're practical and responsible, and I know you will have thought about this. I know your commitment to Beth, too, and that you wouldn't ever take on anything you thought would offer a risk to her.

And maybe, to be honest, I can see how you got here. I've felt trapped by childcare and terrible jobs. With me, it led to an explosion that I still regret – you saw that, and you've made this choice, as an adult, to deal with it differently. I have to respect that.

Please stay safe, my darling. Please.

Oh, I don't know. I wish it wasn't this way and there are some things I can't ever be totally easy with.

But I will always be your
Mum

Heather, of course, had already been thinking the worst for some time. There was no fight there. I saw her in town one day, long after she'd given up trying to call me, stopped sending emails. I was coming straight from a client, on my way to a class. She was on a lunch break, walking down the street crying, unaware of the thousand gossipy eyes on her. I'd got her in my arms before she'd really even taken me in, and over lumpy coffee in the lounge of an old man's bar it all came spilling out.

Heather's fertility problems offered me a chance to put things right. For the past three years, I've been able to reinvent myself as a friend – a real friend, not just so-called on Facebook – and finally pay back her years of devoted service, caretaking our relationship while I was all but absent. This bridge was still unburned, somehow, no thanks to me. I've researched acupuncture and alternative diets for her, gone on yoga retreats and spa weekends with her, held her after each failed round of IVF. I've listened: it's a skill I had to learn, in this line of work. I began to appreciate all the things about her I'd found so easy to shrug off, from her sense of drama to her dogged loyalty. The very basic, good Heatherness of her. That moment when I sat down at a café table, and she said nothing, just slid a sonogram picture across to me with a smile and I knocked the salt and pepper onto the floor flying round to get to her: the sharp beauty of it still makes me breathless. What a thing it is to love someone that much.

I do like to be needed. I've realised that now.

By the time she could focus on anything else, she'd got used to the solid fact of me. That I was there, that I was not damaged, not coerced. She had strange, clear moments of fatalism during her lowest points, totally uncharacteristic, that I still think about.

'It's all very well and good trying to be the ideal, innit, Fi? Yeah. You get married, you go to work every day, you don't break the law. You do all the things they tell you. Bullshit bullshit. Maybe you lose your job. Maybe your body doesn't work like it should. Maybe your sister runs off and leaves you with her kid. Life just keeps bloody happening in all the ways it's not supposed to, and we're supposed to stick to the plan? Fuck that. Fuck that, hon.'

And then there's Claire. I will say this for her: she means well. She means so well. Claire genuinely just wants to look after people. She's honest; no matter how officious the delivery, I can't work up to fury at her. Sometimes I turn it round, patronise her right back, and she bristles at it, writes me off as another made-up airhead looking down on her. But yet we keep coming back to each other.

'I'll think about the job,' I say, finally. 'Send me the details. And let's talk about something else. Anything else.'

This morning's man. His fat, jabbing fingers and his

lazy assumptions about the world, his place in it, and me. I will think about it.

The sun has begun to come out, burning the cloud cover away, and cut out against a very bright blue, the granite towers and crumbling red sandstone blocks of the International Financial District look almost beautiful. I tuck my arm into Claire's: she starts at the contact, then her tendons relax around me, and we walk.

Future

The next morning, she's laid out on the pillow beside you. Sunlight pouring through the white sheet you've hung in the window, singing off the turquoises and pinks of your summer clothes, hung up on the wall and draped over the one white chair that does you for bedroom furniture. The blankets smell yeasty. She moans a single note, tries to pull you back in, and it's as though your body retches. Everything is light and warm and pleasantly coloured, and you've just realised it's repulsing you.

You sit on the floor in the corner, stretching your back at the wall and keeping a wary eye on the bed, in case she moves. You're running the split ends of your hair between your fingers – so much easier out here, to let it go – and it occurs that this may all be by-product. There has not been enough sleep, lately. Your world is fast and chemical and its nights turn daylight all too quickly. It's possible you've only been asleep for a couple of hours, but the alarm clock is on Camilla's side of the bed and you don't want to risk waking her.

Last night, her face up in yours, purple and screaming,

the spit flying. She'd pushed you up against a fence, on the way home. You'd refused to get on the tram with her in that mood, because she would embarrass you. This is the thing with the very posh, you'd said. Nobody ever taught you manners for being out in public, did they? Because you don't truly believe the great unwashed are people, so it doesn't matter what you do in front of them. That was when she pushed you up against the fence, and you remembered your own parents in that sort of position. And probably you knew then, but there was too much static in your head to figure it out.

The baby in the upstairs flat starts crying again, its weird high wail. It doesn't sound like any baby you've ever heard: more like a ghost, or the wind hitting an old building. And she's stirring – you stay absolutely still, every naked muscle frozen against the wall – and she's grunting, pulling the pillow over her head. She'll wake soon, though, and it will force everything wide open again. Neither of you can back down from these things any more. The lightness, the sneering at the world, the complicity that bonded you so tightly in the first place, rotted somewhere. Probably, if you're honest, it had gone before you even got to Berlin.

You pull a faded cotton dress over your head. It was hers originally, but orange always makes her look sallow, so it came to you instead. All your clothes have merged together anyway, now that you're the same skinny size, now that you have the same taste. No bra, no knickers. Time for those later. You move quickly and silently, stuffing roughly half the clothes into your old holdall. You take that blue necklace and the leather sandals. There's enough left there for her, it's fine. You stand in the doorway for just a second, then you turn and you go.

Out in the street without having even brushed your teeth, the breeze drifting lazily up your skirt, cold there. You don't even pause, make your way straight to the main road and hop on the first tram coming, because something in you has already decided you're going to Rene's studio in Kreuzberg. The seat bristles prick your bare thighs, but you quite like it. Perhaps Rene will still be in bed, and you can climb in with him for a couple of hours, the slack warmth of another body.

It had been the stretchmarks. The sly, laughing allusion to your stretchmarks. And you knew why she'd done it, too. She was out of her depth here, Miss Camilla of the air kissing and the cheekbones, the upper-class druggy. The lack of codes and castes amongst Berlin's DJs and artists and hedonists baffled her; stripped of her connections she'd become scared and clingy while you'd bloomed with it. Last night, you'd sat at a table holding court – your German was getting better every day, too – and exciting, intelligent people had laughed at your jokes and you'd felt yourself flying and swooping and soaring, and she'd felt it too, and she'd grabbed for you.

'Careful lovely,' she'd said, ice-voiced as you were standing, gesticulating, warming to your point, 'don't want to bust those stretchmarks back open, mm?'

And in front of everyone, she'd patted your stomach.

That one true thing that bonded you and Camilla together now was your past, and her part in it. Was her silence on it, you realised now: once you'd got through the dark, screaming period you now knew was post-natal depression, she'd known what you wanted without you really having to ask, had adapted herself slickly around the new self you'd decided to be and given no indication she'd ever known different, even when you were alone together, wrapped up in the tenderness of a late-night love. She'd let you think you could trust her, for years, then last night ripped it all open, revealing that she would hold it over you whenever she needed to. Your body had moved quickly this morning because it already knew what your conscious self was still slowly working out. You couldn't ever escape it if she was still in your life.

Rene's studio is at the top of a graffiti-splashed block above a kebab shop, with bikes chained to the rusting banisters all the way up. His door doesn't lock properly, just takes one sturdy push to open, and you follow the smell of frying down the hall to the kitchen space, its basic Calor stove and ripped-out appliances. Rene is grooving on the spot to his own silent beat, spatula in hand and a pair of greying boxers on.

'Tasha! And looking golden like the morning, eh?'

He reaches over and pulls you in for a long, hard kiss on the mouth.

Camilla hates Rene. It's the dreadlocks, you think, the defiance of them, the scummy Kreuzberg squat and the old hippie wisdom. This is a man who will never make enough money to afford your services, not even enough to pay you for the paintings you've posed for, and neither is he cool enough to be of use on the scene.

But he's attractive, even if he is old, and he can always make you laugh. It's healthy to fuck people who aren't paying, sometimes, just because you like them. You shouted that at her last night, too.

In his bed, the rough mattress on the floor, surrounded by the thin, high smell of turps, you map out the possibilities together on his fingers and your thighs. Lisbon, you think. You've heard amazing things about the clubs out there, and Rene has a number of friends who should be able to put you up, at least for the first couple of nights.

'Ah, you will like Lisbon, beautiful Tasha. You will dance through the neon, find a new motion, eh?'

That'll have to go, of course, you're thinking, as you begin to doze off, your head on his hard bicep, just for a couple of hours. Tasha was what Camilla christened you. This new thing you're becoming, this outspoken nomad, moving where the beat goes, this thing will need a whole new name. You just haven't worked out what it will be yet.

AFTERWORD

This is not my world, and I was very nervous about approaching it.

In 2008, I was working as a journalist, and was asked to interview women who did 'edgy, sexy' jobs for a feature. My extensive research (googling) led me to the blog of an escort living in the city where I worked. I'd thought, in my naïve, presumptuous way, that I understood what prostitution was. I'd watched the TV dramas, I'd seen the stock photography shots – fishnet tights and knee-high boots in an alleyway – and I'd read the crime novels where the sex worker character washes up dead to kick-start the plot.

This woman's voice completely undercut all of that. She was articulate, angry and brilliant in her rage. I've since come to the rather horrendous realisation that I hadn't actually thought of sex workers as real people, with their own thoughts, ideas and lives, before. Plot devices, perhaps. Things to be pitied.

She never replied to my clunky and probably very patronising email. However, I realised I needed to know more. I clicked on all the links on her blog – to review sites, and to the blogs of other sex workers. And that way, clicking and clicking, I discovered Laura Lee. Escort, sex workers' rights campaigner, single mother, law student and ferocious, hilarious political powerhouse.

Laura was the first sex worker to agree to meet with me, much later, once I'd realised that I was writing a novel about this world. I'd been following her blog for over a year by then. Laura was as nervous as I was over our lunch; she had good reason not to trust journalists, having been 'outed' before by local papers and forced to leave two small towns behind. She took a risk by trusting me, but she did it because she wanted to get more realistic portrayals of sex-working life out into the public. Whenever I questioned whether I had the right to tell this story at all (this happened a lot), I remembered the risk Laura, and the other sex workers I interviewed, had taken in trusting me, put on my big-girl pants and got on with the job.

With Laura's seal of approval, I was able to break through further; she introduced me to other women she thought I might want to talk to and kept me informed about developments in the ongoing campaign she and her peers had found themselves enmeshed in, for sex workers' rights. She allowed me to use her name as a sort of passport for approaching other sex workers online, enabling me to deepen my understanding of this world and my research into it. She was forthright, was Laura. She took no shit. Formidable, beautiful and armed with the sort of sense of humour that's been forged through fire. She was also one of the bravest, most resilient people I've ever met.

Laura offered me feedback on two separate drafts of *Fishnet*; she attended the book launch and stood up there in front of a room full of strangers, announced herself as a sex worker. 'Be honest,' she said to me later on that evening, after quite a few glasses of wine. 'I'm Anya, aren't I?' I muttered something about Anya being a composite character, which in a way she was. She is younger, looks nothing like Laura did. Their backgrounds were very different. Laura gave me a *look*, then a wink, because she knew. It's all there in the politics and the conviction, and a lot of the ideas Anya expresses, even if I'd translated them into the character's own words. That first awkward conversation in a cafe between Fiona and Anya; that was how I'd felt around Laura at first. Without realising it, I'd created a character who was on paper nothing like her to espouse her ideology and – be honest – her essence, and she saw right through me. And bought me another glass of wine.

The last time I saw Laura, I'd interviewed her for an online magazine. We had cake and tea round at my house, which wasn't so very far from hers, and she hugged me hard before she got in her car. We made noises about meeting up more often, but I was pregnant and she was already heavily involved in the case that would define the rest of her life: taking the Morrow Law (which criminalised the purchase of sex, and in doing so made life much more dangerous for sex workers at all levels) recently implemented in Northern Ireland to the European Court of Human Rights. To do this, she needed to out herself, put her head above the parapet and become, essentially, a public face of sex work. At one point she was even represented by Max Clifford. As *Fishnet* examines, for a sex worker to out herself is no casual decision. Making herself public like this – going on television and radio, putting her face to her social media output, a column with the *Huffington Post* – invited opprobrium, leers from neighbours and the other parents at the school gates, sneering faceless men on Twitter picking at her looks after every TV appearance. If it got Laura down, she never once let them see. She was blazing with fury and conviction by this point; she underwent several traumatic experiences during this time and they all seemed to fuel her further. She fought her case in public fora all over the UK and Ireland, and was ferocious as she did.

The woman the world knew as Laura Lee died suddenly in February 2018. She left behind a teenage daughter, a menagerie of pets and an international network of people who are determined she won't be forgotten. Her campaign to overturn the Morrow Law has been abandoned for now, as her legal team were unable to find another plaintive for the case, but her bravery, beautifully articulated arguments and fierceness have inspired thousands of people and her legacy is still growing.

If you'd like to understand more, please take a few moments to look up the work done by organisations such as SCOT-PEP, The English Collective of Prostitutes, and Sex Worker Open University.

Kirstin Innes
July 2018

ACKNOWLEDGEMENTS

As a good friend of mine insists on pointing out, a book is a group effort (especially when it takes you blimming years to write). So here's a list: Bekah Mackenzie, Ellie Shaw and Kate Robertson have been fabulous, patient and encouraging readers. Caitrin Armstrong has always been on hand with practical advice and support. I am very lucky that an accident of the school system threw us together many years ago, and I love you all very much.

Magi Gibson, Iain Maloney and Rodge Glass all offered essential feedback at various early stages. Bridget Innes helped me through some fallow periods. Nine performed a heroic editing job. My agent Charlie Brotherstone is the world's most charming cheerleader and I'm delighted to have him on side. And huge, huge thanks to Campbell, Alison and the team at Black & White for rescuing this book and creating this beautiful new edition.

None of this would have been possible without my ridiculously patient, supportive partner Alan Bissett. Previous editions of this book were dedicated to him, and had he not pushed me to write, have confidence in my writing and keep writing, it wouldn't have happened.

Finally, I have to pay tribute to some of the brilliant, articulate and inspiring women I met along the way, both online and face to face, who agreed to interviews, read the book to make sure I wasn't barking up any wrong trees, and helped me navigate my way through. N, M and A: a massive thank you to you. Antoinette, you have my sword.

AUTHOR'S NOTE

All the organisations and institutions mentioned in this novel are entirely fictional; however, the background to this book was built up through many years of research and interviews conducted with people who work within the industry.

ABOUT KIRSTIN INNES

Kirstin Innes is an award-winning writer, journalist and arts worker. Her debut novel *Fishnet* was first published in 2015 to great acclaim. She founded the Glasgow literary cabaret night Words Per Minute and often performs at spoken word events and festivals. Her short stories have been published in anthologies and commissioned by BBC Radio 4. Kirstin lives with her family in a village by a loch in the west of Scotland.